M⊕NKSPIKE

Occult Horror

By
S. E. England

ISBN: 978-1-69340-563-1

1st Edition:
www.echowords.org
www.sarahenglandauthor.co.uk

About the author

Sarah England is a UK author. Originally she trained as a nurse before a career in the pharmaceutical industry specialising in mental health – a theme which creeps into much of her work. She then spent many years writing short stories and serials for magazines before having her first novel published in 2013.

At the fore of Sarah's body of work is the bestselling trilogy of occult horror novels – *Father of Lies, Tanners Dell* and *Magda*; recently followed by *The Owlmen*.

You might also enjoy, *The Soprano*, a supernatural thriller set on the North Staffordshire Moors. *Monkspike* is her latest novel.

If you would like to be informed about future releases, there is a newsletter sign-up on Sarah's website. Please feel free to keep in touch via any of the social media channels, too. It's good to hear from you!

www.sarahenglandauthor.co.uk

www.twitter.com/sarahengland16

www.Facebook.com/sarahenglandauthor

'Stars hide your fires. Let not light see my black and deep desires.'

Macbeth IV. Shakespeare.

PROLOGUE

KEZIA ELWYN

At six a.m. Kezia jumped off the bus and waited for the taillights to disappear. The fog was slow to clear in the forest that morning, blurring the veil between dawn and the coming day, but she knew her way of old. Some things, not many, had come in handy growing up here, and the whereabouts of hidden tracks through the woods was one of them.

Sam Elwyn lived in a bungalow at the top of the hill – a decent brick place with several acres, workshops and a yard out back. Well concealed by trees the walk was steep, and Kezia's breath steamed on the air as she climbed. Occasionally she stopped…to watch and listen…resuming a couple of minutes later. Although the path was very rarely used, it terminated at Sam's place. If anyone saw her it would be difficult to explain.

Deep inside the forest it was gloomy, the going underfoot muddy. Fallen trunks frequently barred the way and undergrowth concealed the path. She took care with every step. There couldn't be so much as the snap of a twig or…

What was that?

It had been the smallest of sounds…a soft footfall, a gentle sigh…

The next intake of breath remained lodged in her throat, every muscle tense as she scanned the trees. Tendrils of mist hovered between barren branches.

A few yards away a startled deer had stopped grazing and was staring at her directly. Motionless, relief rushing through her veins, she met its gaze, until finally a sense of calm settled upon the creature. Then bowing its head once more it nuzzled at the damp grass for a few moments longer, before turning on its heels and vanishing into the haze. Nothing else stirred, the only sound that of her hammering heart. Satisfied she was alone again – not something to be taken for granted so close to Wolfs Cross – she continued at a pace, making sure to cover her tracks. Those from the village would know there'd been a visitor if a trail was left – Kade, her brothers, uncles – all hunted at dawn.

Stifling her deep unease, she focused inwardly on her guide and protector. She kept fearful company these days, and creatures like the deer would see who dwelled within and cower, submitting instantly. Humans however, would not, which was why it was vital to work in the shadows until it was too late, far too late, for any of them to do a damn thing about it. People here would know soon enough what they were dealing with.

A few minutes later, Sam's house came into view: the windows unlit hollows, the yard empty, workshops chained and padlocked. Another hour and his labourers would arrive with trucks for the day's jobs. Sam was a wealthy man with a thriving forestry business. Somewhat isolated and getting on in years, he may have been a target for theft in what was a poor area and a deprived village, but Sam had powerful contacts and a team of loggers depending on him to pay their bills. Not only that but he was a short, wiry man with a quick temper who wasn't averse to using a shotgun. His aim was legendary. Back in Wolfs Cross they held competitions for who could hit the most rabbits or wild boar on a shoot, and old Sam would show up and win hands down every time.

She lingered behind one of the oaks for a couple of minutes, moulding her body to its trunk, slowing her breath, acutely aware of the moment, of the steady wash of drizzle dripping onto the canopy above.

At six-thirty precisely a lamp flicked on.

It was her signal.

Darting across the yard like a fugitive she quickly scooted in through the back door, shut it behind her and slid the bolt. Before turning around.

He was standing in the kitchen doorway, dressed in pyjama bottoms tied with string at the belly, and an old brown sweater pulled over the top. She could smell him – the stale sweat of his beer-soaked skin, the dried drips of urine, and the grease of his unwashed hair.

"I thought you'd never come," said the man who churned her stomach. "Kept me waiting, you 'ave."

She threw back her hood, dropping the rucksack on the table and scrabbling for her cigarettes. "Did my best. Anyway, nice to see you too." She lit up. "I could do with a coffee."

"Later," he said, ambling over.

He was staring at her mouth like the lover he thought himself to be. Instinctively she put out her arms to keep him at bay. "I need one now."

The stench of his morning breath caught in her craw,

and she turned her face to one side, swallowing hard as he lunged forwards. One hand was already around her waist, the other tugging at the zip of her jeans. "You definitely do."

Wriggling backwards, she pulled away and forced herself to laugh flirtatiously, to feign a light-heartedness she didn't feel. "Down, wolf. Listen, I want a coffee first and I'm 'aving one. I feel dizzy. Then I'll make it worth your while, I promise."

His eyes flashed to steel and she cringed inwardly, summoning the effort needed to sound cajoling, hating the wheedling tone in her voice as she stroked his arm. "Seriously, I'll be fine in a minute. Have a heart, Sam, I was up at five."

"Right. Well, I need a piss anyway. Get me one as well while you're at it, will you?" He took her cigarette and dragged the tar into his lungs before handing it back. "Two sugars. You can bring them through to the bedroom."

Every bundle of nerve fibres fired and twitched as she hunted in the semi-darkness for cups, filled the kettle and switched it on. *Eye on the prize. Eye on the prize…*

On reaching the doorway however, he paused. "You wouldn't be messing with me would you, Kezia? You wouldn't want to do that, you know – not after all that's been said."

Spooning in the coffee, she had her back to him. "No, of course not."

"I mean, why come up 'ere if you're not gonna…?"

She spun round to face him, forcing tears into her eyes. "Alright, well if I seem a bit off it's because I thought we 'ad an understanding? I've been worrying myself half to death about it. Because the way I look at it, I've kept my part of the bargain – coming 'ere, risking life and limb – but you 'aven't. In fact, I'd say you're leading me a merry dance and not doing what you said you would. I mean, 'ave you thought about what will 'appen to us, me and Gul, if he finds out? If you want to know what's upsetting me, it's that!"

His lip curled. "Oh, right. Well, for your information I 'ave done what I said I would. Did it last week, in fact."

She stared long and hard, watching the expression of suspicion die in his eyes as he walked back towards her, replaced now with what she dreaded the most. Recoiled from.

"Really? Seriously?"

"Course I 'ave. You and Gul mean the world to me, you know that."

She tried not to flinch as he grabbed one of her breasts and began to knead it, grinding his hips against hers.

"Where is it, then? I mean, when did you do it? Only you understand my concern? It's Gul I'm thinking of."

His voice was becoming thick and syrupy. "Later."

She eased him gently away. "Kettle's boiling, my lover. Anyhow, I thought you needed a pee?"

He laughed, showing a row of small, nicotine-stained teeth. "You really want that coffee, don't you? Alright, well bring them through and then I'll prove it to you, alright? Thought you'd trust me, that's all."

She stubbed out the cigarette. "Yeah, I do but—"

"That lad's made a fool out of me, you know that. And now he's gonna pay."

The smile stiffened on her face, his words resonating with the one inside. "Indeed," she murmured under her breath as he wandered out of the kitchen. "Indeed he is."

***

CHAP+ER ⊕NE

MOⅡKSPIKE VILLAGE
March 2019
BELIⅡDA

Belinda Sully rapped loudly on her son's bedroom door, shouting to be heard above the music. "Ralph, your tea's ready."

No answer. Of course, no answer.

"Ralph!"

The bass beat stomp-stomp-stomped into her brain. Music had been the backdrop to her life. From Nirvana to Springsteen and Motown to Soul, it lit her up, made her dance, sing, or bawl her eyes out. She'd partied 'til her feet blistered, walking home shoeless on litter-strewn pavements, still singing, still high. Forty-eight she may be, but on a night out she was always first on the dance floor and last off. Sparky, was how everyone described her – a small person full of zest for life.

She rested her head against the wooden door panel. This stuff Ralph liked though - well, it wasn't even angry punk. That she could understand: each generation had its own stamp, its own energetic zeitgeist that made it an exhilarating place to be. For a while. This wasn't it, though. What he played day and night was a depressing, domineering rant that bore into the mind like a pneumatic drill – a tuneless, obscenity-riddled diatribe of misogyny and hate – every other word, 'mother-fucker,' the theme hard-core drugs, bitches and death. This particular singer, the one he played constantly, had died from an overdose, catapulting him to iconic status. And so the droning litany of doom now resounded from beyond the grave and sounded like it.

She banged hard on the door with the palm of her hand. "Ralph! Your tea's going cold."

A surge of frustration erupted inside her. While she'd been out at work all day and his sister, Essie, at school – he'd languished in bed again. All day. Nineteen years old and lying there playing computer games instead of finding work. Well, enough was enough. This was becoming very unhealthy.

Still no answer.

Right, that was it.

She turned the handle, a tiny smile of victory twitching her lips at the scurry of action emanating from inside. The little sod knew she was shouting and must have fair flown across that room when he saw the handle move. Ordinarily she wouldn't have barged in, but he knew she was there alright and had completely ignored her. He deserved it.

The rising smile however, faded instantly at the sight of him.

She stepped back.

Christ, what was wrong with his eyes?

Confusion blocked her thoughts, rendering her speechless.

Towering over her in the grey hooded sweatshirt he hardly ever took off, Ralph's expression was utterly devoid of emotion – an apocalypse of emptiness – as, like some kind of automaton, he swaggered up close. And then to her profound astonishment, began to manoeuvre her out of the room with his chest.

In a parody of a slow dance…step by step…he backed her out until she was standing once more on the landing. After which the door was firmly slammed shut. A bolt shot home. And the music racked up.

***

It took a minute for the shock to subside. After which her whole body began to shake. A mixture of fury and bewilderment battled for position, as she stood there with half a mind to barge straight back in and give him a damn good rollicking. Never mind that she was half his size.

Why don't you then? Go on…why don't you? You're his mother, aren't you?

Her hand hovered mid-air, the palm an inch away from his door.

Yet something stopped her.

Deep in the shadowy layers of her mind, a hidden and as yet unacknowledged truth lay buried. Her hand dropped to her side. As slowly, she turned around to face the stairs, gripped the bannister rail and plodded back down again – a considerably different woman to the one who had thundered up a matter of minutes ago.

"You alright, Mum?"

She stared down the hallway towards the kitchen. Seventeen year old Essie was pushing food around her plate while glued to her iPhone.

Both teenagers had been deeply traumatised by the death of their father two years ago, dislocating instantly from the haste and habit of their busy lives to plunge into mourning. Where they had stayed. Ralph had ducked out of sixth form altogether, while Essie, fifteen at the time, had needed private tuition to help her stay the course. Meanwhile, the lovely big house in Barons Wood – their much loved family home, which she and Gideon had salvaged from ruins and patiently rebuilt – had to be sold and their belongings packed. The terrace here on Moss Pike Road it had to be said, was considerably less comfortable than what they were used to. On top of that there'd been the gossip surrounding Gideon's death. The last two years hadn't been easy for any of them.

"Mum?"

She jumped, realising she'd been standing at the bottom of the stairs for several seconds, mute and transfixed. "Coming…"

They still visited their father's grave every day without fail. He'd been a good dad. They loved him and found it difficult to come to terms with the fact he'd died at such a young age. Fifty-one. Far too young. Sometimes she wondered if they minded that she didn't go with them, ever, and if they questioned that. Perhaps even blamed her in some way?

The plots were small these days, for cremated bodies instead of interred coffins, but Gideon's marble plaque sparkled, polished and adorned with little carvings and drawings they'd made for him. And like giant ravens his children fluttered and fussed over it in their gothic clothing – Essie in her hooded dusk cardigan, Ralph in the punk-rave long coat he always wore. Both favoured the look of dramatic death, completely opposite to her in looks. Where she was a tiny, freckled blonde, they were just like Gideon – lanky and dark with pale skin and icy blue eyes.

"Mum!"

"Yes sorry, I'm here, coming—"

"God, you look terrible. Literally, you're all like, totally white."

She stumbled to the nearest kitchen chair. The smell of congealing, take-away curry made her stomach swill and she pushed her plate away. "I don't think I can eat that now, actually."

"What's happened? Is it Ralph? Did he say something?"

This was the most Essie had spoken to her in weeks, and she took a good, long, hard look at her daughter. Had she been too indulgent with these kids? Let them wallow for too long? It had been nigh impossible to deny them anything, lest their grief deteriorate into something infinitely worse, something they would not recover from.

Essie's eyes were as heavily blacked as those of Siouxsie Sioux. Piercings studded the rims of her ears and flashed from her tongue. And there was a new tattoo on the inside of her wrist, she noticed, that looked like a witch's sigil. Seventeen. She should have said, 'No'. No to the bloodlust t-shirt. No to the slasher dress she'd worn to Molly's party on Saturday. And if she wasn't mistaken there was the distinct aroma of marijuana in the air. It was all far too dark and far too maudlin. What the hell had she been thinking? Or not thinking!

The sudden slam of realisation was reminiscent of a car crash she'd had twenty years before: while the wheels hung over a precipice and bits of metal lay strewn across the tarmac, her only thought had been how to get to the next appointment. There'd been no feeling in her left arm. People were running to help. Only she had to get to the next client... Was going to be late... Would someone make the call for her...?

No, love, you're not going anywhere. Look, your arm's broken!

And here it was again: the cold, hard slap of reality every bit as brutal and every bit as abrupt. Two years of breakneck coping, selling-up, organising, packing, moving, cleaning, meeting with teachers at the school, fixing meals, running her clinic, attending conferences and appraisals, trying to get back to normal, trying to keep things going...

Christ, why didn't I notice?

"Mum, you're literally freaking me out! What is it? What's happened?"

When she eventually found her voice it sounded thin, wobbling and frail like that of a much older woman. She was falling, flailing in space with nothing to hold onto.

"Essie, have you noticed your brother eyes at all? Is it something he wears – weird faddish contact lenses – something like that?"

Discarding her iPhone, Essie regarded her steadily. A tiny flash darted behind the startling blue of her irises while she clearly decided how to respond, buying time. "Why? Why do you say that?"

She knows what I mean, then! She knows something I don't... Oh, God, what's coming? What don't I know?

A chaos of feelings stirred inside her, as unsettlingly familiar as if they had forever been there, unleashing, unhinging, ready to respond like an echo to a shout. The moment stretched out for all eternity. Here it came... And when she once more found her voice, the words seemed to float between them.

"He...the pupils seem to change shape. They aren't round, they're kind of elliptical like a..." Nausea lodged in her throat along with words that couldn't, shouldn't, be said. Not about her own son. "Like a reptile's... I mean, are they meant to be like that? Is it new contact lenses meant to scare people or...?"

Please God let it be so!

The girl continued to stare at her, the hold magnetic. Until finally she seemed to make up her mind. "Mum, I think there's some stuff you should know."

***

CHAPTER TWO

Later, instead of sleep, the conversation with Essie was to replay repeatedly. If only her busy mind would switch off from the nagging, never-ending turmoil. What had she missed? What was really going on? Finally, at some point in the small hours, her ragged thoughts merged with a slumber so profound it devoured the day, offering if only briefly, some respite.

But before that oblivion came, long before, there came torment. The torment of truths quashed and denied for two long years. Truths which had kept her away from Gideon's grave, and distanced her from the village. Truths which, in the darkest hours of the night, now resurfaced.

This time however, on top of the upsurge of knowledge she didn't want, had never wanted, there came what would be described in a case of physical disease, as secondaries. And the secondaries, as any late-stage cancer patient will attest to, could be the most painful and deadly of intrusions, often expediting a rapid end. They burrowed inside bones and nerves, mercilessly probing and prising apart healthy cells, causing an agony so unbearable that every other facet of normal life receded. Until the battle was either won or lost. So then, here it was - the second onslaught, a pain delivered twice.

Deal with it… you have to…you must face it… you must…

She lay awake, muscles rigid, watching the sweep of car headlights chase over the heavy furniture her mother had once given her and Gideon – cumbersome stuff once relegated to a spare room, yet now all she had. Nobody wanted old brown furniture anymore. You couldn't give it away. Not this sort – a heavy triple wardrobe with an age-speckled mirror, and a chest of drawers so huge as to be almost immovable. Made to last generations, the dark oak sapped both light and space, adding to the closeted gloom in the north-facing terrace. The sun's rays never reached the inside even on a summer's day. 1970s flocked wallpaper peeled from the walls, the odour of mould, wet rot and damp pungent. It needed painting white throughout, she thought, in amongst a myriad of other thoughts. Apart from Ralph's room, obviously, and Essie's… All of which brought her full circle again. Worrying about them. Wondering what could and should have been done differently.

As the silent blackness of night deepened, dropping into the dead hours between three and four, a barn owl screeched from high up in the woods. It twanged at her heart. God, she missed home. When she and Gideon had bought the lodge in Barons Wood twenty years ago it had been little more than an old cabin. Stone by stone Gideon restored the exterior walls, then extended and re-roofed it. Often there'd been no running water or electricity in those early days, but they'd managed. Had brought up their family, put in the hours, the love and the sacrifice in order to provide a nice home. For a secure future.

A collection of moments danced before her with such a force of clarity it transported her straight back in time. The air was freshly scented with spruce and horse-chestnut, and in summer with the jasmine and wild honeysuckle she'd planted, along with old English roses and heady lilac. Back came the pitter-patter of leaves in the breeze and the dapple of light and shade across the lawn. All those years spent creating a garden bursting with colour at every point of the year. Even in winter there were red and purple berries amid the gloss of holly bushes and feathery cedars. But mostly it was the cool hush of the forest she had cherished, and every single morning as she walked down to the clinic to work she'd thanked God for what she had. It was where she belonged and had worked so hard to stay; never understanding, not for the full two years since Gideon had died, why it had ended.

But now, thanks to Essie, she did. Perhaps she always had. Maybe Essie had simply provided that cold slap needed to make her face it. So welcome to phase two, to the secondaries…And, yes, by God it was painful. So painful it twisted inside her gut. It filled her eyes with tears. And it choked in her throat. The grief, the raw and terrible horror of not only having had her life shattered on that fateful golden morning in September, but being forced to recognise that life with Gideon, as she thought it to be, had been an illusion. Something she had still not accepted.

So then, this time there was no choice. No way could it be buried, consigned to history, denied, or bottled and labelled as a mistake. Because this time it seemed the woman had come for her son.

So the question was, instead of lying here a tearful victim, what was she going to do about it? Was she happy breathing in the aroma of passing diesel fumes, and chip fat from The Golden Kitchen over the road after twenty years of hard work building a house someone else now lived in? Content to wake up to the dulcet tones of Monkspike's finest kicking cans, cursing and bullying their way to school? To drunks retching against the wall after falling out of the pub? Great sobs spurted out of her, the whine of a wounded animal howling silently in the dark. How could he have done this to her? How could he? Christ, it hurt so badly. And now this… She pressed the back of her hand against her mouth in case Ralph or Essie heard.

What was it with that woman? Hadn't an affair with her husband been enough? If it was true. Was it? Really? Oh, God…

There had always been just that tiny fraction of room for doubt. Yes, she'd heard the rumours after Gideon's death, but the pitying, questioning stares had her scurrying home to avoid it all. Awful – just awful. Perhaps though, she had closed her ears when it would have been wiser to have learned more?

Pride…

Yes, yes, I know…I know…but it hurt…it hurt so much…I just couldn't…

The hollow of her stomach ached.

But surely, surely she would have heard something, been forewarned, if it was true? Surely? As the practice nurse, she of all people would have got wind if Gideon had been seen with someone else. How come she hadn't known, then? Not seen? Until it was all over and far too late? And even then, even after closing the coffin lid on his dead body, she had still refused to believe the betrayal, had closed her mind to the possibility, and her eyes to the arch if sympathetic glances.

Mum, there's stuff you should know…
Don't tell me…
Kezia Elwyn, Mum.
No.
Ralph's been seeing her.
No.

She found she was grinding her jaw and digging her nails into the palms of her hands, the heat in her blood so intense it was in danger of igniting. So then, not content with screwing her late husband and the consequences of that, Kezia was screwing her teenage son too?

Kezia Elwyn – that skinny care-worker at Temple Lake Nursing Home up the road –married! Oh yes, married, and with a young son, too. Dark hair scraped back from a face so chalk-white it took your breath, she kept her head down walking to and from work along Moss Pike Road, as well she might. Belinda had met her a few times, once when she'd taken a patient up to the Home for admission, but although she knew of her she didn't know her personally. Kezia came from Wolfs Cross on the outskirts of the village at the other side of Barons Wood, a hamlet of one farmhouse and a couple of dilapidated cottages. It didn't have a good reputation. In fact, it had a distinctly dubious one, the farm itself having expanded into a complex of caravans, lean-tos and trailers in order to accommodate more and more family members. Hanging wires were rigged up illegally from one abode to the other, trucks parked haphazardly across a yard littered with half-charred mattresses and discarded furniture. Feral dogs and kids alike ran around with squawking chickens, and gun shots frequently ricocheted around the woods. Social Services were regularly called out; but as with everyone round here those families kept their own counsel and truths rarely leaked out.

Kezia had been one of the few to break ranks, fleeing into the unknown for years before homing back with local forester, Sam Elwyn's son, Clint. The young family now resided on Whitewood Grange, the council estate at the tail end of Moss Pike Road – two minutes' walk if you cut through the churchyard. She wasn't the sort you'd worry about making a move on your husband, though. Most people, men included, gave her a wide berth. Said she freaked them out.

A good ten years younger than herself, Kezia had behaved oddly that day, owlblasting her for some reason, with those unworldly violet eyes. Forearms and fingers covered in tattoos she'd seemed an odd choice to work with the elderly, but care workers, particularly out here in the sticks, were gold dust, and of course appearances could be deceptive. At the time she put her preconceptions aside and gave her the benefit of the doubt. Here, she thought, was a girl trying to do better in life, and all power to her for that.

It was only later she realised just how right her instincts had been, and looking back, yes, those in her care had seemed on edge – gnarled fingers fiddling with chains around their neck, or scratching at the arm rests, tapping their feet in a frenzy of dementia and confusion. One or two jumped nervously at her approach, visibly withering under her gaze, the request for whatever it was they thought they'd wanted dying on their lips.

Recalling the moment she'd stood watching her charge being settled in, observing those in the TV lounge, there had most definitely been an uneasy atmosphere come to think of it. An air of heightened alertness. And now, after all that had happened and knowing what she knew, needles of fear crept under her skin.

Ralph's been seeing her…

Because Kezia Elwyn, word had it, was a Satanist.

***

CHAPTER THREE

SYLVIA

Not often, but increasingly, Sylvia Massey began to wonder if they'd done the right thing moving to Monkspike. At the time, when Mark had been offered a partnership at the Medical Centre with Arran Winter, it had felt as though the gods were smiling on them. Mark had been so excited at the thought of living here, in a forest village he could trace his ancestors back to.

The thing about Mark was, he'd never felt at home anywhere and he'd been ecstatic when he got this job. He knew he'd get it, too – had never been so determined about anything, or so sure it was right. And not long after that, Bel's house in Barons Wood had come onto the market and it all fell into place. Apparently the quick sale had done Bel a favour, enabling her to pay off debts and move on after the tragedy. A good price for a terrific house. Everyone a winner. They'd all been so happy with the move, even Molly, once she realised she'd be getting driving lessons and could go horse riding. And the house was far bigger than anything they could have afforded in Bristol.

Belinda and Gideon, it had to be said, had made a sterling job of the place. He'd been a carpenter – a good one – and she had a hard work ethic fused with an eye for the artistic. Clearly this had been such a lovely comfortable home for them. The large, south-facing, aga-heated kitchen with its bespoke units, had a squishy sofa in a sunny corner, a large kitchen table, an island, and steps leading down to a stunning, Victorian-style conservatory. Then upstairs, all four spacious bedrooms had balconies from which to gaze out at the forest on one side or fields on the other. Yup, a dream come true. For a while…

Now though, a few truths were coming to light, call it a gradual awareness, a collection of whispers and insinuations that had begun to take shape.

Sylvia made a cup of camomile tea and wandered into the conservatory, then lit a few candles and sat down to think. For example, as it turned out there was no way the house would have sold on the open market for the price they had paid. Nowhere near. Possibly not at any price. Which meant if they wanted or needed to sell it would be difficult, and then most probably at a huge loss. Firstly, unemployment here was rife and no one had that kind of money. And secondly, even if they did, they wouldn't come within a hundred yards of the place on account of its reputation, one which remained shrouded in mystery, but would on occasion be referred to in veiled remarks she never quite understood.

Did it matter, though? Did it? Having got to know Belinda at work, they hadn't been able to believe their luck at the time, grabbing the opportunity to buy White Hart Lodge before it even hit the estate agent's books. Stuck in rented accommodation in the nearby town, they were verging on desperate, and since a reputable surveyors' firm advised it was sound and fairly priced they didn't think twice. They certainly hadn't asked if it was haunted. In fairness, she thought, most people wouldn't, would they? And there was hardly anyone in the village likely to educate them on that one, either.

God, they banded together here! Not a word got out to any 'incomer' regarding local business let alone insider gossip. In the three years they'd been here not a single villager had befriended her. Sylvia was a stranger and that was that. Oh, they were civil enough most of the time, seeing as her husband was the doctor no doubt, but friendly? No.

Time, though. Time had unravelled more and more grimy threads of information that now threatened to tarnish the dream.

That evening as Sylvia sat in Belinda's much loved conservatory, now her own zen room complete with hanging plants, herbarium and candles, she closed her eyes in an attempt at meditation. Confusion and disquiet were chattering in her mind, and it was important after the kind of work she did, to release the negativity inevitably soaked up from clients. It sapped the energy and drained her life force. Nobody came to her with love and light. They came to offload depression, anger, bitterness and heartache.

And now it was time to let all of that go.

Although it was still March, the underfloor heating and oil burner kept the room warm and soporific. The dusky evening was slipping into darkness, the forest edge a row of black spikes beyond the glinting reflection of candlelight in the glass. She took a deep breath and filled her lungs, before slowly exhaling to a count of ten. Inhale…exhale…inhale…exhale… There was nothing now except the steady rhythm of her breathing, calming her body, stilling her mind.

Outside a tawny owl hooted, followed by the ke-wick, ke-wick of its call…then a ghostly screech closer to the house…The external sounds receded as she concentrated on the rise and fall of her own breathing, clearing her mind, mentally drawing into herself the free flow of brilliant white light, cocooning herself in it. Getting ready now to expel the darkness…

You're not safe!

The shout had been a male voice directly behind her.

Yet she was quite alone.

She took a moment, heart racing, eyes wide. The skin at the nape of her neck prickled and shivers rippled up the backs of her arms, as if someone had swished past in a long gown.

Fighting the instinct to look over her shoulder, she forced herself to keep calm and close her eyes again, consciously quelling the rising panic. Okay, so something was making its presence known, trying to frighten her. Most likely a low spirit had attached to her aura during the course of the day, in which case she ought to be able to get rid of it. Or it could be from within the house itself - possibly because Essie had been over to see Molly again that afternoon?

Hmm, Essie Sully, Belinda's daughter… If she didn't do what she did for a living it would probably go unnoticed. Most people would accept it as a teenage fad. Well, there was always at least one Goth in every school, wasn't there? But with Essie it was more than that. She brought something into this house every time, leaving a cold vapour trail that accumulated and lingered. And call it coincidence, but whenever Essie had been over, Molly became paranoid about the landing corridor at night, switching on all the lights to run the gauntlet down to the bathroom, and only then if she absolutely had to. Of course her daughter did not make the link, but there were no coincidences in Sylvia's book, having researched and also experienced what she had over the years. And that girl, Essie – she sapped the light.

One autumnal evening last year when Essie had stayed for a sleepover, Sylvia had got up in the early hours to use the bathroom and seen what lurked in that corridor, seen what Molly, thank God, had never seen. On both sides, suspended in hooded shapes several feet off the ground, spectres lined the walls. Although it had been totally dark, the luminous robes had risen out of the umbra and an inconceivable terror had clutched her heart. The power of malevolence rose rapidly as they towered over her, and a low growling, metallic grinding noise began to rumble, and then roar.

She hit the switch, lighting up the upper floor like a football stadium. And immediately the hooded shapes receded, evaporating in a hissing recoil.

The walls were still white. There was the painting of Polperro harbour, there the orchid print, there Molly's bedroom door. But she had glimpsed the dark side that night. And once seen it wasn't something anyone ever forgot.

Rationale and understanding helped, and up to that point she had never experienced such cold terror. Most spirits who remained earthbound had their reasons, clinging to a living person or place out of fear, never fulfilling their own spiritual journey, instead weighting down the individual they'd attached to with the shadow of their death. She had spoken to many through the host, using hypnosis. Some were lost, most were lonely, and all were scared. Occasionally they used bullying tactics to prevent interference, and even more occasionally they were malicious, but it was all part of what she did and rarely did they succeed in frightening her.

Until that night.

Next day she'd smudged sage around the house and made sure to do it regularly thereafter, taking note of the cold spots and chilly breezes in certain places. They were notable in the marital bedroom and here in the conservatory. Frowning, she wondered if it was the house itself, or something Essie brought with her. After all, her father had died in odd circumstances and had been living here at the time. If she could ever persuade Bel to send her daughter for therapy she might find out, but it was hardly a subject easily broached. Her psychotherapy service was by medical referral only, mostly for post-traumatic stress disorder or addiction. Clients seeking spirit-release or past life regression came from the private sector. Those clients however, were never from Monkspike, which was a shame because frankly this was a very sick place. She'd had no idea. Before they came here to live it had just seemed like a gorgeous English village on the Welsh borders.

In her opinion, although definitely not in Mark's, almost all of the illnesses here could be attributed to spiritual attachment: from the alcoholism, violence and drugs, to the depression, physical pain and domestic abuse. Broaching the subject with Mark and Arran, however, was a non-starter. Besides, as both quite feasibly pointed out, spirit-release therapy was not on the NHS. Even in psychiatry it was extremely rare for anything spiritual to be considered. And besides, no one in this village was going to admit to being spiritually possessed, were they? Let alone pay for an exorcism, even if they could. That, most people believed, was firmly in the domain of Catholic priests or horror movies.

Beliefs like hers were isolating. Frustrated, she did her best to work on some of her patients from a distance and incorporate some of her knowledge and expertise into their treatment sessions. Maybe it helped a little and it certainly didn't do them any harm. But the problem here was way too big for one person. Perhaps it was best, as Mark said every time she broached the subject, to simply accept the village for what it was and do her best. Go home and forget about it each day.

And maybe he was right.

Except the oppressive feeling in Monkspike wasn't going away. If anything it was getting worse, almost like an invisible energy field that grew more omnipotent by the day. Sometimes the atmosphere fair crackled. The late afternoon would intensify in colour, trees wavering, grass shimmering in a haze of rose-gold, crows and jackdaws screeching in a frenzy as if a storm was brewing. People secreted themselves indoors, eyes averted as they scurried home and slammed shut the doors.

The question, though, was why? Why was this feeling escalating and why now? Was it since she and Mark had arrived? Or after whatever had happened to

Gideon? Maybe those two kids of Bel's were hanging onto their father's problems? For problems he'd most definitely had.

Of course there was another possibility for the feeling of deep unease this evening. It could be something to do with what happened earlier. Bel was tired, over-worked and struggling with two surly teens still grieving their father, all true. But the woman was also a power house and usually chirpy to the point of brittle. Nursing was her true vocation. In fact, she was one of those small, bustling industrious women who needed to be needed and kept busy. So it had been highly unusual to find her in the distressed, near-broken state she had.

No doubt if Belinda asked, then Arran or Mark would treat her for insomnia or anxiety, and who would question that perfectly reasonable diagnosis?

Once again, if it wasn't for what she did for a living, it might have passed as exactly that. But she had a feeling something was going on in Belinda's family that was far from reasonable. And…here she huddled into her cardigan, rubbing her arms…it was something that lingered in the very fabric of this house.

***

CHAPTER FOUR

She'd found Belinda in the staffroom that afternoon. Already going dark, the day was squally and rain was setting in. Overhead the fluorescent lights buzzed and flickered, and there Belinda was, curled up in an armchair clutching an empty coffee cup, staring out of the window at her own dripping reflection.

Bursting in, Sylvia said, "Penny for them!"

It took her a while, several minutes in fact, as she fiddled with the new coffee machine and the little foil pods, to realise Belinda had not replied. Why did Mark have to go and buy this darned thing? The old one worked perfectly well. Muttering to herself, as yet another fingernail pierced yet another foil lid, the problems posed by today's clients were ticking over busily in her mind. It had turned out to be quite a day at the medical centre, what with a catfight in the local pub, and then yet another call-out to Temple Lake Nursing Home. Despite having been prescribed anxiolytics and sleeping tablets, this particular old lady was now so distressed and in such a high state of agitation that an emergency visit had been requested. And as part of the psychiatric team, Sylvia had gone over to make an assessment.

Ivy Finch, reported to be rambling incoherently about demons looming over her bed and crawling into her mind, completely clamped up however, when Sylvia arrived, resolute in her denial. No, nothing had happened. Nobody had upset her. No, she didn't want a cup of tea, didn't want to wash, and didn't want to lie down. In the end Sylvia had followed her instincts and taken hold of the lady's age-spotted hand. It lay in hers as frail as bird's bones, as she leaned closer and quietly suggested coming back next day to do a calming, relaxation treatment. Within earshot of staff she told Ivy she was likely suffering from extreme anxiety. Then out of earshot whispered she had an idea what the torment was and to please trust her. In return a tacit understanding passed between them. The parchment hand twitched and the large, hooded brown eyes lifted to meet hers. The fear and misery she saw in them told her all she needed to know, and it wouldn't do to delay.

A lot of her specialist work, she'd long accepted, was going to be given for free, but what did it matter? Her family was hardly going to starve, with Mark's colossal salary as a partner, not to mention his part-time work as an associate specialist in psychiatry.

"Bloody stupid machine. Bel, do you know how this works? I'm desperate for a coffee. Oh, and did you treat Maxine Lee? I just wondered how she was. She's been referred to me for stress so I guess that's another one who'll be signed off sick. She definitely came off worst, anyway – incredible seeing she's twice the size of Kezia Elwyn. Honestly though, I mean can you imagine grown women fighting in a pub? Especially over a bloke like Clint Elwyn!"

Another second or two passed before the other woman's silence fully struck home and she swung round.

"Bel?"

Belinda's shoulders were rigid, the muscles of her face twitching as if she was hypnotised or deeply asleep, her lips moving in silent conversation.

"Bel? Are you alright?"

Gradually, Belinda phased back into her surroundings, looking dazed and struggling to focus. "Sorry…Sorry…" She stared at Sylvia as if she had no idea who she was, before putting down her empty mug. "Miles away!"

"Are you okay?"

Actually, now she wandered towards her, it was clear Belinda was absolutely not okay. Her eyes, normally sparkling blue, were dull, scratchy-red and sunken, the hollows of the sockets bruised with fatigue. And although neatly dressed in her practice nurse uniform of navy cotton slacks and tunic, it was clear she had neither done her roots in weeks, or washed the now brassy blonde hair she'd screwed into a topknot. Nor did she wear a scrap of make-up.

It was the latter which was a real surprise, and Sylvia couldn't help but stare that second too long. Never, in all the three years she'd known her, had she ever seen Belinda Sully without make up. Although not classically beautiful, Bel possessed a certain glamour. Her hair was normally shiny and golden, worn either in a neat chignon, or loose and layered around her shoulders. And her eyes, her most striking feature, she made the most of with sweeping eyeliner and mascara. In some ways, and she chided herself for this, Belinda made her feel plain – conscious of her silvery brown hair cut into a bob, the lack of make-up, and her small, tired eyes behind glasses.

Now though, Belinda's lips were chapped and flaking, and her nails were bitten to the quick. Tiny broken capillaries stood out on her cheekbones and around her nose against an ashen complexion blotchy with sores. Even after Gideon had been found dead, later during the inquest, and during the stress of the house move, she had never once let up on her appearance.

This was a woman with chronic insomnia. Perhaps, Sylvia thought, a delayed reaction to trauma? It was a possibility as sometimes the stress took years to fully surface. Her mind began to flick through a checklist of possibilities while she fought to erase the shocked expression she knew was on her face.

"Yeah."

She sat down opposite her. "Well, you don't look it."

"What? No honestly, I'm fine." Belinda stood up and hurried over to the sink to wash out her mug. "Sorry, Sylvia. Got to go, I've a patient waiting—"

"Wait a minute. Please."

Belinda hesitated, one hand on the door handle as Sylvia walked over.

"Has something happened? You know if I can help you, I will."

She'd offered a listening ear many times after Gideon had died, God only knew, but Belinda was a coper, a grafter, and not the type to ask for help. Besides, she'd probably take it as interfering. And when all was said and done Belinda was a local, and the folk here never disclosed a secret if they didn't have to. It took months to get to the core of a problem and the place was riddled with them. There wasn't a single family without at least one member suffering from some kind of mental disorder, and the only reason they turned up for their appointment at all was because they'd lose benefits or sick-leave entitlements if they didn't.

For all that though, professionalism aside, she considered Belinda a friend. And part of her ached that it wasn't reciprocated, not fully anyway. About to give up and apologise for imposing, it was therefore a complete surprise when Belinda apparently had a swift change of heart.

She was gripping the door handle, keeping her face averted when a small cry escaped her. Instantly swallowing it down she blurted out, "You can't help. No one can. You've no idea. I don't know what to do anymore. I just don't know…" Slamming a hand to her mouth, she was breathing through her nose, battling to stop the sobs from escaping.

Sylvia darted forwards. "Oh, my God, Bel, whatever do you mean? What's happened? Come and sit down. Come on. I'll buzz through to Mark and ask him to see the rest of your list—"

"Oh no, he's got enough—"

"You're in no fit state. Please, Bel. Let me help!"

Belinda was dabbing frantically at her eyes, already preparing to batten down the outburst and carry on. "No, I've only got two more. Mark's got enough to do. I'll be alright."

"No. You can't work like this and no one would expect you to." She led her back to the chair. "Stay here a minute. Please. And then we can talk this through.

You're not alone. Whatever it is, I can and will help you. Let me just go and sort out these patients and I'll be back."

She grabbed a blanket from the cupboard and wrapped it around Bel's shoulders. The poor woman was shaking, and now she looked at her properly it was all too obvious she hadn't been eating properly, either. The navy tunic hung from her bones. "Promise me you'll stay here? I won't be long."

Belinda nodded and blew her nose.

"Okay, I'll just tell them on Reception. Two minutes!"

In the end it took ten minutes to sort out Belinda's remaining list, as Mark was mid-patient examination and the receptionist refused to break a lengthy phone call to even make eye contact. And by the time she returned to the staff room, Belinda had vanished.

She stood at the door open-mouthed.

The coffee machine was still bleeping.

The blanket had been discarded.

And a note lay on the table. Hastily scribbled words, which would forever be seared on her mind. Later she would chastise herself over and over and over. If only she had heeded the warning signs. Although no one, not even one such as herself, with all the training and experience she had, could ever have predicted the scale of what was to come.

***

CHAPTER FIVE

KEZIA

That same day, Kezia finished her shift at Temple Lake Nursing Home, changed out of her uniform then left immediately, slamming the door behind her. Hurrying along the path at the rear of the house she cut a thin purposeful figure, muttering to herself as she climbed the hill, the hunch of her back quickly merging with the late afternoon drizzle.

Today had not been a good day.

Crap...crap...crap... At least the rage inside would come in useful later, and that was all that could be said. Because tonight was the night she'd waited for: this most powerful of invocations had to be carried out under a gibbous moon – a time for maximum expansion of will. She had researched the whole thing meticulously, and now finally the correct planetary alignment was in place. Time was running out and so was her patience.

On top of that she'd been humiliated by that pig of a husband yet again. But show him her fury and he'd only laugh and betray her all the more. The man was a self-serving liar and a thoughtless hedonist. Devoid of any emotion bar his own pleasure, what screwed her up more than anything else was the fact she'd fallen for the act. Clint had studied carefully how to gain trust, favours and passion. He knew how to seduce and excite, mirror feelings and put someone on a pedestal. Then discard them. To think she had once thought him a kindred spirit – both outcasts, both lost. He was good, she'd give him that – boy, was he good.

No, her reward was way overdue by now. Way over. Years had passed. But if tonight's efforts failed, what then? What?

Crap…crap…crap…

And that stupid fight in The White Monk on her way to work! Why had she given him the satisfaction? Why? It wasn't even anything to do with him, really. So what had got into her that she couldn't walk right on past and ignore the simpering, pan-faced bitch behind the bar? It wasn't like Maxine Lee was special or the only one Clint shagged when he got bored. But no, she just had to go in there for a word with him about picking up Gul from nursery and end up dragging the woman out by her hair. To be fair, it was the ruby cross earrings that set her off: there they were, filched from her own jewellery box, now sparkling on Maxine's earlobes. That and the sly look Maxine shot her from underneath her false lashes, as in, 'Guess who got me these?'

Well, it had given Clint a good laugh, she supposed, as he stood watching from the side-lines with the chainsaw gang. Sometimes she wondered what possessed her. An almost inhuman eruption had ignited her whole body to a blaze and not for the first time, either. Vaguely she recalled shoving past punters twice her size, marching through the lounge bar with her jaw set and her fingers twitching. What happened next was a blur. Mind you it had to be said - that handful of expensive blonde extensions lying on the pavement afterwards had been a highly satisfying moment, as had the crunch of skull on the inn's stone wall.

It was not a battle though, that she had wished to fight. Especially not if Clint thought for one second it was over him. That was something Kezia Morse would have done back in Wolfs Cross, not the Kezia Elwyn she was today. It had been too public, too vulgar, and a totally unnecessary expenditure of energy. There were far more important matters at stake. And for those it was imperative no one saw her coming until the deed was done.

The voice inside spoke to her ever more frequently now, with every rite, every invocation, spurring her on to the finish. Odd words flew into her head, little phrases, images projected at random. Sometimes hours passed by without any recollection of what she may have said or done. And all the while, the rage simmered and boiled, simmered and boiled, the agitation increasing.

Her nails dug into her palms, her breath coming in sharp rasps as the incline steepened and the dark depths of Barons Wood loomed ahead. Winter was lingering this year. Sleet laced the dusk, spattering into her face, numbing her fingers and toes. Damp soaked in through the soles of the cheap boots she wore, and her thin anorak did little to keep out the chill. Fuck, she hated being poor. Hated the life she'd been saddled with by Clint fuck-face Elwyn; loathed the run-down council house with its cardboard-thin walls, not to mention cleaning up shitty old people with dementia claws and gag-making breath for barely the minimum wage.

Bastard.

At least the job meant being inside Temple Lake House. Gliding around it, touching the walls, and gazing out across the lawns to the woods, it somehow sated the one inside, soothing the restlessness. The scent of a bygone age came and went on the waft of old oak and worn leather; or the fleeting rustle of a silk dress along a corridor - the movement as elusive as the echo of a distant sob. Maybe it was the ghosts. Everyone said the place was haunted.

Yeah well, whatever, ghosts didn't bother her. And anything, absolutely anything, was better than sinking back to Wolfs Cross, especially with Gul in tow. A cesspit of sickness, the skulking stench of incest, insanity and ancient curses had been passed down through the generations, into what was little more than a dingy, dirt-poor campsite constantly fending off the law. Even the humiliation of being married to Clint Elwyn was better than that. No, she had to stick with this, with the pact she had made and the steps taken so far. And trust that at the end of it there would be the reward.

There will...there will...you have to do this...

She checked her watch. Clint was supposed to have collected Gul from nursery. What he'd probably done was dump him with her mother before going straight back to the pub. That's where they congregated, him and the chainsaw gang – smoking out back no matter what the weather, huddled under tarpaulin knocking back ale and whisky chasers, bragging about who they'd fucked, or done over for money. The fact that her mother, Tina, would have been stoned since lunchtime wouldn't even have registered as a concern, his sole intent being to offload responsibility as fast as possible so he could go boozing. By now Gul would be running wild in the yard at Wolfs Cross with his feral, delinquent cousins, while Tina snored away oblivious.

This will soon be over. I promise you, Gul!

Anyway, she could be wrong – maybe Clint had done the decent thing for once and taken Gul straight home for his tea?

Like fuck he had!

This rage never ceased. It pumped through her veins, snatching her from sleep at three in the morning, slamming into her heart at any time of day or night. She couldn't sit, she paced. Couldn't watch a film or read a book. Instead she went walking, for miles and miles and miles through the woods. At half five she'd be on her way to see Sam. At seven she'd be on her way back for Gul, and at nine she was at work. While others ate lunch or dunked biscuits at coffee break, she chain-smoked, dragging on each cigarette until her cheeks hollowed.

Almost at the top of the hill now… nearly there…

Funnily enough it wasn't the sour breath of her rapist grandfather or the filthy, freezing caravan she'd been raised in, not even Clint's mocking deceit and screwing around that focused her rage to laser point. That was just lousy, rotten, stinking luck.

No, what really iced her veins to blinding hatred was the existence of just one woman. And now that woman had been recognised and located, every atom of loathing could be crystallised. The prize was so near…This was the woman who was in the way. So then, forget the ten-a-penny Maxine Lees of the world. They were nothing. No question about it, everything in Belinda Sully's life must turn to blood, bone and dust.

Tell him… have to tell him…

The voice inside was jumbled, vexed, the sounds tinny and far away. But there was a feeling the end was within reach now, and a revelation was coming. Tonight, hopefully. It really did have to be tonight. This was the ultimate and by far the most daring invocation. If it wasn't for the rage, for the sheer force of frustration after all this time, she wouldn't do it. Time might mean little to Spirit, but it was running out for her.

At the top of the extensive sweep of lawns she paused to look down at Temple Lake House, panting hard. She took out a packet of cigarettes lit one, and pocketed the lighter. Took a drag, then another…

When her mind shot to black.

Caught totally unaware, she stumbled, grasping at the air for support. All natural sounds faded, replaced by a single high-pitched screech like microphone feedback, which became louder and louder. It was the nightmare coming again. And there was nothing she could do to stop it. Her stomach plunged, as filled with dread she fainted to her knees.

A wash of sleet whistled across the surrounding fields, lashing the conifers and flattening the grass. Here it came…

She had her head down, hands clamped to her ears. Until the screech faded, the blackness lifted to grey, and the vision played out.

As always, the scene was one of thick fog, in the distance a line of wintry trees. Like an old black and white film, the picture was fractured and the sound crackled, as the camera zoomed towards what at first appeared to be the edge a forest. It soon became clear however, that the line of trees stood alone, a fringe to the barren, howling wasteland that lay behind. The trunks were blackened and crooked, the branches as spiky as giant thorns. A loud caw-caw-caw shrieked out and she looked up. A raven had perched on high, its blue-black feathers sleek and oily, the eyes piercing and bulbous.

Gradually she became aware of a low growling noise like oncoming thunder. It didn't seem to emanate from any particular direction, perhaps it was inside her head, along with the cranking of rusty metal grinding in the wind, words guttural and inhuman beginning to form in her mind. Something was going to appear in front of her, something terrible. It couldn't be seen…*No, no, stop!*

The ground rolled beneath her and she clutched at the earth as if drunk. Until after what seemed like an age, her sight abruptly snapped back to normal, the house reappeared, and the terrible roaring and cranking metal finally stopped.

She found herself on her hands and knees with her nails full of dirt.

Who the hell am I? What am I doing here?

She looked down at her clothes, at the tattooed fingers, and didn't recognise them. Panic lurched until her conscious mind cut in sharply.

This is the nursing home I work in!

Oh yes, of course. Shit! And here she was on the ground.

She grabbed the scattered cigarettes and stuffed them into her pockets. The nightmare normally woke her from sleep. Never had it appeared during the day. Whatever it was, the scene repeated and left a bad feeling, one of cold, menacing isolation.

Struggling to her feet she focused on Temple Lake. On reality. There was the weirdest feeling of having stood here before, staring at this house exactly like now, in this same position, only having long hair and flowing skirts...

She shook her head as if to physically excise the sensation. What was happening to her? Messages and visions were not supposed to occur except when requested. She picked up coincidences or strong feelings, then connected with Spirit and asked for a, 'yes or no'. But this was horrible. How the hell to stop it? This house though, it engendered such strange emotions, an enchanting sight as the sleet began to turn snowy, to swirl and fizz in the air. It was settling quickly now on the roofs and turrets, brushing the cedars and firs in a soft wintry silence. Her face stung with the cold, yet motionless she remained, staring at the house. The feeling of dejá-vu was overwhelming. An ache weighted her heart, along with a memory – was it a memory? It seemed so powerful, so painful. A small face glimpsed at one of the turret windows, pale and quick. A clatter of hooves...

Then just as quickly as the scene flickered into life, it died.

A sharp gust of sleet pelted her face and she jump-started into the present day.

"Fuck!"

Her hair was soaked, her jeans were wet through and it was dark. How long had she been standing out here? More time lost? This was getting worse. The visions were more frequent than ever, each one leaving her floored, wondering who she was and where. And every time it happened she lost another foothold on reality.

Who am I, again?

Oh yes, yes. I work here. I work here, is all. Plain old Kezia Elwyn from Wolfs Cross. A fucking slave, a house-maid…whatever…

She picked up her canvas bag, slung it over her shoulder and made her way towards the gate leading to Cats Hill.

Bloody hate it, hate it, hate it!

She stank of vile excretions and over-boiled vegetables, of fear, regrets, death and detergent. Her body ached with fatigue. And resentment consumed her every waking moment. But her day was coming. Oh, it was coming alright. Her fist clenched over the day's takings – a few hairpins from an old biddy with the Sight, for sure she had it, a piece of broken glass found in the turret stairwell, and an acorn from under the oak outside the dormitory window. These were her eyes and ears. Hurrying away now, she unlatched the gate and crossed over the road into Barons Wood. There was work to do and then she must get home.

Once inside the woods the air was still and the whine of the wind instantly dropped. Swiftly she swept between the trees making up for lost time, the darkness amassing in shadows behind her, like courtiers trailing her robes. The public footpath skirted White Hart Lodge where Belinda Sully used to live, and on drawing level she paused to glance at the sight of the candlelit conservatory. Six-thirty already, and there was that silly therapist burning incense. Now that was a joke. Bet she had no idea what was hovering around her yearning to step in? Mind you, she would undoubtedly have been spooked a fair few times in that house.

She grinned. There would be cold spots aplenty in there, with all the lower entities she'd sent over to keep Belinda Sully company at night, not to mention disturb her peaceful plant room – the place she liked to rest in on a sunny evening or chat away to friends on the phone. When she had friends, that was. For a fact, Belinda had caught movement in the woods as she'd looked out back at dusk, for that was exactly the time Kezia chose to watch the house and its residents, to find and lift into her pockets a pebble here, a strand of hair there - those precious eyes and ears the demons needed.

So now it was Sylvia Massey's turn to peer into the darkening woods, to be suddenly chilled and wonder who or what had brushed against the back of her neck. To stare at her own flickering reflection and have that feeling of being floodlit on a stage, unable to see into the black pit of the auditorium.

What was she doing? Kezia narrowed her eyes. It looked like meditating. Yes, well she'd need to after dealing with Monkspike's nutcases all day. It made her laugh to think the woman had to sit and listen to all their garbage. It must be like being on the Jeremy Kyle show for a living. Whose brother had shagged whose daughter and whose boyfriend had copped off with whose mother? That was about the size of it. And most of them smoking spliffs, drinking all day, still in bed at three in the afternoon and letting their kids run wild.

Well, the therapist was welcome to White Hart Lodge. For a while. Doubtless she wouldn't be staying long. Belinda had been removed and so too would Sylvia. Fact.

With the surge of angry malice her mind blacked once more. She tried to swallow down the rise of nausea. God, she was going to be sick. The dark canopy of trees whirled overhead.

Whoa…surely not again…?

This time there was no warning before an image flashed straight into her head, as clearly as watching a movie on the big screen.

A horseman with long cloaks flying around him was galloping towards the old oak door of the lodge. On reaching it, he turned the horse around and violently kicked a spurred foot into the iron-studded wood. The horse reared up and the door flew open…

The vision cut.

A millisecond flash.

Yet it left her reeling with an emotion so raw it physically hurt. She doubled over with the agony of it: a lightning flash of euphoria followed instantly by a sense of loss so great it was unbearable. The pain ripped through her body, blinding her with tears.

This isn't real…it's just a trip…a message…

She held onto the bark of a tree behind her, desperately trying to erase the emotional pain. Working with the occult was not simple. Instructions came in pictures, with strong intuition, or repeated signals that could not be coincidence. But these flashbacks to another era were not only random and unbidden, but baffling. It was like having lived here before, but she didn't believe in all that. There was nothing high or noble about humans in her opinion, no development of spirit through reincarnation. And what she raised were demons that had never lived or been human. The only credo she subscribed to, based on experience and results, was demonolatry because frankly demons delivered.

Along with Clint and the others back in Gloucester, Satanism had been a thrilling ride for a while, with drug-fuelled highs and black masses in a run-down house on the outskirts of town. It had been a great outlet for all the despair, disappointment and frustration of life so far. Hardly any of them actually believed in it but they sure as a high-road-to-hell enjoyed the sex and wild trips. Sometimes dreams had blurred with reality, so naked people massaging each other in blood could have happened, or not... Most of that time she had since blanked out as being so debauched and base as to be unspeakable, with many of the acts performed so disgusting as to bond those taking part with each other forever. Whoever broke the vows would be avenged with murder and nothing less.

Murder...yes...rape and bondage and torture... It had all happened. What she hadn't seen she'd heard about. And police, mundane people, knew nothing. Nothing at all. About those who stepped outside the confines of human boundaries.

But then one night when she had been lying alone, gazing out of an upstairs window at the full moon (she must have been in the first trimester with Gul? Something, certainly, had permitted her to be exempted from the black mass) she had received a visitor. It wasn't clear if it was a dream or not, and she had felt no fear. His eyes were brilliant blue, as dazzling as light refracted by a cut sapphire, and he was staring down at her as she lay on the bed. Handsome and muscular he possessed a sharp, square jaw and angular cheekbones. And as she gazed at him in confusion, trying to figure out what was happening, a blue aura appeared to shimmer around his whole body – the hazy dark blue of dusk in summer.

Her first thought was that it couldn't be due to anything she'd smoked because she'd been feeling ill all day and hadn't taken anything. Her second thought was that she must be in a locked dream because it was impossible to move. Her limbs were paralysed and her voice stuck in her throat. Unable to utter a word she blinked, then squeezed her eyes tightly shut and then opened them again. Yes, he was still there. He continued to stare at her intently and it was then that a small stab of fear pressed into her stomach.

I've seen you before…

There was a strong, heady scent about him impossible to place, and when he spoke the voice didn't seem to fit the form. What had she expected? Certainly not that of a very crusty old man with a fifty a day habit. The voice was raucous, sharp and raspy. Inhuman. She was to go home. Go back.

Never, no, I hate it!

A picture had then come to her, of a house with a long conservatory, of a handsome boy fully grown, and a moonlit garden stocked with herbs. She saw herself moving around this garden, the sound of ravens screeching from nearby treetops as she hummed to herself, unpegging washing from a line.

And when she woke next day it was with a powerful conviction. She woke Clint.

"I want us to go back to Monkspike."

"Are you kidding me? Fuck's sake! Go back to sleep."

But the nagging conviction grew and grew until it became an obsession that could not be ignored. It made her ill, nervous. That was when the pacing started, and the chain-smoking. Muttering to herself she would rage at passers-by in the street and began to lose weight alarmingly. Meanwhile Gul was on the way and growing daily. Finally, the idea came into her head to apply for a council house and just before Gul was due, she got it.

By then Clint was becoming tired of petty theft and insanitary conditions in the squat, and his eyes had sparked at the news of a place to live along with a range of benefits. After that, just as the man with the blue eyes had promised, everything fell into place, including the care worker position at Temple Lake. In fact, they were so desperate for staff none of her forged documents had proved an issue – they barely glanced at them.

Lest there was any doubt in her mind as to whether or not another force was behind events, a cataclysmic moment happened shortly after moving into the new house. Six month old Gul contracted a fever, and she'd rushed him over to the medical centre. Belinda Sully was the nurse, a woman she'd vaguely been aware of growing up and never taken much notice of. But there she was that day while Kezia waited outside the doctor's office with Gul. Her blonde head was bent towards the doctor's.

Whispering they were, having left the door ajar. The two of them. And the sight caused such a riptide of jealousy inside her it was all she could do not to fly in and push them apart. Pained for a reason she could not understand, she was still struggling to quell the horrible feeling, when all of a sudden a peel of laughter ricocheted around the room, so loudly it caused her to nearly jump off the seat.

Behind her the corridor was empty, the receptionist chatting quietly with a patient at the glass window. So the source was not from there. Puzzled, she stared at each person in turn in the waiting room. Surely they could hear that person laughing?

And then it registered. No one real was making the noise. The guffawing, nasty raucous laughter was all in her mind. Only she could hear it. This was madness – voices in the head! Vaguely aware of a hum of chatter in the background, she sat rigid with shock, the breath tight in her chest. And only the fact that Gul was wailing miserably had she snapped out of the trance.

She turned to pick him up. Immediately the laughing stopped, reality came spinning back with a sickly, technicolour lurch, and at that precise moment Belinda Sully looked up and noticed her. She didn't smile. Nor did she speak. Neither of them did. Instead they stared at each other for an unnaturally long time. Seconds ticked slowly and methodically by, the fluorescent lights buzzing, a phone ringing on and on…As if both had just seen some terrible apparition and didn't know how to react.

Later she realised that had been her first sign.

It took a while to understand, but soon a pattern formed. The one inside seemed excited, flashing images of the woman into her dreams and waking visions.

She'd be walking Gul to nursery when Belinda's name was shouted into her ear, or dropping off to sleep when that moment their eyes met replayed in her mind. Acceptance came quickly, along with relief that it was not insanity but the subtleties of the occult. And from then on each tiny break-through, either by thought or deed, was validated or rejected by communing with Spirit. She threw the dice: Yes or No?

She was on the right path, being led, knew why it had been necessary to spend time at the satanic cult and began to practice all she had learned. Disregarding the pomp and ceremony, all the godhead assumption and dread lords at the watchtowers – all that crap – she worked alone. All the stuff about protection was ridiculous. There was nothing to be afraid of; demons did trade and made deals just like humans did. You just paid a higher price if you didn't deliver, that was all. It also took time, months if not years, to bring an objective to fruition. In the spirit world time was an alien concept, and this was one of the most difficult and frustrating aspects.

What kind of a message was this one, though - the wrench to her heart at the sight of the man on horseback? So was she correct in her assumption, then? Tonight would be the culmination of the whole journey? It seemed that way. Her pulse quickened. She wasn't mad, not insane at all. This was real.

Deep in thought, and about to walk on past White Hart Lodge, she caught a sudden movement from within the conservatory and paused. Sylvia had sat bolt upright, her glasses glinting in the candlelight as she looked about in alarm. Had something spooked her?

Hurry...hurry...

Bending down to collect an item that had fallen into the undergrowth on the edge of the garden, a thought popped into her head. Oh, yes, of course. Sylvia's daughter was the arm-linking best friend of Essie Sully, wasn't she? And this looked like a teenaged girl's lip salve if ever there was one. Cherry flavoured. Kezia smeared some on to her own lips, then dropped it into her coat pocket.

But now she must hurry indeed, or it would be too late. This was the night she had waited for. And afterwards there would be no going back. Life would never be the same again. Not for anyone.

***

CHAPTER SIX

The way to the old monastery cut through the deepest part of the forest, well-off any right-of-way. Known as Winters Dipple, this side of the hill was muddy underfoot with no discernible track. Few knew it was here, and as such the thicket was almost impassable. In the dripping darkness it could quickly become disorientating, the only indicators being the presence of ancient landmarks.

The first of these landmarks was a large oak less than ten minutes north of White Hart Lodge. Its huge trunk blocked the way, arms outstretched like one of Tolkien's ents. And quite as if capable of walking, the roots rose from the ground, giving the impression of prising out of it on a dozen or more gnarled legs. They called the mound from which it grew, Hangman's Tump, on account of this being where criminals in bygone days were brought up from the village by cart and hanged. Skirting the tree, she hurried past. It was not a place to linger.

Never has been…never has…

A little further on, a narrow track forked to the right, and Kezia looked out for it now. Marked by a strangely formed yew tree, the pathway zig-zagged down to the witch's altar she normally used. Tonight though, for this most important of invocations to the high demon and his legion, it had to be performed at the monastery ruins – a place of mass death and severe trauma, where few ventured even in daylight and which would possess far stronger energy.

The yew loomed out of the darkness more quickly than expected. Entwined into the crease of a limestone outcrop, it presented an eerie spectacle, like that of a man climbing a rock, with one knee bent higher than the other. Almost upon it before realising, she started at the sight thinking for a moment she had company, then breathed a sigh of relief. Jack, she called him – as in Jack and the Beanstalk, climbing up to the skies. At least this was definitely the right track and it was now safe to pick up pace.

At the top of Winters Dipple, where the forest floor abruptly gave way to a perilous cliff edge and the steep descent to the valley below, came the final marker. This was an outcrop of scowles indigenous to the area. Huge pointed rocks full of iron ore, stood haphazardly among caves and crevices as if dropped there by giants. Covered with feathery moss and tightly-coiled ferns, dead trees grew out of the sides at odd angles, the twigs and branches coated in soft grey lichen that resembled furry fingers.

Untouched, this part of the forest had remained the same for centuries, frequented only by deer, wild boar, squirrels and hares. The poachers in Wolfs Cross never came here, the only part they refused to hunt in. Folklore had it this was a sacred place, where the majestic white stag had been sighted, and it was a sin both against the Crown and God if that magical beast was ever to be maimed or killed. Those who had seen it were left in awe, swearing the stag radiated white light and possessed antlers five feet high or more. The black witch was reputed to have seen him standing on the very ground on which she built her hovel – the house now known as White Hart Lodge.

Those tales were of course, nonsense. People liked, Kezia thought, to make their ancestry and home town sound important even when they weren't. The truth was that they were fireside tales to keep strangers out of a forest where secrets were kept and misdeeds appropriated. And misdeeds were most certainly appropriated here.

On reaching the scowles, she stopped to get her breath and peer over the edge. Her eyes sparked. The monastery looked as if it was lit from within. The stones shone white despite the absence of moonlight or stars, the site shrouded in ethereal mist.

St Benedict's was one of the first Cistercian monasteries in Britain. Built by the French, it was situated on the bend of a river and now lay in ruins. Clearly the building had once been magnificent, with a church of cathedral stature, a chapter house, cloisters and dormitories, along with kitchen gardens, stables and outbuildings. Sometimes, when she stood at the head of the path as she now did, if her visit coincided with one of the hours of prayer, she imagined she could hear bells tolling across the valley. How they rang and rang, those bells etched with crosses, warding off the devil and the wrath of his storms, scaring away the demons.

Here in the woods, as dusk closed to night, it was time for the Office of Compline, the End of Day readings and prayers. She stood quietly, leaning against one of the great boulders, waiting... Yes, there it was, the faint peel of bells, rising and falling with the patter of rain.

It seemed as if time had not only stopped but rewound hundreds of years, the atmosphere vibrating into another age with the precision of a tuning fork. Closing her eyes, she breathed in the wood smoke, lowland vapours, and the damp miasmas of rotting undergrowth. Here in this hidden shadowy place another realm was opening up, a far, far darker one than anything previously experienced. Dusk heralded night. And night was much feared by the monks for being the time when the devil was most active: fear, that most powerful of primitive emotions, the one perversely guaranteed to feed the dark ones and bring them even closer.

She blinked and blinked again, swaying slightly, the trees beginning to whirl around and around. Another vision... She took a deep breath.

And this time the transition was seamless.

White monastic robes glided across the lawns, sweeping indoors as a sharp wind whipped up and the bells echoed as far as the woods. Candles were being lit at one window followed by another then another. Earnest prayers carried on the air...

'Farewell, O Fair Lady and pray for us to Christ...'

How terrified they were, lying wide-eyed on beds of straw wondering what evil the night may bring. How fragile their faith, how paralysed with dread, and how pitiful the knowledge of their fellow men. From sunrise to sunset they toiled in near silence, took meagre meals, and prayed fervently seven times a day.

'*Do not forsake us, Oh Lord, Our God…*'
Silence now… silence til dawn…

Yet the devil moved among them all the while, singling out one here or another there with the demon of distraction, an acedia which rendered them suddenly and unaccountably frustrated beyond measure with cloistered life, either crippling them with inertia or sparking them with mischief. Many rose again at midnight to fend off the omnipotent evil, praying for salvation and safe delivery to dawn.

Like lambs, she saw them trembling in the darkness at the thought of Satan circling the monastery in an ill wind, come to plague their dreams and render them insane. It was pitiful. Contemptible. The devil was there already yet they could not see. He lived in the treacherous one who whored in the village, while professing to sympathise with widows and suffer with the poor. He lived in the one who meted out punishments yet lied in confession to escape it himself. And most of all he lived in the one who sold his soul for power, riches and fleshly pleasures while forcing hard labour and indoctrinating fear in the lower orders. Oh, the devil did well here in the monastery. Very well indeed. Although, and here she paused to concede the point, he usually wanted paying.

There was a feeling here though, that this devil lingered. Perhaps that was the real reason the place remained unspoiled? Despite it being a rich hunting ground even her own tribe avoided it. A heavy oppression weighted the atmosphere, one which lay leaden in the head and chest, giving a sensation of sinister foreboding. On the stillest of days, a whistling breeze would stir in the treetops without affecting the air below, a whispering canopy of silken sways. Buzzards circled and crows cawed as if a storm was coming; and a strange blue haze hovered off the ground.

If ever a place held a powerful telluric energy it was this one. Perhaps that was why the Cistercians had chosen it in the first place? Now though… now there was an added, almost malignant feel to it. And that made it both electrifying and terrifying in equal measure.

A belt of rain spattered against her face, and exhilarated she ran down the slope and across the fields towards the ruins, passing through what had once been the formal gardens, before stepping over the foundation walls and into the core of the monastery. The chapter house where long ago monks had confessed their sins, was east facing, and here the walls were still several feet high on one side, with the river cascading past on the other. And at the back, on the far side, a flight of steps led down into a small, enclosed chamber. This was where she headed now.

Over the years, with this being the only private and covered area, local teens had held séances and Ouija sessions here for a dare. No one came anymore. Said to have once been a punishment room of some sort – a misericord – iron rings remained bolted into the moss-coated wall on the north side, where horseshoe bats now hibernated. Occasionally they could be heard squeaking, and were often seen flying around at dusk; yet even conservationists were reluctant to visit.

A man from the national conservation society had been once to record the flurry of nightly activity, but when he returned to the pub he'd been visibly shaken. The recording hadn't played back what he'd seen. In fact, he'd been so overcome with a terrible sense of dread he couldn't explain, he had apparently given up after less than twenty minutes here, convinced someone then pursued him across the fields and the dark country lane back to the village. After a stiff drink at the bar, he finally plucked up courage to play back what he thought he'd recorded, only to find the whole recording had flipped upside down, and there on camera, amid a horrible growling and scraping noise, a series of sinister, unearthly images had flashed onto the screen.

Inside the chamber the air was icy as a crypt and utterly still. It took a person with little or no sensitivity to enter without any trepidation whatsoever – especially if they'd heard the stories – or one swaggering with drunken bravado.

Yet armed with only the text of an ancient grimoire she could barely decipher, and a few basic tools, Kezia stepped inside.

***

CHAPTER SEVEN

BELINDA

After fleeing the medical centre Belinda had rushed straight home. For a moment back there she'd been close to cracking, the proffered help from Sylvia overwhelmingly tempting.

But she couldn't tell her. Mustn't tell a soul. Besides, Sylvia would be duty bound to take action, and in the same position she would do exactly the same. So how could she possibly divulge what was in her head, let alone say what was going on with Ralph? The consequences would mean an end to everything she'd ever known; were unthinkable.

No, she had to deal with this herself, keep it in the family until one way or another it blew over. All things passed, right? Given time everything, as her mother always said, came out in the wash. 'Fifty years from now,' she'd say, 'and no one will even remember.'

After hurrying down Moss Pike Road she arrived at the genal between her terrace and next door's, thankfully without meeting anyone. The tiny backyard still housed a pebble-dashed coal bunker from a bygone age, and what had once been an outside toilet, now served as a shed. A clothes line had been strung up by the previous owner, the grimy nylon beaded with raindrops. Moss coated the stone walls and the slate tiles were slimed with a coat of green. Putting her key into the backdoor she paused to glance up at the bathroom window, eyeing the row of cleaning fluid bottles silhouetted behind the frosted glass.

Would he be in? She wavered. Oh God, to be frightened of your own son… If only Gideon was here…

Well, he isn't is he?

Her hands shook as she pushed open the door.

You lousy stinking bastard, Gideon Sully. And to think I loved you all those years – wasted years living a fucking lie! How could you? How bloody could you?

Letting herself in, she shouted, "Ralph? You in?"

An overflowing heap of unwashed dishes lay festering in the sink, cereal bowls and empty milk cartons strewn across the worktops. The kitchen stank of old fry-ups, baked-on grime and unemptied bins. Was this her kitchen? Had she left it like this?

He was in alright. From upstairs heavy Goth metal music thumped through the ceiling, reverberating around the walls, relentlessly pulsing through the very fabric of the house. There wasn't a single room in which to escape its screeching metallic rant.

She closed her eyes. Tears burned the retinas. As she stood there with her back to the kitchen sink, put her hands over her face and cried until she was sure her ribs would break. A great overspill of fatigue, worry and despair erupted in breaking, racking sobs – everything she hadn't wanted Sylvia Massey to witness. Tears poured down her cheeks, soaking into her hair as, crumbling to the linoleum floor, all the remaining energy she possessed drained out of her. It was just too much, all too much.

How long she stayed there she didn't know. Half an hour? An hour? But the light had faded when she finally raised her head.

Essie was standing over her in the semi-dark, a look of mortification on her face. "You alright, Mum?"

Christ, did she look alright? But Belinda did what Belinda had always done, and smiled through the swollen blur of misery. "Yeah, sorry," she said, dabbing at her eyes. God, she must look such a mess. "Sorry, love. I just had a bad day, that's all. I felt sick and came home early. Must have picked up a bug or something, I expect. Mind you, I'm not surprised in this filthy kitchen. We need to have a huge clean-up. Sorry, sorry."

Essie stared, squirming slightly. "Do you want me to make you a cup of tea or something? I'll bring it up if you, like, want to go to bed or whatever?"

She held out a hand to be pulled to her feet. "That's very nice of you. Actually, I might take you up on that, if you don't mind." She held onto the kitchen table, fuzzy with tiredness. "Can you manage to get your own meal tonight? Just this one time? There's a frozen pizza in the—"

"Yeah, no probs. Mum, you look terrible – literally all blotchy."

She sighed. There was no one like a teenager to make you feel decrepit and revolting beyond words. "I know."

"What about Ralph?" Essie asked, as Belinda headed towards the stairs. "Shall I make him something, as well?"

Without turning round she stopped with her hand

on the newel post. Hesitated. The very mention of his name made her stomach flip. And then a thought which had previously not occurred to her, did so now. Had he behaved towards Essie in the same way as to herself?

The notion paralysed her. *Oh, dear God!*

"Mum?"

But her daughter appeared unperturbed, her manner chirpy enough. There wasn't a hint of anything untoward. Even so, until she'd got to the bottom of this it would be better if Essie didn't go knocking on his door. "By the look of the kitchen, I'd say he's not going hungry. No, leave him be. Just see to yourself, love."

And lock your door!

She glanced over her shoulder, but Essie had already stuck her iPhone earplugs in and was heading back to the kitchen. No, Essie was fine. There were no signs of distress. It seemed Ralph's malevolence was directed at her and her alone. Perhaps he blamed her for his dad's death? Or maybe Kezia had put thoughts into his head along those lines? Whatever that woman had done to him though, the resulting behaviour crossed all boundaries of what could possibly be classed as normal human resentment.

She bounded up the stairs to the bedroom. That damn bloody music, would it never cease? He never used to be like this. Never. He hadn't been brought up to be so selfish. Would always consider others in the house and put earphones on. It was as if he was going out of his way to torment, like he knew it would bother and annoy her, grind into her psyche and wear her down. It wouldn't affect Essie, who had her own music in her ears. No, this was just for her. He knew she valued peace and quiet at the end of the working day, or a TV programme while she ironed, and had deliberately set out to make her suffer.

Shutting the bedroom door, she began to undress. Insomnia. That was the root cause of her irritation and intolerance: why she couldn't think clearly or seem to help herself. Insomnia due to anxiety.

And the hallucinations? Did it cause those too?

Yes, well those would be due to psychosis, which often came as part of the parcel with depression and anxiety. And no wonder. Who wouldn't be depressed having lost their husband to suicide, found out he was having an affair, discovered they were penniless, been forced to vacate the home they'd spent twenty years building...and then to crown all that...believing they'd steered both children through bereavement had just been told their son was sleeping with the same woman his father slept with. Who just happened to be a Satanist.

You couldn't fucking make it up! She was thumping the pillows and whipping the blankets into shape with every syllable. No wonder she was falling apart.

And the nightmares?

She clambered into bed and pulled the covers up to her neck. Those! Yes, well, they were the worst. The worst imaginable. All of which brought her back to insomnia. And the paralysing fear of falling asleep - the one thing she needed more than anything else on earth. If she could only sleep then it would be possible to cope, heal, come through this, and help Ralph.

There were no tears left, just trickles that traced from the outer corners of her eyes and rolled into her hair.

The sheets were cold and she cursed herself for omitting to make up a hot water bottle, for having to lie here frozen because she hadn't the energy or the inclination to get up again. Bone weary, that's what she was, with a fluttery little heartbeat and a thumping headache. As soon as Essie had brought up the tea, she'd pile on more blankets, wedge the door shut with a chair, then take a couple of paracetamol. They usually knocked her out for a while. There was some cotton wool somewhere too; yes, if she stuffed her ears with that it would muffle the bass beat and hopefully, pray to God, allow for a few hours' sleep.

"Mum? Can I come in?"

"Yes, love."

Essie set a mug of tea down on the bedside table without taking out her earphones.

"Essie, I need to ask you something."

Taking out one earphone, Essie sighed. "Yeah?"

"Is everything okay? School?"

"Yup."

"Friends? Homework?"

"Yeah."

"At home? Are you sleeping okay?"

Essie screwed her face up into an expression of disdain that she should be asked such a thing.

"What about Ralph? Has he spoken to you about anything? You know, after what you told me last week I was wondering if—"

Essie shook her head. "Haven't seen him." She stuck her earplugs back in.

"Wait! Nothing at all? Anything about, well, about—"

"No, Mum. Honest. Sorry, pizza's burning."

Belinda nodded. Okay, so this was definitely just between her and Ralph. It was personal. Not some kind of general sleepwalking problem, but targeted.

Although relieved Essie was not involved, in other ways it puzzled her even more. Ever since he'd backed her out of his room and shut the door in her face, it felt as if the animosity was increasing at a meteoric rate. There was an air of oppression like a storm was about to break, strange noises came from his room that sounded like an old man laughing to himself, and sometimes there were heavy rumbling noises like furniture being moved around. Could be she was imagining it…Like everything else…

Perhaps this was insanity? That's what they'd say - Sylvia, Mark, Arran, her mother, the neighbours… *And no wonder, look at what she's gone through!*

She took a sip of tea then got up and wedged a chair underneath the door handle. Since the incident the other night there was no taking chances. It was not something she was ever likely to forget or wished to be repeated. In fact, if she ever managed to erase it from her mind it would be a blessing.

It haunted her constantly. And probably always would.

A couple of nights after Essie's revelation, she had been woken in the early hours by a slight draught on her face. The bedroom door was opening. A strip of silvery light stretched across the carpet, and there in the doorway was the outline of a man. Just standing there watching. She had lain with the breath frozen in her lungs, confused at first as to who it was.

Her mind scrambled around. Gideon's ghost? A burglar?

The figure seemed then to float towards the bed.

Every muscle in her body tensed for flight, her eyes wide, straining to see in the dark. Then just as she was about to leap from the bed, an image took shape. Not that of a burglar or a ghost, but of her son – made distinctive by his floppy dark hair, the shapeless zipped sweatshirt and swamp pants. Relieved, she let go of her held-in breath and began to prop herself up. He must be sleepwalking. God, he hadn't done that since he was a child…

"Benedicta?"

"What?"

His voice nearly stopped her heart. It wasn't Ralph's, but deep, and intoned with a slightly foreign accent.

The moment of confusion cost her. Now there was no longer time to get to the light switch or the phone. Who the hell was it? Not Ralph, not her son…who? "Oh God, what do you want? Money? My watch? Take it all, it's—"

"Ah, Benedicta!"

Too late. Bending over the bed he was peering quizzically into her face and she jumped sharply back against the headboard, scrambling to get out. She had seen him clearly though, quite clearly, and it was definitely, indisputably, Ralph.

"Oh my good God, you scared me half to death. I think you're sleepwalking—"

He was climbing onto the bed, crawling closer. "Benedicta, I have found you, after all this time."

"What? Ralph, I'm your mum. You're sleepwalking,

love. Dreaming."

Doing her utmost to keep her voice steady, she glanced at the digital clock. It was two in the morning. She began to inch away from him and out of the other side. "Come on, let's get you back to bed. You're in a dream—"

What occurred next happened so fast she still had only had a vague recollection, but one moment she was preparing to help him back to bed, the next a hand had lunged for her throat and he'd hurled himself on top of her.

In the struggle to escape she cracked her head on the bedside table, but managed to spring out and scrabble to the far side of the room, keeping her back to the wall like a wild, caged animal. In the neon light emanating through the crack in the door, presumably from his TV or computer, the eyes challenging hers were oil-slick black and no longer almond shaped but small and round as marbles. And was it a terrible hallucination or was his face really distorting before her very eyes? No longer soft skinned with the downy trace of a moustache, his complexion looked deeply lined and reptilian in texture, the nose triangular and flat, the mouth that of a craggy old-man's. She stared in horror. It was as if another person's image had superimposed onto her teenage son's face – like a double exposure. Transfixed, her brain fought to find a logical explanation, a way through the adrenalin rush of panic.

Holding out both her palms to face him in a placatory gesture, she forced herself to keep calm. Whatever was happening he seemed to believe she was someone else and that made him very dangerous indeed, not just to herself but potentially to Essie. Her glance flicked to the bedroom door and the landing, as slowly now, and carefully, she crept around the perimeter of the wall, keeping her voice as steady and soothing as possible.

"Ralph! Listen to me, I'm your mum. Ralph, this is a bad dream you're having. Come now, come with me, let's get you back to your room. This is just a bad dream, come on…"

He stood motionless and immovable, and it took every scrap of courage to reach out and touch his arm as over and over again she reminded his subconscious mind who he was. "Ralph? Ralph?"

Confusion reigned. But after many minutes of explaining and cajoling, the blackness of his eyes began to shift and lighten. Still the pupils were abnormal, altering shape, his expression fuzzy and unfocused.

She held her nerve, thinking only of her daughter in the next room. "Come on, Ralph. Ralph! This is your mum, Ralph."

The situation, she realised, could go either way.

"You're sleepwalking, sweetheart. Having a dream. Let me take you back to your room like I used to, hmmm? Remember when you were a little boy and we'd go and read that favourite story of yours. What was it? Can you remember?"

Thankfully, he'd let her lead him back to his bedroom, after which she'd barred the door with a chair. And next day the music was back on full volume and she hadn't slept for more than an hour since, and that was now getting on for a week. Although there had been no repeat of the incident she'd instructed Essie to use the lock on her door because Ralph was sleepwalking like he did when he was little, and it could be frightening.

During the day he rarely emerged from his room, obviously only creeping out when she'd gone to work. Once or twice she knocked on his door to ask if he was alright, and sometimes she swore he was in there talking rapidly to someone in another language. Other times there came manic laughter from within, even though he was alone. Explaining it away to herself she'd rationalised he was perhaps on the phone. But she knew, deep down, that she was kidding herself. The laughter was of a caustic, nasty variety and lasted for many minutes, sounding much as she remembered from the psychiatric unit of her training days.

It was going to come to a head, of course it was, but day by day she did her best to monitor his behaviour whilst feeling increasingly fatigued and confused herself. No sooner had a thought or decision formed in her head when it dissolved and she couldn't for the life of her remember what it was. Her head ached with a pain that cramped up through the skull, her surroundings fuzzy and vague. Voices echoed and mumbled in a background hum, the level of concentration needed just to function more and more of a strain. The days blurred into one another, whipping past so that now a week had gone by and here it was, getting worse.

Slipping back under the icy sheets, she downed the tea Essie had brought, then swallowed a couple of paracetamol and an antihistamine. With a proper night's sleep it would all look different in the morning. That was all that was wrong with her. What Ralph needed was professional care and it was her job to take him because this could not go on. It had to be someone he would open up and talk to because he sure as hell wouldn't talk to her. Perhaps she could ask Arran? Oh God, no – far too old-school and condemnatory. Ralph would be sectioned with schizophrenia in a heartbeat and then the village would know. Mark, then? Could it be kept secret? It would mean Sylvia being involved too though, and for some reason…

For some reason, what?

She shook her head, trying to clear the clouds that had once again massed into brain fog. One solid night sleep was all that was needed, and then…then… she could think things through… sort it all out like she always had and always would. Just one night sleep without interruption, intrusive thoughts, or nightmares …please…please…

This couldn't go on, it just couldn't. But then again, how did it end? None of this must ever come out, not in a place with a history like this one. Just look at where those who went mad ended up?

So how then, did she get help?

***

CHAPTER EIGHT

Mid-dream and someone was running a brush through her hair. The sensation was pleasurable yet at the same time sinister, the person wielding the brush attempting to lull her into submission.

Relax and just let go… come on… let it happen…fall, fall…

Progressively becoming aware of slipping into danger, her conscious mind suddenly interjected. She was still asleep. Must wake up.

No, stop, no, I don't want this! No!

Forcing herself awake, she immediately reached to the back of her head and stroked her hair. Softly she ran a hand down its length. It felt fly-away, as if indeed it had recently been brushed. Well, that was weird, the dream so real.

Heart still thumping hard, she peered into the darkness. How long had she been asleep? At least she'd had some. Was it morning yet?

An amber glow from the streetlight shone through the curtains, and a squally belt of rain splattered against the window.

Something didn't feel quite right.

Her glance flicked to the door. The chair was still wedged underneath the handle.

But something was definitely amiss, a sensation of

not being alone. Unease crawled over her skin as slowly she scanned the room inch by inch. The silence was deadening, the smell of damp wallpaper and mould spores more pronounced than ever. It was seriously freezing in here. The bedroom was always cold, especially so in March when the months of winter had not yet relinquished their grip, and this house with its thick walls preserved the chill like a morgue. But this was more than simple cold and damp. It was icy.

Her breath clouded on the air as gradually the mists of her dreamlike state cleared, her eyes adjusted, and the outline of her mother's heavy oak furniture loomed from the shadows. A streak of bluish light from underneath the door suggested a computer or television was still on, but the house was absolutely silent.

So why then, would every instinct, every nerve and every cell of her body, be on high alert? A cursory glance at the clock told her it was quarter to three in the morning. And she was definitely alone in here.

Perhaps it was a carry-over of fear invoked from the nightmare? They could be very real and leave a feeling of being deeply disturbed for a long time afterwards. In vain she tried to capture the essence of it, but had only the vague fluttering impression of being watched. Watched as she slept. Her eyes burned into the darkest corners of the room, examining every item. The hooks on the back of the door…yes, those were just robes hanging there not ghouls floating above the ground. The music box on the chest of drawers, which had been hers as a child, given to Essie then salvaged in the move. Would it pop open and play 'Swan Lake'?

Stop it!

And the wardrobe…had the door creaked open another inch? Had that flowery arm of a blouse been sticking out like that when she went to sleep?

Stop it!

Unable to tamp down the rising panic, her eyes pierced the darkness until they ached. The thing was, the horrible, horrible thing, was that the temperature seemed to be plunging rapidly, plummeting to that of a deep freeze. Her teeth began to chatter in her head and despite the weight of the blankets her back was frozen to ice.

It couldn't be blamed on Ralph this time. The feeling of being stared at from the darkness had followed her out of the dream into reality, and was now impossible to shake. Almost like the presence of another, the shadow of another being brought forth, about to manifest…

Slowly, carefully, still scanning every inch of the room, she began to shuffle towards the bedside table, her hand reaching out for the lamp. Damn, where was it? She found the wire and clutched at it, pulling it towards her. In the blind scuffle a mug fell to the floor and for a fleeting moment she turned to locate the switch. Which was when something tugged, deliberately and quite hard, on her hair.

Flying out of bed she ran towards the light switch on the wall yet. Nothing happened. It wouldn't work. Why? Why? Swinging back around she stared into the darkness of the room. There was absolutely nothing there. Nothing. Her heart thump-thump-thumped in her ears and burned into the pulse points. And then unbelievably she heard her own voice say, "Gideon?"

Instantly she regretted that.

Stupid, stupid.

Tears of fear and pain stung her eyes.

Alright, Bel, calm down. Deep breaths. This is not your husband's ghost. This is just fear. A nightmare and a bad time with Ralph. Tiredness and depression and…

A short, sharp breath of air blew onto her cheek. A small puff of air from someone standing right next to her.

This was a serious night terror. A dream from which she must wake up.

But her eyes were open. Wide open. And then with a mighty bang in the centre of her chest all became clear.

In front of her, as she stood shivering and terrified, was the personification of her nightmares. No more scrabbling around trying to recall the face that watched her as she slept. This was him. He'd chosen precisely when to reveal himself, and when to sear the image onto her mind.

Wearing a white cowled robe, a man of peculiarly inhuman appearance stood, or hovered, she couldn't say which, before her.

And then he was gone.

Leaving behind an image so distinct and so disturbing, she continued to see him long after the room began to thaw by degrees and her heartbeat steadied. Beneath the hood, round black eyes had glinted from an empty abyss; the flesh the pallor of a corpse a day or so before it decomposed. His nose was wide and triangular with gaping nostrils, the skin wizened to hide, and the mouth blackened with diseased gums and rotten teeth. An ugly man he had most indisputably been, but neither that nor the fact he had appeared as a ghostly apparition were what chilled her the most. It was the eyes. They were so profoundly unsettling it was nigh impossible to look into them without the dread of somehow being corrupted, of falling.

Fall…let it happen…fall, fall…

Burdo.

The name. A sigh. A whisper from the corners of the room as if the essence of him still lingered.

How? Why would that name come to her?

'Because it is my name, of course,' said a deep, accented voice that resounded from inside her head. 'Enchanté, Benedicta'.

***

CHAPTER NINE

SYLVIA

After she'd found Belinda's note on the staffroom table, Sylvia had hurried over to Mark's office.

"Belinda's gone," she said, sitting on the chair just vacated by his last patient.

Still tapping away at his computer he didn't look up. "What do you mean, gone?"

Trying to keep her voice down in case the patients in the waiting room overheard, she shook her head in frustration. "Gone, as in upped and left. What do you think I mean? Here, look!"

Mark took the note she thrust under his nose, read it and handed it back. "So she's not feeling herself! I'm sure she'll ring tomorrow morning. Look sorry, Syl, but I've got seven more patients to see now instead of five, and I should've knocked off half an hour ago. And there are two home visits."

"Two minutes won't make much difference, then. And this is Belinda we're talking about. Just hear me out, will you? Please? It's just that Bel wasn't just, 'not herself,' she was extremely unwell. I mean, mentally and spiritually—"

"Oh, for fuck's sake. Look, can't we talk about this later? I mean, how urgent is Belinda's spiritual health exactly?"

"That means shut up and don't mention it again. But this needs to be discussed. I'm really worried about her. So when later?"

"I don't know—"

"Exactly. So it was a fob off. When do we ever talk these days? If you're not here you're at a meeting or over at the hospital, and if you've got a free moment it'll be the bloody golf course before me. When do we ever actually discuss anything?"

"Please don't do this here."

What infuriated her the most, was the more irate she became the more he adopted the quiet condescending tone of a parent trying to subjugate a rambunctious child.

"I'm not doing anything here. My voice is barely a whisper. I simply need to talk to you, but it seems I have to not only make an appointment but justify the need for one too. How dare you talk down to me as if I've come in here for a domestic! I'm trying to tell you that there is something badly wrong with Belinda – our nurse and our friend – and I think with her daughter too. And since I'm on the subject, and you know this is true because she's told you as much, there is something scaring the crap out of our own daughter at home. Something in that house. And then there are patients up at Temple Lake who, one after the other, are telling us they're frightened half to death, seeing demons and having night terrors —"

"Yes, and I've prescribed anxiolytics and sleeping tablets for every single one of them, they're winding each other up. You of all people should know that hysteria spreads—"

"Oh, I see, just zonk them out so they don't cause a fuss. Great answer and easy as piss for you to sort." She stood up. "Alright, it'll keep for a bit longer, I suppose, but I do need to talk to you properly, calmly, rationally. And sooner rather than later, okay?"

He turned once more to face the computer screen, his mouth set in a grim line. "I'll look forward to that, dearest."

The temptation to slam the door on her way out was overwhelming. Instead she smiled breezily at the waiting patients before walking briskly down the corridor to her own office at the far end. Hers overlooked the church, with Barons Wood behind it, and was the quietest part of the medical centre. Private clients never came here. They would be seen at the various clinics to which she travelled for the express purpose. This office was for NHS referrals for a variety of psychological pathology. And there was one more to see that day.

Sitting on a chair outside her office, Paige Morse was waiting. Paige hailed from Wolfs Cross on the outskirts of the village, although Sylvia guessed that as soon as she saw her. Outside in the carpark, visible through the venetian blinds, a man was waiting for her in the driver's seat of a dilapidated truck. Cigarette smoke fugged the cabin as, with a baseball cap pulled low over his face, he slid down in the seat.

"Sorry to keep you waiting. Would you like to come through, Paige?"

On all the documented accounts Paige was down as being eighteen. Truth was she was fifteen, and heavily pregnant. Tapping into the computer, Sylvia scanned reams and reams of notes as quickly as possible, much of it in bold and heavily underlined. Paige had scoliosis, rendering her back twisted to one side, and her facial symmetry was out of alignment, with one eye slanting downwards at the outer corner and positioned significantly lower than the other.

"When are you due?"

"June."

Clearly there was no point in asking who the father was or why she had absconded from various places of refuge over the past six months. Social Services had visited her many times, but ultimately Paige was adamant she wanted to stay in Wolfs Cross with her grandfather, Kade Morse.

"Is that your grandfather waiting outside for you?"

Paige nodded.

Medical tests showed the baby was healthy and although there were many question marks beside her stated age, with medical examinations and outward appearances suggesting she must be considerably younger, the girl insisted she was eighteen and the professionals were wrong. Unfortunately, many of the births at Wolfs Cross went unregistered and it seemed Paige was another who'd slipped through the net, at least until her first hospital appointment when she had presented with a twisted spine.

Her father was violent towards her, she said, and her grandfather had volunteered to take care of her and the child.

Paige answered each question monosyllabically and without interest. Although she'd attended the special-needs school in the village, those attendances had been rare, and as a last resort tutors had been sent to her home, although they were subsequently refused entry. It was doubtful the girl could read or write.

"So tell me what's been happening, Paige? The doctor says you've been behaving oddly, feeling violent and flying into rages?"

Paige stared at her.

"Is that true? Do you often feel angry?"

"No."

"When do you feel angry, would you say?"

She shrugged, and looked away. Towards the truck in the yard.

"Paige? The police arrested you for assault last week. Your, erm, sister, was she?"

"She ain't moy sester."

"The other girl isn't related to you? It says here she lives at Wolfs Cross, her name is

Courtney-Ann Morse and she's fourteen. Are you sure she's not related?"

"Cousin or somethin'.'

"So why did you become angry with her? Do you want to tell me what happened?"

Paige shrugged again.

"Okay." She read out loud from the report in front of her. "It says here, and I quote, 'She exploded into rage, baring her teeth and growling like a wild animal. I thought I was going to die. One minute my sister was calm and the next she'd smashed a glass and attacked me with it. I had to have stitches in my face and she fractured my jaw.'" Sylvia turned to face her. "Are you seriously telling me you don't feel angry?"

Paige stared at her for an uncomfortably long time, her expression glacial and distracted.

Sylvia took a deep breath. This wasn't going to go anywhere. It was always the same – usually cat fights and sexual jealousy, or drink and drugs. About to ask about the latter because of the unborn child, it therefore came as a total surprise when Paige's whole demeanour began to change, from her voice and facial expression, to her personality. The lax muscles of her face tightened incrementally like that of a marionette pulled by strings; the mouth hardened to a peevish line, and a spark fired deep within the dullness of her eyes. The transformation from 'no one home', to alight with spirit was so rapid it caught her completely unaware. A totally different person had emerged.

And when she spoke it was with clipped, quick-fire hostile retorts, albeit with the same vocal chords, "What the fuck is it to you? You should leave her alone and stop prying. Go fuck yourself."

Sylvia reeled back, quickly adjusting to the new situation. Did she have dissociative identity disorder, she wondered? It was possible, seeing as child abuse had been likely. Certainly the possibility of this being an alter personality had to be ruled out before anything more sinister could be suspected.

"Who am I speaking to?"

The voice snickered nastily. "Oh, so you see me, do you? That's interesting."

The accent was not a local one. It sounded, if she wasn't mistaken, slightly French.

"Who are you? Do you have a name?"

"You should leave that house in the woods. You don't belong there." The girl's eyes bored into hers. "If you don't they will make you."

For a second or two she hesitated. Okay, so this wasn't an alter personality, but an infesting spirit. He or she knew about her home and was making threats. She had neither the time nor the necessary privacy for a spirit release session, but it was worth a try. "Whoever you are, you're doing this young girl a lot of damage, preventing her from—"

"She's a fucking half-wit. And besides, I like what she gets and I intend to stay." The eyes glittered and the mouth puckered with amusement. "If you know what I mean?"

Sylvia nodded. It would be unethical to continue this any further without Paige's consent. "Let me speak to Paige now."

"Don't ask her anything more! If you persist you will be very sorry. Extremely sorry. Or your daughter will. She looks like you, with light brown hair and glasses, yes? Ah, she's so pretty and small…But she hitches up her skirt on the way to school, then pulls it down again on the way home through the woods. Didn't you know? Yes, she takes the short cut even though you told her not to. And she wears her hair high up, like so?" Here Paige demonstrated a ponytail on the top of her head.

"Enough. Let me speak to Paige."

"Yes, you can imagine Molly – it is Molly, isn't it? – walking down the dark corridor to the bathroom, alone at night without her glasses…You can see her blanch with a terror she will never forget… the scream etched on her face the moment her heart stops—"

"Paige? Can you hear me?"

Sylvia's pulse began to race. This girl had no understanding or control over her conscious mind, and there had been no warning or preparation for this.

She raised her voice to a command and repeatedly called her name. "Paige, talk to me! Paige!"

Eventually the shadow lifted from the girl's face and the muscles relaxed. She blinked and turned to look at her. "I feel sick."

Feeling rather queasy herself, Sylvia reached for a receptacle and plonked it on the desk in front of her. "Do you need to be sick right now? I'll get you some water."

Her hands were shaking as she filled the paper cup. That attachment knew about the dark spirits inside her home, how much they frightened both herself and her daughter. Was it all connected? She tried to focus on the job in hand. Whether it was a lower entity or a demon, and it was impossible to say which it was, they would bully and rage and threaten, basically do and say anything, to avoid leaving the host. They knew how to scare and went all out to do so. Frankly, on this occasion it had worked. The important thing was to recognise it for what it was and make sure this girl was treated properly, and soon, so she could be saved from what would inevitably drain her life force and destroy the unborn child too.

"Paige, do you find you lose time? Like you suddenly realise a lot of time has gone by but you don't remember anything?"

"Yeah, that happens a lot."

"I'm guessing you don't remember fighting Courtney-Ann or losing your temper, then?"

Paige shrugged. "She's lying."

"No, she ended up in hospital and there were

witnesses. But I do agree with you that it's possible you don't recall doing it. Okay, here's what I think we should do. I think we need some therapy sessions and we need to start as soon as possible. I can help you but I need you to work with me on this, okay? You must come to the session, it's really important."

"Does that mean I'll get signed off from Jobseekers? I can't work, I told them."

"Yes, but you must come to the treatment session. Look, we need to…" Here she took a deep breath because what she proposed had to be off the record. "We need to do some calming sessions – meditation – and if you're agreeable, hypnosis. I think it will help."

"If I get moy money, that be alroight, I s'pose."

Sylvia nodded. A tiny snag of fear caught and lodged in her gut. There was no way she could simply go home and forget about what was happening in this village. Sorry, Mark! But this girl was an innocent and so were all the others with spirit attachments. The old lady, Belinda, and Essie were all cases in point. Nothing, she was absolutely convinced, was coincidental. Everything had fallen into place far too easily; from the vacancies for hers and Mark's positions, to the house coming onto the market at precisely the moment they needed it. Yes, she was here for a reason, alright. And the full horror of what she may be facing was only now beginning to dawn.

She flicked through her diary. "Friday alright for you? Three o'clock?"

"Yeah."

"Good." Handing her a reminder card, she added. "I can't stress enough how important it is that you attend, do you understand?"

"Yeah."

"Will your grandfather be bringing you?"

"Yeah."

"Okay, well please tell him that you must be on time and that we will need at least two hours."

Without answering, Paige put the card in her jacket pocket and stood up.

"Do you understand, Paige?"

The girl had the door open before she swung around and spoke in another voice entirely, this time that of a much older woman with a local accent, "You don't know your 'usband very well, do you, moy lovely?"

The whole encounter had left her with a lingering darkness, which shivered underneath her skin like a virus. The hypnotherapy session with Paige would not be one to look forward to any more than the old lady's at Temple Lake. And exactly as had happened after leaving both the nursing home earlier, and then Bel less than an hour ago, an image flickered in and out of her mind, so fleeting it was impossible to grasp. Yet this time she acknowledged the presence.

A flash of white. A face gone as quickly as it appeared.

Who are you?

Her question was followed by a void of darkness. And the silence of a tomb.

***

CHAP+ER TEN

You're not safe...

There could be any number of things causing this unease, she thought, looking around the candle-lit conservatory. The day had left in its wake the strangest sensation of being watched from darker realms, as if she had been noticed. It had happened before. She was communing with spirits, and the lower entities hovering around the living didn't like it. Interference was rarely tolerated by those who had no intention of being moved on, and she knew just how malicious they could be. How they could grind you down with fear and madness.

The threat regarding Molly's mental health had been particularly worrying, followed by seeds of doubt and jealousy regarding her marriage - just to remind her how low and dirty the dark side played. Mark's attitude hadn't helped, either. A lack of belief and support never did, serving only to increase her sense of isolation.

There was something in this house though, and the spirit residing in Paige Morse knew it...

Overhead, creaking floorboards suggested Mark was heading for his study. He did have a pile of work to do, that was true, so it was probably best to give him another hour before she went up for a word. For a word they most definitely needed to have.

He was the one who had craved this rural idyll and

gone after the partnership here. Adamant about how fantastic it would be to go back to his roots. How brilliant for them all to breathe fresh air and go to sleep listening to the owls in the woods. All fine and she'd agreed right the way down the line, never uttered a squeak of protest. So, he could bloody well listen now to the only concern she'd ever raised the whole time they'd been here. And it involved their own family, for God's sake. What had got into him?

She'd known him pretty much all her adult life, and in all that time he'd never been anything other than honest, kind and loving – even boyishly exuberant. Mark loved being a doctor. When she'd met him he was still an SHO contemplating a career in psychiatry, but many years later, after a stint as a registrar, he switched to the general practitioner course. Financially it made more sense, he said, as well as offering more freedom in terms of location. Plus, it would still be possible to work as an associate in psychiatry, to keep his hand in. Wouldn't it be great to bring up their family in the place his great-grandparents had lived? *Just think…imagine…what if… and how magical…* She'd been caught up in his infectious enthusiasm, never hesitating for one second.

Tears stung her eyes like hot needles recalling how things used to feel between them. Had always been until they came here. To this place. And this house.

God, was she losing him?

Something had changed, incrementally and surreptitiously, yet now she recognised it, it seemed sudden. Again a shiver worked its way up her spine to the nape of her neck, and she brushed at the cool spot of skin with her hand. *Something else here was at play.* Definitely. Something bad was coming, and if she wasn't supremely careful it was going to undermine everything she held dear.

Many would dismiss this feeling of trepidation as a fertile imagination – if they couldn't see something it didn't exist – but she knew better than to ignore the signs. Spirit phenomena, as she repeatedly tried to convince every medic she'd ever met, was beyond the senses and artifices of mental cognition. As a result of general disbelief however, a great many people were not only unable to get the correct help they needed, but were in terrible danger of losing their sanity, as well.

She reached for the bundle of wrapped white sage she kept to hand, lit it and let it smoke for a while, then proceeded to walk around the room smudging and cleansing the air. Afterwards she relit the smudge and repeated the process throughout the house, lingering in the corridor leading to the bathroom, unable to erase the thought that had been placed in her head - of Molly's small face frozen in terror.

"Air, fire, water, earth…Cleanse, dismiss, dispel!"

From within Mark's office there came the sound of tapping on his computer keyboard and the drone of a documentary. The house now reeked of smoky sage. It should have dispersed the negative energy though, and with that thought she crept past unheard. Back in the conservatory she placed crystals all around her and then sitting down once more, forced herself to concentrate on meditation, breathing deeply in and out, drawing in a powerful white light that filled her body and enveloped her aura.

In and out … In and out…

The method transported her gradually into a trance state, anxiety receding, the only sound that of her own breathing and the occasional squall of sleety rain on the glass.

Then something, a tiny incongruity – she couldn't say what – began to pull her out of it. Like a sparkle in the sand, it caught her attention and once seen she could no longer deny its existence. Slowly, unable to help herself she emerged from meditation and opened her eyes.

There! The stealthiest of movements outside!

Heartbeat on hold, her eyes bored into the darkened windows.

Someone was there.

She blew out the candles and waited for her sight to adjust. Only the outline of the forest was visible, the spears of treetops black against the cloudy sky. It seemed unearthly silent. That was the first sign all was not well. The second was a wink of movement at the far end of the lawn where it bordered the woods. There were heat-sensor lights at various points along the perimeter fence, usually and frequently activated by foxes and rabbits. Whoever was there however, was not a creature but human; the length of a distorted outline flashing briefly across the grass as they darted between the trees.

From west to east.

Sylvia frowned. But that old path didn't lead anywhere. Neither she nor Mark had ever used it, but when they'd first bought the house an ancient right of way had been pointed out, one that eventually emerged at the monastery ruins. But that was a good mile out of the village, even if you did want to go there on a cold, sleety night in March.

Someone was there, though…

It left her unsettled and a little afraid. And then unspeakably angry. She needed to talk about this. No matter how bizarre it sounded, if she was frightened and Molly was frightened then Mark should bloody well give a damn. He should care that people in the village were sick in their droves, that the elderly were frightened in that nursing home, and his own daughter was terrified in this house. Oh yes, and that their marriage wasn't only the last thing on his list but didn't appear to feature on it at all.

And why was he so scathing about all things spiritual, when he knew it was what she did, that it was her passion? Why wouldn't he even discuss anything to do with the village, and most particularly anything to do with Belinda? They had always talked.

You don't know your husband very well do you, my lovely?

She gripped the armrests of the chair, then sprang upright. Right, that was it. It was time to have this out.

***

CHAPTER ELEVEN

Kezia

The chamber, as she stepped inside, was both freezing and coal-face black. The stench of bat droppings was noxious, and the tomb-like space quickly closed in around her. A peculiarly icy breeze seemed to emanate from the smaller room at the back, along with a low hum like a wind tunnel.

Steeling herself, she strode into the middle and slipped the canvas bag from her shoulder. This must be done. It had to be. She could not and would not take much more. The indignity, humiliation and poverty were grinding her down. Clint's mocking expression, the smirk on Maxine Lee's face, the misery of vomiting in the sluice this afternoon, all replayed in her head. So now here she was, in the arctic chill of this horrible place, about to discover what everything had been leading to. She gritted her teeth together to stop them from chattering as she knelt to unpack what she'd brought.

The torch did little to illuminate the chamber, its dim orb bobbing around the walls, picking out dripping moss, a low ridge of crumbling stones – presumably the dividing wall between this and the misericord at the back – and in the corner the flick a rat's tail as it fled the light. The wall on the east side had been sketched with something, and she leaned closer. It looked like a widdershins spiral from occult practice, the vortex unsealed. Drawn long ago it was faint, but as she traced her finger over its mark an odd tingle raced up her arm and she jumped back.

The cold blackness seemed to crawl up her back, damp seeping through her thin clothing in an icy shiver. Her breath misted on the air as she set down the torch and began to prepare for the rite. Never before had she dared to summon the demon, Malphas, himself. And certainly not in a place like this, with so much power. The atmosphere crackled with static, the energy intense. Little wonder with a history like this one. To date she had used the witch's altar and paid homage to him, requesting guidance and validation But enough was enough. It was now time to bring this to a conclusion.

The one inside fizzed with excitement, making her palms sweat and her fingers shake. Images were flashing into her head of Belinda Sully's face, of sores spreading across it, weeping and full of pus; of hair rinsing down the sink in great, swirling clumps, of night terrors blighted by the one who snooped and spied in the forest. The one whose eyes followed the women who dared walk alone, whose lips wetted as he stalked and watched and waited.

Rage and revulsion rose from inside as she worked, setting out the tools needed as if she had done it all her life. And coherent thoughts tailed away as the one inside took over.

How thee blighted my life! How disgusting I found thee. Go haunt her now, go infest her dreams, do what thou will, but be gone from me…

Her facial muscles had set to stone, jaw grinding as she set a black candle at each of the four compass points. Taking pains to follow the grimoire precisely, she adorned a makeshift altar with an inverted pentacle, incense of storax, and libations of herbs and mead. These were the preferred gifts for raising Malphas, as was the planetary alignment of Mercury in Libra. In sorcery, each of the seventy-two demons had an exact list of preferences and must be communicated with personally and worshipped accordingly. Everything had been planned for this rite.

Now for the all-important sigil. According to the grimoire, a demon must always be called by their name, and the sigil, like a coat of arms, had to be perfect, copied meticulously and with no small detail incorrect. For this was the most powerful tool a sorceress had – the name and identifying mark of the demon she wished to invoke. By focusing on the name, the demon should by all accounts present himself. This was drawn on a scrap of animal hide and carved into each of the burning candles; all of them over-scribed with her own blood.

As she worked, a feeling of oppression began to build, pulsating and powerful, the candlelit cavern flickering with shadows. And the hands seemed alien to her: these were not her hands with black marks on the fingers. They seemed inept and clumsy. Yet the rush of anticipation felt as the hands took hold of the etched ink sigil, and took out a blade, was real enough. A thousand memories poured back in. The deal was about to be sealed.

A surge of excited glee erupted inside at the sight of

the knife.

Do it!

She cut deeply and diagonally into the tender flesh of her inner arm. It stung and smarted. The skin spliced open in an oozing weal. She stared at the gaping wound, watching as the blood beaded and glistened before pulsing out of the tissue in arterial spurts. Immediately a surge of euphoria flooded her body, the sharp sting fading as the elation of release took over. Life drained away and it was glorious. Ruby red globules ran down her arm and dripped onto the sigil. And it was all she could do to not let it continue.

She heard laughing. Was it her own laughter ringing around the room?

Tearing herself away from the sight, and the sensation of intensely pleasurable relief, she pressed on a dressing pad taken from the nursing home, and wrapped a bandage around her arm, before burning the blood-soaked sigil and dropping it into a glass jar of devil's claw, stinging nettles and elderberries. These were her gifts to Malphas, laced with her own fresh blood. She offered them to him, then picked up the mead and drank, setting down the rest for the demon.

Every detail was now correct.

She stared defiantly into the candlelight, her voice sounding peculiar to her own ears, as if it was very far away.

"I'm doing what you ask, and you can have my pathetic soul, but you have to give me and my son a life worth having. Give me my dark desires. And then you can have my soul and welcome. But not…hear me…not before I get what I want!"

The smell of dirt, animal excretions and damp rapidly became more prevalent, and all four of the candles fluttered and danced.

"Right," she said, feeling less sure. "Let's do this."

With the torch trained on the grimoire she began the conjuration. Citing the words loudly, her voice echoed like a bell into the abyss. Her own tiny figure she saw as if looking down from on high: a girl cross-legged on the stone floor, head bent, the pale neck so fragile.

"I do invocate, conjure and command thee, O' thou Spirit Malphas, to appear and to show thyself visibly in fair and comely shape, without any deformity or tortuosity…"

The text was long and difficult, and as she read the first bite of night's chill sank into her skin. Only the candles, which periodically flattened and spat for no apparent reason, lent any orientation at all. On and on she read the ancient script, at times feeling as if she was flailing around in space, with no concept of where the walls or roof or floor were. All reality dropped away, her own voice resounding in her ears as if it was a foreign tongue, the whole experience strangely dislocating.

Until finally she finished and became aware of herself in her own body once more. "Wherefore, come thou, visibly, speaking with a clear and perfect voice, intelligibly, and to mine understanding."

He should now appear.

She stopped reading, put down the grimoire and switched off the torch. The darkness hissed, the candles fizzed, and rain pattered solidly on the grass outside.

"Are you here?"

The answer lay in the silence. In the utter emptiness

of a deserted ruin in the rain.

An icy gust blew with force onto the back of her neck, and she shuddered all over.

"Are you here?"

Minutes passed. The rain intensified, firing like millions of pieces of shrapnel onto the stones above.

Nothing's happening. Nothing.

Grabbing the torch she flicked through the pages, ignoring three further required rites and going straight to the penultimate conjuration, the one to use if the demon did not appear. After that lay the ultimate, threatening curse. The wording was strong and doubts flooded in, even as her hands shook with disappointment and rage. This stuff had probably never truly worked. The whole thing was a stupid lie! Why had she even come here? Drugs, false hope or madness? Alright, so Belinda Sully's husband was dead and the woman now lived in a stinking terrace on a main road, but that was because he'd been a sucker for an easy lay and was heavily in debt. The matrimonial bomb was going to drop anyway. Nothing to do with her raising demons! She'd been kidding herself. And there was nothing in this for her.

But you saw Malphas…he spoke to you… Stay with it…

Shut up! Whoever you are, shut up!

Would the voice inside of her ever be still? Always telling her what to do, even taking over so she couldn't remember who she was or where she was.

Angrily she took a deep breath and shouted the words of the final conjuration with self-righteous authority.

"I do by the power of these names the which no creature is able to resist, curse thee into the depth of the Bottomless Abyss, there to remain unto the Day of Doom in chains, and in fire and brimstone unquenchable, unless thou forthwith appear here and do my will–"

There was a rustling noise nearby. Was someone there?

Ralph?

Silence.

Pray it wasn't that dumb wit boy! Had he followed her again?

She waited a few moments.

No, there was no one there.

Picturing Malphas now as she had last seen him, focusing on his image and his name with all her mind, she continued, "And therefore come thou peaceably in these names of God, Adonal, Zabaoth, Amioran; come thou; come thou, for it is the King of Kings who commands you–"

There. The noise came again. And her heart lurched.

A large raven had flown into the chamber and now regarded her from the entrance.

***

CHAPTER TWELVE

The raven hopped inside the chamber. A singular bird appearing incongruously at night, with apparently little apprehension at approaching a human being, it cocked its ebony head to one side and studied her rudely before hopping closer.

Her heartbeats lumped into a ball of lead and stopped her breath, the power of the moment electrifying. She stared, violet eyes wide, mesmerised.

What the fuck?

Within the flame-flickering chamber the air was smoky, the rain drip-drip-dripping monotonously outside, pitting the earth, swelling the nearby river. The coldness of the stone at her back and beneath her feet was as frigid as the grave, her breath hot on the air. Yet it was here, in this damp, freezing cold dungeon, that confirmation of another world was about to be glimpsed. It really was. And it was mind-blowing.

She held her breath. If this was truly magic then the majority of the human race was both ignorant and woefully arrogant, because they knew nothing. And here was she, a trailer trash ex-junkie the world looked down on, endowed with a power that exalted her beyond anything they could even begin to imagine. She had been chosen. And the enormity of it surged through her veins – of what she was about to see; of what she could have. Another realm, a door, was going to open!

The bird's eyes were glinting black diamonds as it hopped up close. Perilously close.

This had never happened before.

An image, words or thoughts conveyed, was all.

Reaching for the grimoire, she read in hesitant spurts, constantly eyeing the bird. It had to be a sign or a messenger. There was a blue haze around it.

"Malphas, I have called thee through Him who has created Heaven, Earth and Hell…"

Unable to tear her eyes away from the raven to read properly, she floundered.

"I bind thee, that thou remain affably and visibly here so long as I shall have occasion for thy presence; and not to depart until thou hast duly and faithfully performed my will…"

The bird began to skip away, its back to her.

She raised her voice. "By time pentacle of Solomon have I called thee. Give unto me a true answer!"

The bird had now merged with the shadows.

"You will do my bidding. I have given you my life's blood. And I will give you my spirit and my soul. But I command you now to speak to me as a man. I want what you promised me …And then I am yours."

The raven spread its broad, ebony wings, stretching them out in a crepuscular quiver before moving into the back of the dungeon, towards where the bats were hibernating.

She stared after it and her mouth dropped open.

It was just a bird! Not a messenger… just a bird…

She threw the book at the wall, half crying, half screaming. Pushing herself up onto her knees she scrabbled for a handful of stones and threw them at the raven, then raising her arms to the ceiling shouted, "Give me what I asked for! I have come here in the dark through the forest on my own, and done exactly what you said. But it's been three long years and I'm fucking pissed off. And no, I'm not insane. I know you're there. I saw you. Where are you now? Why do you let me down?"

The raven hopped back in and she glared at it.

"So you were just a figment of my drug-addled brain all along? Well, all hail fucking Satan for the load of crap it all is! Okay, we'll do a 'yes' or 'no' session like usual, and then I'm out of here. I can get what I want with or without you anyway. Sam will see to that."

She took a dice from her pocket and shook it. "All those stupid Satanist meetings," she told the bird. "They were just drugged up orgies. People with no beliefs in anything but their own egos. Reading prayers backwards and all that shit - load of tossers. Right, gonna roll the dice. Are you, Malphas, real or not?"

It would be one or two for a negative, three or four for a neutral, five to six for a positive.

She rolled the dice. Six.

The bird hopped around the edges of the wall, periodically vanishing into the umbra of the shadows.

"Coincidence. Right, here we go again." She rolled the dice.

Six.

"Right. I get it – six-six-six. Hey, tell you what, Demon, let's go for a hat-trick. If I get another six, plus you speak to me I might believe in you."

She rolled the dice at the same time as the raven flew

out into the night air.

Six.

And all four candles snuffed out.

***

Coincidence!

Nevertheless, she began to scramble her things together with a degree of urgency. The night air was heavy with a sodden chill, and from somewhere within the woods a vixen screamed. The snow of earlier had turned to sleety rain, drumming the ground, drilling holes into the mud, pebble-dashing the trees.

Only now did she become aware of the hunger churning her stomach and the numbness in her muscles. The whole thing tonight was a crashing disappointment. Three years now. Three. And all she had promised to do for Malphas, all that had been silently injected into her head, she had done without thinking and without question: Belinda's husband, business, house – all gone. And so too had she brought down Belinda's son, Ralph, infesting him with dark spirits. That he was ill, she knew without doubt. The boy rarely left the house let alone came to spy on her at the altar in the woods anymore. It had been easy, with him mourning his father's grave, racked with grief and confusion. Yet Belinda was still going to work, her daughter still went to school. And she herself had nothing. So here she was, out here in the dark and the cold with her son at Wolfs Cross.

Stuffing her belongings into the canvas bag and mumbling to herself, she found her hands were trembling violently, the fingers white and numb. Cold had cramped her legs and stiffened her back, and the night was as black as an eclipse. Wiping miserable tears from her face, she was about to stand up when the ominous feeling from earlier suddenly and quickly intensified to such a point it felt as if a weight had descended on her head. Her chest laboured and her limbs became leaden. And the hissing silence became a high-pitch whistle.

Please no…not the vision again…

She crouched, stock-still, waiting.

All rage had dissipated in a heartbeat. The atmosphere pulsed. Someone had their eyes on her, breathed…no…more than one…A whole crowd seemed to be circling, closing in, a draught created by the movement of long robes or gowns.

She shone the torch around the walls.

"Hello?"

The temperature plunged further, as if a freezer door had opened. Shrouds of black hovered around the edges of the room, swallowing the shadows and extinguishing the light.

Urgency kicked like a rider on her back. She stood up, turning around and around. The smell had changed too, from damp earth and incense to that of mould, sweat and…she couldn't say… resonant of bad meat. There was something else too - a low continuous hum like bees in a hive, fading in and out.

Grabbing her bag she hurried to the exit, making it as far as the steps before the humming noise amplified dramatically, and against her better judgement she turned to see. From within the depths of the cavern, the darkness appeared to be separating into dozens of light grey shapes. The air stirred with movement, the curious murmurs now more discernible. They were whispers and prayers. More than prayers, no these were pleas of terror and shame, guilt and remorse. The chamber was filled with beseeching and begging, the feeling of dread mounting rapidly as the noise grew louder by the second, filling her head with a monotonous, escalating drone.

Fuck, these are the monks!

People had said they'd seen the ghosts of monks here but no one ever believed them. These weren't just ghosts though – there was something horrible about them.

Tearing out, she ran across the rubble and leapt over the low walls. *Someone was following her*. Two seconds to get her breath and then she was racing uphill to the woods. Whoever it was had followed her out of that place and was on her tail. Right behind…

Ahead, at the top of the hill the heavy firs bobbed and swayed, wind whining through the canopy. Soaked to the skin, her face and hair dripping, she panted hard on the last part of the climb, hot and shivery in equal measure. The thing was gaining on her. She struggled up the muddy field, gasping. It was about to draw level, to clamp a hand on her shoulder. The presence was burgeoning, a towering mass looming over her head. What was it? This couldn't be happening.

Keep running. Don't stop and don't look back… don't look behind!

The one inside was back. And this time was welcome.

It's him… don't look!

Hadn't this happened to that conservationist? The story revisited her instantly, of how he'd sworn someone had followed him all the way back to the village, of the recording full of moans and roars!

The border of the forest was in sight. She clambered up the bank and raced towards it, grabbing at the nearest branch to expedite the climb. Then finally, with her spine against the trunk of a large spruce, she swung around to face the pursuer.

There was no one there.

The cathedral stillness of the woods immediately eased the onslaught of wind and rain; evergreens steadily dripping into the cool, shadowy undergrowth. The forest had its own voice, a taffeta rustle and pitter-patter of drips and breezes. She held onto the solid wood behind her, checking it was real, that this was no dream, not a hallucination. She was clean, had taken nothing in weeks. So what then, was this?

She squeezed shut her eyes and reopened them.

Below, the ruins of the monastery had vanished through the veil of rain - gone the moss-covered grey stones, the arches reclaimed by ivy, the crumbling remains of walls and sunken foundations. Now the building shone in all its former glory, a similar vision to the one she'd had on arriving. The stones radiated with an ethereal glow, and silent white-robed monks hastened across the lawns to the toll of bells. This time however, they were not simply uneasy but visibly agitated. As soon as they had filed inside candles were lit at every window, and Evensong rose into the air along with the fragrant scent of incense.

It gave the impression they were keeping vigilance,

protecting themselves like soldiers in a citadel. The scene was playing out again, but why? And why was she being shown this after the disaster of this evening?

Deep in thought, she jumped at a sudden noise behind, coming from within the trees.

Someone was here. So they had followed her!

With her heart hammering she strained to hear.

Nothing. Only the trickle of raindrops from the oak's bare branches, and the soughing of wind in the canopy.

Again. There it was again. A sigh. Followed by a footstep, lighter than air.

Don't turn around!

Prickles worked their way up to her neck. This was him, wasn't it? The one she had sent to Belinda's nightmares, the one so feared and disliked by the one inside. The one everyone in the village said visited you just before you went insane.

Don't turn around. Don't look at him.

Unable to prevent it, she shuddered from head to foot as his presence moved ever closer so that he breathed into her hair.

They are afraid, yes?

His freezing touch sank through her thin jacket, ice slipping underneath her skin, burrowing into her veins, a feeling of being explored as if he had slithered inside her very soul, and could see every part of who she was.

I have a little, shall we say, surprise for you, Witch!

Revulsion rose inside her, at the rank smell of mould and decay smothering her nose and mouth until she could barely breathe. A crawling sensation had wormed into her mind, probing her thoughts with all the odious writhings of a maggot infesting an apple.

She clutched her temples. *Get out of my head. Get out of my head…whoever you are!*

His lips grazed the nape of her neck. *Better be careful, you wouldn't want to lose him…twice…*

A white hood, beneath which black eyes glared with malignant contempt, flashed briefly into her mind, then vanished. The electric energy cut to grey, and the vision dissipated, the scene below replaced once more by a dripping forest, muddy ruins and a curtain of squally rain.

Immediately she looked over her shoulder. Already knowing he would not be there and never had been. She moved in dark realms these days and the feeling this was not going to end well occurred to her for the first time. Why had she really been brought here?

Cold, starving hungry, soaked to the skin and now extremely late to go and fetch Gul, the fear of what was transpiring began to worry her deeply. She wasn't powerful at all, was she? Far from having struck a deal and able to demand a reward, it was beginning to look as if she'd been used. Without even knowing why.

God, what had she done?

You wouldn't want to lose him twice…

The white hood, the black eyes – just as described in stories passed down through the ages, told by those who'd seen him, those who ended up in Wolfs Cross.

Gul! Had he been referring to her son?

She had to get back. The need was now urgent and she broke into a run. He mustn't stay the night at Wolfs Cross under any circumstances. She rooted out the mobile phone while running. No signal. Nothing.

Speeding up, the ground thudding beneath her feet, she was half way back before the phone beeped into life with a missed message. Bent double with stitch, she stopped and squinted at the screen. Her mother had sent it at six to say Gul was with her.

"Okay!" She sighed, well hopefully she'd be there in time to get him home before bedtime. She checked the time.

What? No freaking way!

She flew downhill so fast her legs were in danger of buckling. This could not be right. What the fuck? She must be losing it, going mad. Time was missing…hours of it…

It was three in the morning.

***

CHAPTER THIRTEEN

BELINDA

There was no way she could get back into that bed and sleep. But standing shivering in the dark with her back against the wall was not an option either. Should she go downstairs? She hesitated, recalling the incident with Ralph. Besides, sitting up in that chilly, dismal lounge at half past three in the morning was a depressing thought.

No, this had been a horrible nightmare, that was all – a hallucination at worst. There was no external force, no ghost and no demon. Gradually, reluctantly, she crossed the room and got back in. This time the lamp worked just fine and she left it on, pulling the covers up to her neck.

Wide awake, she lay staring up at the ceiling. *Burdo…Burdo…*

The name would not stop repeating in her mind, and it was impossible to stop it. If it was simply a nightmare, or night terror, then she ought to see Mark about it and ask for an SSRI. This had to be down to extreme anxiety, surely?

So why wouldn't the light come on, then? The lamp or the main switch?

She deleted the question from her head.

Burdo…Burdo…

And the cold? Why did the temperature drop to sub-zero, yet now it's okay?

It was a thin-walled house on a wet night in March. It would be warmer when it had been painted and the heating was fixed.

Burdo…Burdo…

Still she lay awake, exhausted but with her brain still firing…on and on and on…his name. It was like Tourette's Syndrome, the words she dreaded speaking the most were the ones that shrieked inside her head.

Burdo… Burdo…

Don't say his name, it will be worse. It's as if you're calling him!

Yet on and on it went, her own mind chanting the name in mockery at her lack of control. *Burdo, Burdo, Burdo…* and the more his name was repeated the more he grew as an entity, a character, a person.

I don't want to know who you are. I don't want to see you. Go away, I don't want this.

This couldn't go on – not even for one more day. Tomorrow she would ring in sick and book an appointment.

Burdo…Burdo…Get out of my head, out of my head, out of my head!

Perhaps it was sheer exhaustion but finally sleep came and the incessant mind chatter cut to black. Later she recalled the strangest dream, of floating on a deep, dark ocean tide, miles out to sea on a small boat, and that it had seemed natural to be rolling on the swell of the water. But then one end of the boat became weighted down, as if someone had joined her.

Yes, someone was sitting at the other end of the boat,

so heavy it was letting water in. Her consciousness lifted a little until she became aware that she wasn't on the ocean but in bed at the terrace on Moss Pike Road. It was a dream, that was all.

Her consciousness lifted a little more. The lamp should be on but was not. The room was dark… all dark.

And she should be alone but was not.

With that thought her heart slammed in her chest and she snapped awake, keeping her eyes tightly shut. She could not see, did not want to see, who she knew would be there. Every muscle seized tightly. She lay rigid with her heart firing bullets.

The edge of the bed had dipped on one side as if a large dog had settled there, and a strong waft of mould and decay cloyed the air.

It's been such a long time, Benedicta. Are you not pleased to see an old friend?

No, no, I don't want this. Stop!

A low chortle and a strand of her hair gently smoothed from her face. *Come now, what is, how you say, good for the goose is good for the gander.*

Burdo, Burdo, Burdo…

To her horror, her eyes opened.

He was sitting on the side of the bed watching her with ebony eyes that bore into hers, his reptilian skin cracking now into a grin of rotting tombstone teeth.

Shrinking so far back into the mattress every spring coil pained her spine, her bladder loosened and hot fluid trickled down her leg. *Oh God, oh God…*His face was terrible to look at – riddled with some kind of horrible skin disease, the breath so fetid it made her gag, eyes burning with malevolence. He seemed to move closer in short, sharp bursts, so that with violent haste he was but a hair's breadth away. The black eyes were searching her mind – looking for a way in.

She screwed her eyes shut.

Yet still could see him. His face continued to probe hers even inside her mind's eye. There was no escape. He was gliding into her consciousness, the coldness of his spirit walking right in.

No, no, no, stop!

The white monk's face was now poster-billed on her mind – his pinprick eyes searing onto her retinas. The wide, triangular nose spread across the wizened bones of his skull so closely she could see the pores stretching into crater scars. The stench of decay crawled down her throat as with panic she realised she was suffocating, his bloodless mouth descending on her own.

In vain she tried to turn her head to one side but found she could not.

There was no way of switching off the vision, of preventing the clammy coldness infiltrating her skin, or the crawling fingers from stroking her breasts. Slowly, inevitably the carcass of bones lowered onto her in the parody of a lover... the small, round black eyes never wavering as they bored into hers. As silently and seamlessly his whole being entered hers. And they became one.

No!

Ice rushed into her bloodstream. Nausea rose up in a wave of bile.

And then it was over. The heavy weight lifted, the air cleared and the image faded.

She sat up in a cold sweat, weak and dazed.

The lamp was on exactly as she had left it.

Another nightmare, then. A continuation of the same. Shivering violently, she grabbed the covers and wrapped herself up tight. That had to be the worst fucking dream she'd ever had in her life. At least a dream or night terror, whatever, was all it was.

Lying back again, she tried to calm herself. It lingered though, the image of his face…and his name…

***

CHAPTER FOURTEEN

"Mum!" Essie was shouting and frantically rattling the bedroom door.

Roused far too abruptly from a deep and blissful sleep, Belinda tried to surface. It was still dark and it took a few moments to register.

"Mum! Mum! Why's the door stuck? Mum!"

Oh God, that was Essie! Flinging back the covers she flew across to the door and moved the chair wedged under the handle.

Essie's face was ashen. Without Goth make-up and still in pyjamas, her daughter looked childlike. And extremely frightened.

"What on earth is it?"

"Mum! Oh God, Mum, it's Ralph. There's something badly wrong with him. I think he's gone mad."

Belinda grabbed her dressing gown. "What's happened?"

"Oh my God, I don't know what to do."

"Essie, what on earth is it? Tell me."

"I just don't know what to do."

She reached out, "You don't have to do anything, love—"

Essie pulled away, "You've no idea. I've kept the worst from you but I should've said. I should've done something. This is all my fault." Her breath was hitching in her throat as she struggled to contain her distress. "Oh, Mum, it's been going on ages, but...but...I just thought..."

Belinda reached for her again and this time hugged her tightly. "Alright, alright. Now just tell me properly, what's happened? What do you mean, he's gone mad?"

"I couldn't tell you, I just couldn't. But when you asked about his eyes, I had to say about Kezia. I didn't want to have to tell you but I had to. I'm so sorry, Mum. Everyone at school is talking about it. But you took it so badly about dad and I didn't want you to worry anymore about us - me and Ralph So I just thought it would get better and that...and I wouldn't have to...but...I think, well... I think he's...I think he's possessed!"

"Possessed? Oh, Essie, I—"

"Yes! He's been saying stuff, like weird things before, but it's really bad now. And then this morning..." Her eyes widened and she stepped back, staring at Belinda, searching her face. "He's scaring me, Mum. Really, seriously scaring me."

Belinda quickly tied her robe. "Has he hurt you? Or threatened to hurt you? Tell me the truth."

"No."

"Has he ever frightened you before now?"

Essie shook her head. "No."

She tried to keep her voice low and level, to keep her own rising panic in check as well as Essie's. "Alright, now tell me what's different about him this morning. What makes you think he's possessed?"

"Okay, well I know he was trying to connect with

Dad. Oh God, I can see by your face you're going to go ballistic—"

"Just tell me, Essie."

"Right, well he's been with Kezia Elwyn, up at the witch's altar in Barons Wood – doing satanic rites and stuff. We got talking to her in the churchyard and she told us she could help, you know, speak to the other side. We only wanted to know what happened, you know, why Dad–"

Belinda paled. "What? But that's—"

"I knew what you'd say, you see, but we were desperate to know why Dad died and what he was doing with her, with Kezia. She said she missed him too, and she did tarot and Ouija to connect with spirits and could help us. Then Ralph started, you know, seeing her properly. They'd go up to the altar. Anyway, after that I didn't go because I think it was, you know, like sex magic or—"

"Oh, Christ!"

"And I know she made him kill things, for the blood–"

"Oh my God!"

"I know, and so that's why I couldn't say anything, especially to you. Everyone's scared of her and I didn't know what to do. I suppose I hoped it would all stop, just be okay… But now he's acting like a different person. He's not himself – he's like, laughing to himself, sniggering even though there's literally no one else there! And you're right about his eyes, the pupils change shape from square to oblong to oval, and he looks really ill, like the colour of ash. But before there was a lid on it, as if somehow it was under control. But now the lid's off and he's shouting and saying things about murdering the whole village. He's covered in blood and dirt and he's banging on the walls with his fists. And there's all these drawings pinned everywhere. Like he just went mad in the night. And now he's going to kill everyone in the village, saying we've all got to die for what we've done. "

"*Kill* everyone?"

"Yes, and when I told him to calm down, to sit down, he shouted a load of insults in my face. Called me vile names, and he knew personal things that he couldn't have known – stuff I hadn't told anyone, not even Molly. I never wanted to tell anyone, not ever. So how could he know? How?" She started crying again, burying her face in her hands.

"Alright, listen, Essie. We'll talk later, but right now I want you to go to your room and stay there. Your brother's very ill and I need to call the doctor out urgently. So please go to your room, get dressed and keep the door shut. Promise me?"

Essie was shaking her head. "It's all my fault—"

"No, no, you really must stop that. It isn't. If it's anyone's it's mine because you clearly felt you couldn't talk to me and that was wrong – you should be able to tell me anything. Now listen, this is not your problem to solve. You are not the problem and you have not caused it. It's just a shame I made you feel you had to keep it to yourself all this time, but you've told me now and it was the right thing to do. So please do as I ask. I'm going to talk to Ralph and we'll take it from there. Your brother is ill, not possessed, alright? None of that demonic stuff exists outside of the movies, it's not real.

We're going to get him well again, okay? And it's me who's in the wrong. I should have tried a hell of a lot harder."

Her voice sounded a lot stronger than the way she felt inside. Her empty stomach hollowed out, and her heart thudded sickeningly as she walked along the landing towards Ralph's room.

He's saying things about murdering the whole village…

Having been jolted from a deep sleep, the terror of last night only now began to replay – of the white monk lowering his disgusting corpse onto her body, exhaling foul breath into her lungs, the ice slicing underneath her skin… It was all coming back, the full horror of it.

She knocked on her son's bedroom door.

No answer.

"Ralph?"

From within came the sound of a furtive, unnatural giggling.

Before going in, she took a moment to picture her son as used to be – the floppy-haired boy with clear blue eyes and the kind of smile that lit up his face. There was one particular day, he must have been about nine, when he'd run into the kitchen at White Hart Lodge with a sparkling emerald dragonfly that had been stuck in some netting, and together they'd gone to release it by the wild pond. That was her Ralph. The little boy who had watched in wonder as it flew like a jewel into the summer sky. He'd grown into a young man showing every sign of emulating his father with carpentry skills, his hands steady, an eye for symmetry and beauty, and a work ethic straight out of her own book. It had been nothing less than tragic that he'd been the one to find his father that day.

Again she rapped on the door. How could she not have noticed the rapid changes in him: that he'd started to avoid not just work, but friends too, not to mention any interaction with herself? At the very least she could have persuaded him to see Mark. It was just that at one point he'd seemed to be coming out of it. It had, after all, been two years since his father died, and she'd moved heaven and earth to help them both through the trauma. Thought, perhaps, that the worst was over and this latest phase was self-indulgence.

She shook her head. As if though, as if he was ever going to get over something like that! Who was she kidding? It was only herself who buried pain and grief and carried on smiling, insisting time was a healer. Time did no such thing, it simply replaced older memories with newer ones.

No, she should have done more and she should have noticed.

"Ralph? Can I come in?"

The sniggering had stopped.

She reached for the door handle and turned it. "I'm coming in now."

She stood in the doorway. And the shock took her breath.

He was crouching in the corner, hands clutching what was left of his hair, the scalp matted with blood and scabs, clumps of black lying on the floor. His nails were embedded with soil, which was also smeared all over his face. And wearing a long, charcoal overcoat he sat on his haunches softly rocking back and forth, the room around him a state of utter chaos.

Belinda reeled back at the overpowering assault of ammonia, and the sweet, metallic smell of fresh blood. Fouled clothing lay strewn across the floor, the bed was stained and unmade, littered with empty bottles, food wrappers and discarded videos. She scanned the scene. Wallpaper had been gouged off as if by a wild cat, and all the doors of both wardrobe and drawers were wide open, their contents spilling out. A frenzied burglary could not have made more of a mess. And as Essie had said, there were drawings – hundreds of them – black ink-smudged scribbles on page after page of notepaper. They lay like confetti on the bed, scattered across the floor, pinned to almost every square inch of the walls, even the curtains. And all of them exactly the same.

She stepped inside.

He was peeping through his fingers, watching her, the demeanour having altered from nasty hilarity to curiosity.

And when he spoke it was with a French lilt, "You left us?"

For a second she stood quite still, her response lost in a fog of confusion. She swayed slightly. The room darkened by degrees, the noise of the traffic outside dulled, and the boy looking at her from far, far away, was not one she recognised.

"Burdo? Why did you leave? Did you find Benedicta?"

The voice emanating from her throat was not her own. "Do what I told you."

"Will you come back?"

"Do not question me. Do what you must. Do it today."

"All of them?"

Her fists clenched and her jaw hardened to steel. "Yes, make them pay. Except for *her*. Don't touch her. I like to—"

At the sound of a floorboard creaking, the voice froze in her throat.

The room once more came into focus, the traffic roared into her head, and dazed, she turned around.

Essie's face was ashen.

"Mum?"

***

CHAPTER FIFTEEN

SYLVIA

The sound of whirring helicopters woke her from a disturbed night's sleep. Following the huge row with Mark last night her eyes were bleary and sore; she must have had less than three hours. At quarter to seven the light was still dull, and her head throbbed with an ominous ache just over the right eyebrow. She reached over to the bedside table for a paracetamol. Never before had they argued like that. Never had such contempt and loathing disfigured his handsome face, not when looking at his wife, anyway. Her head might hurt but it was nowhere near as much as her heart.

Damn, and there was such a full day ahead. Not only that but it was so important to be in a good place for the hypnosis sessions ahead, to be full of energy and light, to have nothing about her that was weak or vulnerable. Stupid to have had it out with him last night. Bloody stupid! What in God's name had come over her that she couldn't have waited until the weekend? She just had to go stomping upstairs and fly at him. It wasn't the way to go about things, as she told her patients day in and day out – railing at someone, accusing them. It only ever got their back up.

Blinking back tears of fatigue and regret, the empty

space beside her gave an added jolt, remembering Mark had chosen to sleep in the spare room. That was a first, too. And it was lonely as hell.

In the grey half-light with the soft wash of rain against the windows, she was rummaging in the bedside drawer for tablets, thinking it was going to be a long, long day...when there came a sharp tap at the window and she stopped mid-search.

What was that? A bird?

Motionless, she strained to listen. The house was quiet, everyone fast asleep for a little while longer. Then it came again. No mistake - rap-rap-rap!

Someone was at the bloody window! Flinging back the covers she hurried over. Hesitated. Then peeped between a tiny gap.

Christ!

She leapt back. Essie Sully's ghost-white face was flat against the pane.

Sylvia's hand flew to her chest, her heart rate zipping through the roof. The girl's normally spiky black hair was plastered to her skin, rainwater dripping down her cheeks as she clawed at the window. Alabaster white, with yesterday's eye make-up smeared into the hollows of her eyes, she was clearly undaunted by Sylvia's obvious fright, banging harder now at the glass, half screaming, half crying.

Unable to decipher a word she was saying, Sylvia made placating gestures while scrambling frantically into the leggings and sweater she'd cast off only hours before, and rushed towards the stairs. What on earth could be the matter? It must be Belinda. Something to do with the odd state she was in yesterday?

She'd told Mark. Bloody told him, and now look! But for Essie to come here, and at this time in the morning, it must be really serious.

Watching her race past, Mark was standing at the doorway of the spare room, his hair ruffled in that rooster look he had when he scratched his head in the morning. Part of her ached a little, but she tamped that down in one fell swoop. Just how and when had he become so bloody superior, so know-it-all and condescending? Was it being a doctor in a small place like this, where hardly anyone else was educated? Was it earning ten, maybe twenty times what anyone else here earned? He'd never been like this before, and certainly wouldn't have dreamed of speaking to her the way he did last night. Did he get off on criticising and condemning her like she was an idiot? Her nostrils flared and her teeth ground together at the sight of him.

"What's going on?" he said, in a tone suggesting that whatever it was it must be her fault.

Sylvia, who would normally have taken a second or two to explain, shot past him without answering. *Fuck you!*

"I said, 'What's going on?'" he called after her.

On reaching the kitchen she pulled the door closed behind her, then hurried over to the outside one and unlocked it. Peering into the morning mizzle, she called out, "Essie?"

Footsteps crunched on the gravel path and Essie turned the corner. "We need the doctor!" Essie was yelling as she ran towards the open door. "Please! You've got to help us! Where is he?"

Sylvia caught her as Essie bulldozed straight in.

"Whoa, hold on!"

"Doctor Massey! Please, you've got to help!"

"Alright, alright, steady on, I've got you. Sit down, Essie." Sylvia tried to steer the girl towards the kitchen table. "Sit down, come on."

"I don't want to sit down—"

Both swung round as Mark strode in. Already dressed in jeans and sweatshirt, his mouth set in a grim line, his face hard.

Behind him, Molly was hovering on the stairs. "What's happening, Dad? What's going on? Is that Essie?"

"I don't know yet," he snapped. "Go and get showered and dressed. I'll be up in a minute." Closing the kitchen door behind him, he glared at them. "Alright, what's going on? And try to keep your voice down, Essie. I don't want Molly upset any more than she already is."

Sylvia gazed out of the window to avoid having to even look at him. The forest edge stood as a wall of sentinels guarding its silent interior, an ethereal morning mist hovering over the lawn. So the all-out screaming match last night was all her fault, was it? Of course, arguing like that when Molly could hear was a disgrace, of course it was, and it had never happened before. But if he was wholly blaming her, trying to lay the lot at her door he could fuck right off. She took a deep breath and turned to face Essie.

"Try to keep calm. Tell us clearly what's happening so we can help."

"It's Ralph! He's done something terrible, I know he has. He's gone mad. He's been acting weird for ages, but now he's pulled out all his hair and he's covered in blood and dirt, and he's saying he's going to kill everyone in the village. There are hundreds of little drawings pinned to every inch of his room, all over the walls and the curtains and the floor. He's in a terrible state and he's speaking in a weird voice and saying horrible things. I think he's possessed by the devil. I told Mum this morning but now she's acting weird too, and I'm scared."

It was all Sylvia could do not to turn around and say, 'Happy now?' to Mark. She knew this was coming. Belinda hadn't been sleeping, she looked awful and her note had quite definitely said she didn't feel herself. She'd told them more than once that her children hadn't coped after Gideon's death, and that they spent an unhealthy amount of time in the graveyard. Clearly the woman had been to hell and back trying to keep the family on the straight and narrow, and now Ralph had become unhinged. It could all have been predicted. And, as she had desperately tried to tell Mark last night, there was a bad feeling in the village as a whole, with a lot of people sick and not just physically. There was a brooding malevolence here, and more and more people were feeling it. Belinda was affected, the old people in the nursing home, Paige Morse, and now Ralph. There were earthbound spirits everywhere here. She could hear them, see them, feel them. And by the day they were amassing, as if a door had been opened from another realm, and in they had filed.

A line…heads cowled…white cloaks…

Sylvia shook her head to clear the unbidden image.

This was something she couldn't share. Especially

not with Mark.

"I don't want to hear any more of this dogs' bollocks," he'd said last night. "Stick to psychology because there are enough problems here for you to be getting on with without all this incense burning crap. Let me sort out the meds, and you can hold their hands and regress them to their fucking childhoods, because believe me they are fucking fucked- up."

"And you think I don't know that? You think I was born yesterday? I'm just saying, before you dose everyone up and have them all carted off to psychiatric units forever more, at least let me try to do some spirit release—"

"Sylvia, I don't mind you indulging the well-to-do and ripping them off for a hundred smackers a time, but—"

"You lousy bastard."

"But you don't bring it to my door. You do not start saying our house needs a fucking exorcism and our friend's daughter needs spirit release. Is everyone fucking haunted in your opinion? Is that your answer to everything? You're obsessed and unwell—"

"Do you have to swear every second word? And you know damn well I've trained for the best part of twenty years as a psychologist, hypnotist and regression therapist. I've lectured all over the world. How dare you put mc down and try to make out what I do is nonsense, whereas you—"

From the other side of the house there came the sound of a door closing and a toilet flushing. "Oh well done," Mark said. "You've woken Molly."

The worst of it was, she'd gone against everything

she ever advised – rising to the argument, defending herself and continually pushing home her point. It just wasn't like her. It's just that it was impossible to get through to him. He was so damned aggressive and, frankly, angry. It was like he hated her.

Tuning back into what Essie was now saying, she realised Mark had already made his diagnosis. "Sounds like your brother's depression has tipped into something a little more serious," he was saying. "Has he ever threatened to harm anyone before?"

"No."

"And you say he's been talking to himself for a while? Is he hearing voices?"

Essie nodded. "I tried to keep it from Mum because she has enough to worry about, but the other week he pushed her out of his room, like literally, and I know she's been scared of him since then. She asked about his eyes and—"

"What about his eyes?" Sylvia interjected.

"The pupils change shape like a reptile's. It's weird but I thought it was because he was doing drugs with that Kezia—"

"Kezia Elwyn?" Mark said, the colour draining from his face. "But she's twice his age! And married! With a child!"

"Yeah?" Essie said, reverting briefly to her normal self. "And?"

"And doing drugs? Please tell me you and Molly haven't—"

Essie jumped up. "I thought you were a doctor. You gonna help us or give us a lecture? My brother is promising to twat the whole fucking village and you're bleating on about your precious daughter doing a spliff! Listen, I'm telling you I think he's done something terrible, really bad. He's covered in dirt and blood. He's been out during the night because he's filthy, and now there are helicopters everywhere. Can't you hear them?"

"Essie, is he in a fit state to come to the surgery?" Sylvia asked. "What was he like when you left?"

"No, he's not. And worse, my mum is talking to him as if he makes sense, like telling him to get on with it, like she's in on it! They were saying stuff like, 'Do it today.' I heard—"

Mark frowned. "In on it? In on what?"

"On the plot to kill everyone." Essie stared from one to the other. "Oh my fucking God, you think it's me that's paranoid? Well, come over to our house, then! Come and see. Come and see the drawings he's done. Come and hear the voice he uses and ask him who he wants to kill because I'm telling you it's everyone. And it's going to be today. If he hasn't done something already, that is. You've got to help us. Please!"

Both Sylvia and Mark were reaching for coats, boots and phones.

Sylvia shouted upstairs. "Molly?"

Her daughter peered over the top of the bannister, glasses on, long brown hair tied onto the top of her head in a swinging pony tail just like Paige Morse had described.

"Something's come up. An emergency. Can you get yourself breakfast? One of us will be back soon but if not, just go to school as normal, stick to the main road, and text me when you get there, okay?"

Molly nodded. "What's going on, Mum?"

"Essie's brother's not well. We don't know any more, so this morning we could do with your help, okay?"

"Is Essie alright?"

"She's fine. Alright, now we have to go. Hopefully one of us will be back in time, but if not, go straight there and don't take the path through the woods. Walk down Cats Hill and stay on the main road like I said. Text me when you're at school, okay?"

Molly was trying to see past her into the kitchen.

"Molly, did you hear me?"

"Yes."

"Promise me you'll do exactly as I said?"

"Yeah, yeah…"

Overhead the helicopters sounded as if they were circling wider now. It happened occasionally, that someone went into the forest and didn't return. Like Essie's father. And the sound of them had the girl's eyes wide and haunted. She was peering through the blinds.

"I wonder who they're looking for…"

***

CHAPTER SIXTEEN

Minutes later all three jumped into Mark's Audi Estate, with Essie in the back.

Fastening her seatbelt Sylvia said, "I wonder why the helicopters are out?"

"Oh God!" Essie wailed.

"Try not to panic, Essie. I doubt it's anything to do with Ralph. Your mum's with him and she won't have let him leave the house—"

"Actually, she was the one telling him to get on with it."

Mark accelerated down the drive, swinging the car out onto Cats Hill amid a screech of tyres.

Sylvia switched on the radio. "Let's see if there's anything on the news. Don't worry Essie, we'll be there in two ticks."

"He was covered in dirt. I mean his fingernails were ingrained with it, and now all these police helicopters are out, so what if—"

"I've got to ask," Mark said. "Does he have access to any weapons? A shotgun, for example?"

"No, but they've all got them at Wolf's Cross. Kezia's got one. Clint's got one. Oh, and I just remembered the names Ralph and Mum were talking about: a woman called Benedicta. I've never heard of anyone called that, but they both seemed to know who she was…"

Mark turned left onto Moss Pike Road and put his foot down hard.

"And he was speaking in a French accent as well, asking about this woman, Benedicta. It's weird - really, really weird."

Mark was accelerating full throttle down the middle of the main road, his knuckles white as he gripped the steering wheel.

"For Christ's sake, Mark!" Sylvia shouted above both the engine and the radio "Try not to kill us all en route!"

Hitting the brakes, he swung the car into a parking space outside Belinda's house and jerked the car to an abrupt halt. About to unclick his seatbelt however, he stopped on hearing the first line of the seven o'clock news, and turned up the volume.

'A three-year-old boy has gone missing in the Monkspike area. The alarm was raised at around four this morning and police helicopters are out searching, as yet with no luck. Gul Elwyn is described as having deep blue, violet eyes and blonde hair, is wearing a navy puffa jacket, and was last seen at Wolfs Cross on–'

"Isn't he Kezia's son?" Sylvia asked, turning towards Mark.

His reaction however, left her stunned. Jumping out he slammed the door so hard it shook the car, before turning to face the wall of the house. With one hand on the wall, the other covered his face.

Sylvia's jaw dropped. Anyone would think it was his own child that had gone missing. His own in danger. Why in hell's name would he act like that?

Alas, this was no time for questions. If they didn't get to Ralph quickly, who knew what could happen?

It took an effort to concentrate on the job in hand, with so many mixed-up feelings of her own. "It looks like a little boy's lost in the forest," she said to Essie as they got out of the car. "I'm sure they'll find him soon. Come on, let's go and see your brother."

"Shit, I hope Gul's alright," Essie said, following Sylvia to the door. "I've seen him a few times trailing after Clint, miserable and snotty, poor kid. No wonder he's wandered off. I've seen him on his own a few times as well, and he's only three—"

Belinda answered on the first knock. "Essie! Where the hell have you been? I've been worried sick!"

It was then she noticed Sylvia, and her expression hardened. Ushering Essie inside she began to close the door in Sylvia's face. "I wasn't expecting visitors. I'm sorry about yesterday if that's what you've come about? Only I didn't feel well. Honestly, you needn't have bothered, we're fine—"

Mark joined Sylvia on the step, having composed himself.

"Oh, goodness! Mark, as well! What's going on? Essie, what have you been saying? Look, I'm sorry I can't let you in, the place is a tip."

"Mum, I had to get help. I was scared—"

Belinda flushed, her eyes glittering. "And I told you to stay in your room," she snapped over her shoulder. "That I was dealing with it. Essie, how could you?"

"Bel, please don't be cross with her. She was worried about her brother and ran all the way up to get us," Sylvia quickly explained. "And it really doesn't matter about the housework. Look, she's told us Ralph's ill, that he's been threatening harm to others, and she was worried sick, frightened half to death that he might do something rash. It's probably a good idea if he's assessed so we can help him. Can we please come in? I know it's hard for you but—"

Belinda seemed in two minds. "I told you he's fine. I had a talk with him and—"

"I think it's best we see him," said Mark. "If he's been threatening to kill people we can't just leave him here, can we? He needs help, Belinda."

She stared at him, a conflict of emotions behind her eyes.

Overhead the helicopters were back, this time hovering over the village.

"Or do we call the police and have him sectioned that way?"

Her eyes flashed. But she relented enough to open the door and let them in. Glaring at Essie, she hissed, "You had no right. No right at all."

Essie pounded upstairs and slammed the bedroom door shut behind her.

Addressing Mark, Belinda said, "I think there's been a terrible misunderstanding. He had a bad dream, that's all, saying things he can't even remember now. It's true he's been depressed and I should have brought him in, but I don't want him sectioning, do you understand? I just couldn't cope with that… everyone will know. Please don't…"

Mark began to head up the stairs.

Before their eyes, Belinda had switched from openly hostile to pleading and wretched. Close to tears, she was wringing her hands and visibly shaking as she called after him, "Please, just don't tell people here... I mean... you have no idea..."

Sylvia reached out but before her hand touched Belinda's arm, the other woman shot her a scathing look and shrank back. The bright and chirrupy, can-cope-with-anything Belinda she had always known, had taken on the persona of a down-trodden woman. This one was a timid, head-in-the-sand type from a bygone age - a woman afraid of her husband and expecting a beating.

"I just don't want him sectioned," she whimpered. "Please!"

"Alright, alright!" Mark snapped as he reached the top of the stairs. "I heard you." Then under his breath, "Three   fucking   times." "I told you it was a bad dream, sleep walking, and it's over. He's fine now."

With one hand on the newel post, Sylvia regarded her steadily.

The hallway seemed particularly dismal, and despite the glare of an overhead lightbulb a murky cloud hovered around Belinda's aura. She appeared to be in the grip of a terrible anxiety that had her sleepless, and so agitated as to be unable to keep still.

But as she regarded her, Belinda's persona suddenly flipped back again, to her stronger self.

"I can manage perfectly well. All he needs is a course of antidepressants. I know I should have brought him in before now, but that's all he needs. I will not agree to him being hospitalised, though. I'll look after him. I'll take some time off and we can sort it out as a family. This should be private."

Again Sylvia tried to reach out, and again Belinda flinched away.

"Come up with us, Bel. If he's poorly we're only here to help, you know that." She glanced upstairs. All was quiet. "We do need to see him in order to make an assessment, and I can assure you we'll do our best for him. For you too. Are you coming?"

She was about to turn and follow Mark upstairs, when an accented, slightly deeper voice spoke directly into her ear.

"Get out of my house, you fucking bitch!"

***

CHAPTER SEVENTEEN

KEZIA

At quarter past three that morning Kezia had burst onto the main road after sprinting down the hill. And at twenty past, was fumbling frantically with the key in the front door, her fingers so numb they barely functioned. The rain was torrential. It poured off guttering, swirled into drains and bounced off the tarmac. Her face was as wet as if she'd been swimming, and her feet squelched in the now ruined, cheap shoes.

Once inside, she kicked them off and sprinted straight upstairs to Gul's room. Clint had to have picked him up from Wolfs Cross, surely? He knew what the risks were up there. He bloody knew!

At first it was too dark to see, but not wanting to switch on the light in case it woke him, she tiptoed across the floorboards to the blue dolphin rug that matched Gul's blue dolphin duvet and pillowslips. He loved dolphins. Loved all animals. The only reason she hadn't let him have a pet so far was because his many cousins loved destroying and torturing them. He wasn't yet big enough to defend either himself or a much-loved creature, and he was far too young to have his little heart broken. She leaned over the bed, still not sure if he was in it or not, amongst all the soft toy creatures he liked to sleep with.

Closer…closer… The cold horror of pre-knowledge slicing into her heart moments before she put out her hands to gently touch his forehead… that he wasn't there.

The bed was cold and empty.

Fuck!

The bastard had left him up at Wolf Cross. All fucking night!

Adrenalin blocked out all further thought. With her senses on fire she marched across to the front bedroom, clinging to one last thread of hope – that he just might possibly be in with Clint. Praying he would be. Already knowing he wouldn't.

The wet snores of an unrousable drunk were reverberating through the walls. She pushed open the door. Flat on his back, Clint lay spread-eagled across the whole width of the bed with his mouth open. No sign of Gul.

She switched on the overhead light, spotlighting him in its full surgical glare.

"Where's Gul?"

Greasy in sleep, he murmured a few expletives before rolling noisily onto one side and pulling all the blankets with him.

She raised her voice. "I said, 'Where the fuck's Gul?' Wake up, you lazy bastard! Where is he?"

With no response she walked around to the side he was facing, roughly shoved him back over and yanked the covers off. "I said, 'Where the fuck is Gul?'"

For a second he was dumbstruck. Eyes like red pinholes blinked in the light. "What're you doing, you crazy bitch?"

Screaming, she lunged for him, shaking him and thumping his chest. "Gul! Where's Gul? He's not in his bed. You've left him up at Wolfs Cross, haven't you, you thick selfish bastard? Don't you know how dangerous that is? You stupid, stupid pig!"

He swiped her away. One movement and he'd stood up and thrown her against the wall. "Get off me, you mad bitch. I need a piss. And where've you fucking been anyway? You're hardly a model mother, are you?"

"Just tell me," she yelled, following down the landing. "Is he still up at Wolfs Cross? You left him there? You didn't go back? Christ, you just couldn't wait to dump him and get to the pub, could you? It's not often I ask you to look after him."

Slamming the bathroom door shut, he shouted over the sound of his bladder emptying, "Can't go and pick him up when I'm pissed, can I? He's alright up there. Anyway, where've you been? It's fucking shit o'clock in the morning."

By the time he exited the bathroom however, still mid-curse, she was gone.

It didn't matter what time it was, no child of hers was going to spend the night at Wolfs Cross. Her own memories were still so vivid they chased her into nightmares and hunted her down; the worst being the one which started with the caravan door opening, and her grandfather standing there, swaying and stinking of beer. The sole reason she'd started drinking at fourteen and cutting herself at fifteen, had been to try and obliterate them. No amount of hard drugs had ever set her free from the torment, and the cause of that had started at three years old, maybe even younger. Her grandfather had not been the only abuser, either. It was a place for bad people, her mother slurred into her ear one night after her sobbing woke her up. Tina had stroked her hair and said she was sorry, that bad people came here and they did bad things.

Heading for the kitchen she grabbed a tea-towel and quickly dried off her sopping hair, then shoved on wellies, grabbed a padded anorak and scarf, rammed on Clint's Barbour hat that he used for hunting, took his truck keys and shot out of the front door. How could she sleep knowing her son was up there?

***

At four am she parked the truck outside the farmhouse gates and got out. Wolfs Cross consisted of one farmhouse, two dilapidated old cottages, and several static caravans. The gypsy camp, as she called it, squatted in drizzly darkness. Just one dog, an Alsatian trained to attack, prowled back and forth behind the gate.

"Here, boy! Here, Loki!" Crouching to the dog's height she called him over. There wasn't an animal she'd encountered yet that wouldn't come to her. It had always been thus. Now though, that power was amplified, and there was no doubt the dog would obey without question.

Whining a little, Loki lowered himself onto his hindquarters and dropped to the floor, crawling over on his belly.

She rooted in the jacket pockets and found some crumbling biscuit pieces, holding out her hand to the dog. She always kept biscuits for Gul and sometimes forgot to empty out the remains. It came in handy anyway, and Loki duly licked the sugary treat from her palms.

"Now, do me a favour and I'll return it three-fold," she whispered softly.

The dog gazed intently into her eyes, the look she found in them both adoring and afraid.

"Let me in. Let me climb over the gate and don't make a sound. Once I've got to the house you can go wake Kade. You won't get into trouble, I promise. Now, go sit in the woodshed where it's dry. Wait! Until I'm in!" She pointed to the wood store by the house. "Go. Quiet!"

Retaining a submissive posture, Loki slinked away in the direction she pointed, before trotting faster into the shadows with his tail tucked in. Once he'd reached the wood store, he sat watching, alert yet docile. As if hypnotised. Only the light in his eyes was visible.

Satisfied he was not going to stop her getting to her destination, Kezia sprinted over to where she knew Gul would be, and then hurled herself against the door. Her mother, kicked out by her father, Kade, now squatted in one of the condemned cottages. It should have been razed to the ground many moons ago, but far from having been demolished, the place had electric wiring rigged up from the main house and a satellite dish stuck on the wall.

She banged on the door with her fists. "Mum! It's me! Have you got Gul? Mum! Wake up!"

Not a sound came from within.

Kezia kicked the door repeatedly with her boot,

shouting, "Wake up! Wake up! It's me - Kez! Mum!"

A light came on in one of the bedrooms over at the farmhouse.

"Shit!"

Waking Kade was akin to poking a sleeping cobra with a stick. But adrenalin had the upper hand, and besides – the uncoiling, spitting serpent of her own was rearing up for one hell of a fight.

She stepped back from the cottage door, rain lashing her face as she stared across at the house. Kade's lanky figure was in the doorway, loading a shotgun.

A click sounded, followed by the sound of the slide pumping backwards then forwards, charging the chamber to fire. "Who's there?" The voice was thick and syrupy with sleep and liquor.

"Kade, it's me, Kez. I'm here for Gul. Is he here"

She walked a few yards closer, revealing her identity.

"Fuck's sake, Kez!"

Behind him a heavily pregnant girl lumped into view. Wearing pink pyjamas her bump seemed enormous, an incongruous contrast to the frailty of her curved spine, which caused her to slump to one side with the weight.

Kezia cringed inside. Twenty years younger, Paige Morse was both a niece and a half-sister – one of Tina's offspring like herself. She shuddered. The girl hadn't yet turned sixteen, and as far as she knew was unable to read or write. Wolfs Cross never changed.

"I need to find him urgently. He's missing. Have you seen him? Has my mother got him?"

He lowered the shotgun. "What d'ya mean, missing?"

"Clint left him with Tina. He should have collected him but he didn't. I need to know where he is."

"Stupid bastard."

"I just want to know if he's here or not. I can't wake her."

"Funny that," he muttered. For a second he disappeared, then re-emerging he shoved on boots and ran out into the yard. "Here - spare keys. Let yourself in and take the kid 'ome. Just keep it down alright, or you'll wake the rest of 'em up."

"Thanks."

"Where's my fucking dog, by the way? What you done to 'im?"

"He's fine. Whistle. He'll come."

They stood in the rain for a minute eyeing each other. She'd never called him, 'Dad.' He left her mother when she was a baby, and after that there had been many different fathers. All she knew was that Kade seemed to rule the camp. Raindrops beaded on his eyelashes and in the oblong of light from the farmhouse doorway he looked much older than she recalled, heavily grooved around the mouth and across the forehead, his mouth a grim line.

Eventually he nodded and she knew that for now she was dismissed.

Lamps had been switched on in several of the caravans now, including her mother's place.

"I 'ope he's there," said Kade.

"Me too."

Marching over to Tina's cottage, Kezia rapped hard on the door, turned the key and walked straight in.

***

CHAPTER EIGHTEEN

Disorientated and dishevelled, Tina Greenwood was ambling down the corridor from the bedroom at the back of the cottage when Kezia burst in shouting for Gul.

"What the bleedin' 'ell's going on? Who is it?"

The house reeked of bad plumbing and greasy cooking. Almost treading on a mouse that shot across the floor, Kezia jumped back and grabbed at the wall to steady herself, noticing just in time the huge spider she nearly put her hand on.

"Oh my God!"

The mouse skittered under a skirting board as she flicked on the torch. Covered in rodent droppings the linoleum was filthy, the kitchen at the end little more than a rusty stand-alone cooker and a fold-down Formica table. Not a spare inch remained that wasn't piled high with empty cans, bottles, dirty clothing, and over-loaded carrier bags full of decomposing rubbish.

Kezia grimaced. This wasn't where she'd grown up – that had been either in the main house or one of the caravans. This hovel was something the others had rigged up for Tina, a drunk who'd taken to lying under a bush if she couldn't make it home before passing out. Long before she'd reached this state though, Tina had given birth to eleven children, most of them with Kade Morse, but also with his brother and his father, Kezia's grandfather. The latter now deceased. The static caravans were occupied by various members of the Morse family, with most of the men working for Sam Elwyn, or providing local butchers with wild game.

"You're living in a right mess," she said, trying not to gag as her mother lumbered closer. "It's disgusting in 'ere. You pissed again?"

"What?"

"God, you stink like a dead badger. When did you last 'ave a wash?"

"Well, that's a blurry cheek, tha' is – bursting into my 'ouse at God knows what time… What time is it? Wha' you want, anyhow?"

"Gul. I've come to collect Gul," she shouted. "I can't believe Clint left him 'ere. I mean, look at this place! Where is he?" She was stomping from room to room, calling him. Damp glistened on the stone walls like sweat, the floorboards bounced with rot, and rain pummelled the iron roof. Strangely hypnotic, the sound instantly triggered one of the worst flashbacks - a particular night when she'd lain awake having been roused by the ferocity of a storm. Her bed at that time must have been in a lean-to, she couldn't remember exactly, but what she did recall, in all its stark, gut-wrenching detail, was the stab of fear as the door to that room cranked open and her grandfather's wiry form stood silhouetted against the inky night sky, a silvery veil of torrential rain behind him. That had been the first time.

"Gul? Gul? It's Mum!"

Every room was unfurnished, some with window panes missing. Behind her, Tina seemed to be ranting about something but it was incomprehensible. She tuned her out. All she wanted to do was grab Gul and get him out of this hell-hole.

Tina's own room was the very last, at the end of the corridor.

She barged in slamming back the door. Not once had she ever left Gul with her mother. On the days when she worked late shifts and couldn't pick him up from nursery, Clint was supposed to do the parenting. He'd only lie on the sofa watching TV, or more usually loll around in bed, but at least Gul was safe. Why the hell did he bring him here? He had strict instructions - if there was ever a problem with him doing his bit, he was supposed to ask Lindsay next door. Lindsay who was sober and washed properly, and had two well-fed, clean kids of her own.

Grumbling to herself while trying not to inhale the overpowering stench of body odour and stale alcohol, she lunged towards the grubby bed in the corner and stripped back the duvet with one swoop.

"Gul?"

The sagging mattress was stained and lumpy, dipping in the middle where Tina had been lying.

Where was he? Why wasn't he here?

"Gul? Gul? Where are you?"

"I keep tellin' yer–"

Panicking, Kezia ran in and out of all the other rooms, searching each one again. All were unfit for habitation. Some had missing chunks out of the floor, others were open to the elements. None had any furniture.

She tore back to her mother's room again, unable to accept he was most definitely not here. As if he would be silently hiding from her.

Finally she stopped running, and turned to look at her mother. "Where is he, then? Where's he gone? I don't understand."

"I dunno—"

"What do you mean, you 'dunno'? Did Clint drop him off tonight or not? We need the lights on. Fuck it if the others notice. I'm beyond caring." She reached for the switch.

"Don't! Don't put the light on or you'll get electrocuted in this weather."

"What? And my boy was here? Oh my fucking God." Her heartbeat had escalated to near fibrillation. "Mum! Listen!" She shook her by the shoulders in a futile attempt to sober her up. "Was Gul here this afternoon? This evening? Try to remember. Did Clint drop him off? I need to know if he definitely came here."

Tina's small, bleary eyes, half-blinded with cataracts, seemed unable to focus – darting around in her head like pinballs in a machine. In the bobbing torchlight her face bulged to grotesque, rolls of wobbling fat trembling beneath her chin, the hair a nest of yellow and white straw sticking out in all directions. "Oh yeah, he was 'ere, alright. 'E were playing out in the yard, 'appy as Larry 'e were."

Kezia's face twitched with distaste. Chicken poop and sadistic little cousins who never washed – what a country idyll!

"That's right." She reached for a packet of cigarettes, lit one and offered it to Kezia.

"No…"

Tina took a drag. "Yeah, 'aving a whale of a time, he was." A vague smile lifted her slack features, and Kezia resisted the urge to shake her so hard her remaining few teeth jiggled out along with the cigarette.

"And then what? When it went dark did he come in here with you or go back inside with someone else? What happened. Is he in one of the caravans? Try hard to remember exactly."

Tina's features screwed into concentration. "Well, that's just it. I came in 'ere and must have dozed off, I suppose. Anyhow, when I woke up and came out to call him, it was dark and he wasn't there no more. One of the other kids said a man had come for 'im, and they'd gone off 'ome through the woods…Oh yeah, that's right – he said a man from the church!" Her face brightened. "So 'e was taken 'ome, see? Through the woods!"

A man from the church…

Kezia backed out of the room, then sprinted down the hallway and out into the rain. It was blowing sideways now, spraying her face as she whirled around and around. *Where was he? Out here on his own in this weather? A man had come for him… Oh my God, oh my God…*

On the periphery of the camp the woods towered black and impenetrable, with not a glimmer of light. From this direction there were no paths to the village church or anywhere else. She knew this absolutely, from all the days spent hiding from her grandfather and his brothers. No, the only building you'd find if you ventured through there would be the monastery.

***

CHAPTER NINETEEN

SYLVIA

Stunned, Sylvia turned to stare. Belinda's normally vivid blue eyes were devoid of expression, her face a robotic mask. Yet the voice emanating from her throat was loaded with malice.

The mouth curved into a nasty smile. "You have been fighting again, n'est pa? He does not like what you do, does he? But…" Unexpectedly Belinda stepped right into her personal space and Sylvia drew back in alarm. Belinda's face was less than a couple of inches away. "There are things he has not told you." Her eyes penetrated her own, searching for a reaction. "Ah yes, I see now – he didn't tell you anything, did he?" The lower lip stuck out in a parody of sympathy. "Oh, poor you." She stroked her arm, smiling. "So… how you say… ignorant!"

Despite her rocketing heart rate, Sylvia forced herself to breathe slowly in an effort to calm her nerves. It was one matter putting a client under hypnosis and speaking to spirits who were lost or confused, it was quite another when they jumped out and targeted you personally without any warning. And this was twice in less than twenty-four hours.

So what was it she didn't know about her husband? What hadn't Mark told her?

Belinda was watching her closely, the spirit inside her reading her mind and revelling in the discomfort she saw there. For a moment, a little too long, she had fallen for the trick, allowing herself to be needled, and the focus to be shifted onto herself instead of dealing with the problem. From upstairs raised voices, and what sounded like a roar, kick-started her into action.

"Belinda! Can you hear me? Belinda?"

Belinda's eyes flickered into semi-recognition.

"Grip my hand if you can hear me, Belinda."

The other woman's hand closed on hers, as she swayed and sank onto the bottom step of the stairs.

Sylvia squeezed her shoulder. "Okay, wait there. We'll talk later. Right now I have to help your son."

When she got to the top of the stairs, Ralph's bedroom door was wide open and Mark was standing in the doorway, barring the exit.

From behind him Sylvia took in the scene. Essie had not exaggerated. Every available inch of wall, curtains and bedding was covered in pieces of paper scribbled with black ink. Airless and littered with dirty washing, videos and used cups and plates, there were also signs of dark arts practice: black candles, a pentagram hung upside down on the wall, a Ouija board and partially burned sigils on scraps of cloth and paper. All this she took in with one swoop. Because most notable of all was the boy himself.

Ralph was up on his haunches like a wild dog, about to spring from the bed. With teeth bared, his eyes were rolling into the back of his head as, with torrents of abuse, he raged at Mark in a chorus of wheezing, mocking bass tones that had her prickling with cold all over.

"He's got schizophrenia," Mark was saying.

"I don't think so—"

At the sound of their voices, Ralph stopped springing up and down on his haunches and cocked his head to one side. "Ooh! Arguing again!"

Sylvia froze.

The accent, like the one Belinda had used, was French, and the knowing accusation the same. With a lance to the heart, she registered for the third time now, that here was something intensely personal. She and Mark were deliberate targets. She looked back at the boy who was now staring at her intently, awaiting a response.

"Who are you? What's your name?"

The smile was a venomous sneer that twisted his mouth and hardened his eyes, as ignoring her he turned to Mark. "You should not let her answer back like that, you know? You hate it, don't you, big man? That's why you're an…" Here he stopped to savour the word, before delivering it with a relish that made him salivate, "…adulterer…"

You don't know your husband very well, do you, my lovely?

He didn't tell you anything, did he? Oh, poor you…

She wavered, refusing to look at Mark. Never in all her twenty years as a hypnotist had she ever encountered the demonic, but it looked as though this could be a first. If it wasn't, then whatever earthbound entities were involved here, they were hate-fuelled to such an extent they could be equally dangerous.

The words of a professor she'd once worked with

151

came back to her. 'Forget anything else I may have taught you, Sylvia, but not this: Should you ever come across the dark side, it is absolutely essential you do not show fear or it will feed them like a drug. They will do anything to make their victim feel terror, guilt or shame: lie, cheat, abuse, make you think you're insane – and from that fear they will grow until their presence becomes more powerful than you. They will bring you down. Their mission is to destroy the human spirit. Don't ever, ever, forget that.'

Her voice sounded tremulous. "Ralph, can you hear me? It's Sylvia."

"Of course he can't hear you," said Mark. "He's psychotic and speaking in tongues. I'm going to ring Brody and put him in the loop."

Doctor Brody was the Consultant Psychiatrist Mark worked with at the County District Hospital. According to Mark he was an out-dated pacifist who did 'fuck-all' for a living. He would however, need to be called in order to have Ralph admitted and sectioned immediately.

"Yes, go. Go now," she said.

As Mark turned to leave, Ralph broke into a giggle, bouncing up and down excitedly. "She doesn't know, does she? She doesn't know you're screwing…" Again he stretched out the deliciousness of the word he was about to impart, watching closely for the effect it would have on them both. "…Kitteeeee."

"Shut up, that's enough!" Mark walked out. "I'll ring Brody. And we need an ambulance."

His footsteps thundered down the stairs, leaving Sylvia alone in the doorway.

Ralph's face had contorted into a near unrecognisable, gleeful malevolence. Blood had congealed on his ravaged skull like lumps of tar, a strange ring of hair left intact. With a start she realised it resembled a monk's tonsure. His pallor was grey and drawn, the hollows under his eyes bruised. Sores had broken out on what had been healthy skin, similar to a heroin addict getting zero nutrition, and he'd bitten his lips so badly the flesh was chewed. That he was terribly ill was without question. That she had so little time to prevent an incarceration which would quickly result in his death, was the issue at stake. He would die in days. Whoever was inside him would make sure of it.

Christ, please help me!

Her heart lurched and her stomach twisted into knots, as silently she offered up a prayer for protection and began to surround herself with white light. Here she stood alone, on a dismal morning in March, looking evil directly in the face. Most of the modern world would say Ralph had schizophrenia, or dissociative identity disorder, or anything else that had been categorised and put in a medical text book. But the one diagnosis a doctor would never give would be what it really was. How well dark spirits were protected by western society. In many other parts of the world, those places considered by the west to be primitive or inferior, the true diagnosis would be made and the boy saved. Alas, the residing spirits in Ralph knew precisely what this situation entailed.

And now they were waiting for her next move.

Already his lungs were weakening, his breath rattling and laboured. A map of veins had appeared on one cheek and was spreading across his face. The arteries in his neck bulged.

"I repeat, who are you? What is your name?"

"He's fucking…Kitteeeee…"

"You should not be in the body of this boy or any other living being. You are dead and should go to the light to continue your spiritual journey. I can help you. Now tell me your name or names."

"Oh. Interesting. Hmmm…Let's think… No, Mrs Psychologist, let's talk about your husband instead. Yes, let's talk about that. It's faaar more interesting."

The boy's eyes were alight with fiery enjoyment, the pupils morphing from ellipses to squares to diamonds, the irises jaundice yellow.

"Tell me your name!" Sylvia repeated.

"Did you know your husband meets her in the woods? They go to the altar. Do you want to know how he fucks her? He spreads her out across it, on her belly, and pushes up her skirts…and she screams for more…"

She had to turn this around and reject the images bombarding her mind, or she was done for. But it was difficult, so damned difficult. Imagining a suit of armour made of mirrors facing outwards, she used the power of her imagination to deflect them. "Tell me your name or we have no deal," she said sharply. "No exchange of information, no nothing."

The malignant snickering stopped dead. "No deal? What deal?"

"Tell me your name. I cannot do business when I don't know who you are."

The sound of a rapid phone conversation coming from downstairs heightened the urgency.

"Tell me right now or we have no chance of a deal, and I can offer you something a whole lot better than what you currently have."

"We don't believe you."

"Okay listen, this boy whose body you are inhabiting will shortly be taken to hospital. Once there he will be restrained and given strong drugs, but because you are draining his energy he will rapidly lose strength and die. What good is that to you? Don't you understand? I could set you free from your miserable dark chains and take you to the light, where you–"

"The light burns us. The light is a lie. It is not there. We prefer to be here."

"Us? How many?"

"Burdo told us to stay here. We have to stay."

"What are your names and who is Burdo?"

"We have to stay. The light will burn us."

"No, listen to me. You were human, weren't you? You once lived, did you not? The light is pure love. It's real, I have seen it and it's beautiful. It is your destiny, your right as a human spirit to go there. Come with me, let me show you. Or you will descend to that dark place again, from where you will never be free of fear and hatred. Every time you attach to a living person's spirit you sap their life force and drag them down. You ruin their life. Meanwhile you are not progressing on your spiritual journey. You are lost and in pain. Listen to me – if there is light for me there is light for you too. Don't you want that?"

The boy's eyes burned into hers. "Such lies. You know nothing. You are fed lies. There is no light. Only ash. We have been disciples of God, but it's all lies…

lies…"

Her confidence wavered. *Disciples of God?*

At the sound of a door slamming, Ralph suddenly leapt down from the bed onto the floor in front of her, and she couldn't help but spring back.

"You lie. All of you. Lie. But we're back now. The door has opened." More than one voice curdled in his throat. "And they will be repaid for what they did to the disciples of the Lord."

It looked as though he was going to attack and with her back to the wall she was about to shout for help, when abruptly he crumpled to the floor, rolled onto his side, and lay with his limbs jerking as if he was fitting.

For now, the energy force was spent.

She fetched a pillow and placed it under his head, as the fit subsided, his eyes closed and he appeared to fall asleep. He'd been such a handsome creature – tall and raven haired with the same forget-me-not blue eyes his mother had. She would not forget the day he'd found his father hanging in the woods. Seventeen-year-old Ralph Sully had apparently cut the body down with an axe before cradling his father in his arms, sitting there on the forest floor stroking his hair for hours before they were found. Belinda had tracked him down after becoming worried. Gideon hadn't come back from his morning walk through the woods to the newsagent, and Ralph should have been in school.

His forehead was damp and a fever burned. The infestation had exhausted him, and as such it would be safe to physically move him to hospital. That he should go was without question, but she had to speak to Brody first, before Mark got to him. If Mark had his way

Ralph would be in a psychiatric unit for the rest of his life, and somehow she didn't think that would be long. Brody though, being the consultant, would have the final say.

With her hand on his forehead she spoke directly to his unconscious mind. He must be strong. He must believe in the light and walk in the light. She would move the spirits on to a more appropriate place as soon as possible. They were beginning to show signs of engagement, of confusion.

"Stay strong, Ralph. I don't know how this happened to you, but I know you can hear me. Your thoughts are not your own just now but your soul is. And I am talking to your soul. Hear me and know I will help you all I can, okay? Stay strong! Hang in there, okay? You're not alone. I can and will help you."

Reciting the Lord's Prayer quickly and quietly, she then prayed to God for her own strength and guidance. There would have to be an exorcism. There appeared to be a whole nest of seething entities inside him, with the leader, Burdo, having vacated by the sound of it. It was often the case – when the strongest, leading spirit abandoned the others, the remaining nest of spirits would have to be dealt with one by one. Only there wasn't enough time.

This could be too much for one person. A colleague may be able to help, but the nearest was in the next county and the situation was an emergency. What about Brody? If not, she was on her own because as soon as the medication went into Ralph's system he was lost. Once a patient was deemed as having hallucinations and delusions, these same beliefs were subsequently ignored and treated as false, a figment of a sick mind. As such the infesting spirits were laughing, safe in the knowledge no one was ever going to remove them. The host would get sicker – cutting and starving themselves – whilst alienating all those around them, and degrading, debasing, their own image and memory. At least for the moment the spirits were quiet and the boy was sleeping.

As she sat stroking his forehead, there were a few minutes to reflect.

We were disciples of the Lord... A door has opened... Burdo told us to stay...

Had the infestation happened while he sat with his father in his arms for all those hours? Or was it in the graveyard? But he had to have invited this in. She glanced at the Ouija board and the black candles. Had Kezia Elwyn opened this door?

It's a lie...there is no light!

There was a history here in Monkspike, wasn't there?

Picking up one of the many hundreds of scraps of paper scribbled in dark ink, she frowned. Then selected another. And another. Then a handful. They were all identical! She stood up, snatched them off the curtains, from the bed, stuck to the wardrobe doors, even glued to the ceiling – all the exact same image: that of a small, wiry man wearing a hooded robe, the features heart-plunging in their photographic detail. Far from being the fraught scribbles of a madman, these were artistically precise, as if sketched by a talented artist, or even photographed. And the man was quite distinct, his pock-marked, pitted nose triangular and wide, the spoon-shaped mouth cracking into a decaying grin, the drum-tight sheen of skin pulled taut over the cadaverous bones of his face. What clutched at her heart with horror though, was the expression in the blackest coal-hole eyes imaginable. Look into those too long it would be to fall headlong into the abyss.

Christ, this boy had to be saved.

Hurrying downstairs, panic ripped through her. She had to speak to Mark and Belinda before the ambulance arrived. Let them agree to her seeing Brody immediately, to stall any form of treatment until she'd spoken to him.

Brody was her best shot. Mark referred to him as an incompetent fool, but then he referred to everyone like that at the moment. But Brody was no fool. He'd been a psychiatrist for forty years and seen it all. Not only that but he was a deeply spiritual man and by far the more likely of the two to understand, or at least listen, to what she proposed.

She walked smartly into the kitchen.

Mark and Belinda were seated at the table, their chairs pushed close together. Belinda was sobbing, plucking at his arms, his shirt – tearfully pleading with him. In turn he was holding her at bay, his expression set in a mould of irritation. It was quite as if they were the squabbling husband and wife: he dominant and aggressive, she submissive and weepy – a washout of the confident, positive woman she really was. Abuser and abused were the words flying into Sylvia's mind as she stood in the doorway with her mouth open.

Something was panning out here that she couldn't see. Something obvious right under her nose. Yet hidden. All she knew for sure was that it hurt like hell.

***

CHAPTER TWENTY

"The boy will have to be sectioned," said Mark, quickly adjusting to her presence. "I've just been telling Belinda there's no other option."

"Right."

"Naturally she's upset. Maybe we could put the kettle on, Syl?"

"Sure."

"While I go and ring Brody," he added, making a swift exit.

Her words trailed after him. "I thought you'd already done that."

Belinda watched him go. And Sylvia observed her doing so. Frankly, if logic didn't dictate otherwise, she'd swear Belinda Sully was in love with her husband.

Her heart panged and tears stung her eyes. Were they seeing each other, then? Oh God, this was unbearable. Mark had definitely been distant and snappy for a while now, almost itching for an argument, never agreeing on anything. And was that why Belinda had never wanted to be friends? Was that the reason - Belinda, the glamorous blonde widow, who should be with the handsome doctor instead of herself, the mousy, bespectacled one? Shock and misery engulfed her, and it was all she could do to inject enough doubt into that assumption to speak, to function.

"Ralph's much calmer now," she said in a thin, distracted voice. "Asleep. He'll be alright for a while. Enough time for us to make arrangements, anyway."

Making a determined effort it seemed, Belinda switched her attention from Mark to herself, the beseeching expression on her face draining away, replaced with one of confusion. "Ralph?"

Sylvia turned to face the tiled kitchen wall, reaching for the kettle because she needed a coffee very badly – a strong one with a lot of sugar in it. Her voice wobbled with emotion as she spoke. "Your son's asleep."

"Yes, good."

"What about Essie? Ralph's going to be taken to the General for assessment and you'll want to come with us."

"I can't. I'll have to stay here and tell people he's broken his leg or something. They mustn't know!"

She spooned coffee into the cups with shaking hands, desperately trying to focus. Why the hell hadn't Belinda noticed how ill her own son was? And what was this crap about caring what the neighbours thought? It didn't fit with everything she thought she knew about her. There was something going on here that would explain all of this; she just had to work out what it was. Keep her head. Right now it was important to do her job, stay practical, and get as much information as possible. In less than an hour her wits were going to be pitched against spirits who knew far more than she did.

Instead of remonstrating with her, she changed tack. "Belinda, who's Burdo?"

Behind her the other woman stiffened and the atmosphere changed. She'd already picked up the boiling kettle, was about to pour water into the mugs, when she noticed Belinda's reflection in the steel and almost dropped it.

It was a hall of mirrors moment. Belinda's face had distorted, the forehead bulging and the jaw dropping to reveal a gaping mouth dislocated from the joints, like that of a snake about to devour prey several times its girth.

It's a trick…just a trick…like looking into the back of a spoon.

Overhead the kitchen light flicked on and off, on and off, then completely off.

She slammed down the kettle. The bang of steel on wood crashed through her bones, searing through nerves. Swaying, she clutched at the work unit and fought down the overpowering need to pass out. A heavy weight was pressing down on top of her head, her heart hammering so rapidly that pain radiated down her left arm and thumped into her throat. This was a heart attack. Oh, dear God, whatever was in this house affecting this family, it meant to annihilate her. There was no way it would allow interference.

Fighting with every ounce of strength she had, silently she pleaded with God. *Dear Lord this is my moment of great need. I beg you to send me your divine light. I beg you to let me help these people, only please dear Lord, save me now. I need your love and strength.*

The worst washed over her in a wave of nausea. She lurched to the sink and leaned over, dry-retching and sweating profusely, her face burning while her back shivered.

Belinda's voice was tinny and remote. "Are you

alright?"

Her eyes were streaming. Nodding, she gasped. "Not sure what came over me. I'm so sorry."

"You'll have to lay off the wine at night."

"Yeah." Dabbing her eyes with a piece of kitchen roll, she slumped onto the nearest chair. It was like the worst hangover ever. Her head pounded along with every pulse beat. "I just need a glass of water. I haven't had anything to eat yet, that could be it."

She had never believed in God until she'd worked in spirit release therapy – a career path prompted by a client who under hypnosis had begun to talk in another voice. And although not affiliated to any religion, she had found power, strength and release with her personal belief. We are after all, she thought, only human, and with that came fear and weakness. No one had all the answers.

"I'll make us some toast. If Ralph's left anything, that is." Belinda had switched to her usual breezy persona as if nothing had happened, chatting rapidly while finishing the coffees and sticking bread into the toaster. "You sit down," she said, grabbing butter and marmalade, plates and knives. "It's going to be a long day and it's been a rotten start. We've got to keep healthy. If he's asleep I suggest we get some sustenance while Mark's ringing Brody. I've got to get dressed yet, as well."

Sylvia took a sip of coffee, trying to keep it down inside her sea-swell of a stomach. It would be a safe bet that Bel knew nothing about the malicious spirit infesting her. Very probably she simply lost time and had no recollection of what she'd said or done. Could be she was unaware of her behaviour around Mark, too. Although, that one didn't make sense at all.

She frowned. "Thanks. Yes, you're right."

Belinda, sitting opposite, began to butter toast.

"I need to know a few things though, if I'm going to help Ralph," said Sylvia. "And I'll be honest, I'm not in total agreement with the doctors on this. I mean, yes, he will have to be sectioned and I think you know that, but…" She leaned closer, lowering her voice so Mark would not overhear should he barge back in. "I don't think he should have any medication of any kind. Not yet. Not until I've had chance to talk to him. Look, I know this is going to sound crazy because it always does, and what I'm going to say to you is something you might well reject but I—"

To her astonishment, Belinda leaned across the table and grabbed both her hands. This was the same woman who'd broken down in the staffroom yesterday, only far more desperate. The words flew out in a torrent as if she had only seconds. "You asked who Burdo was? He's a monk! Or he was. I see him, Sylvia, and I'm scared to death. He's dressed in white and he's in my dreams and in my mind, and it's so, so real… Oh…oh…"

Her words trailed away and her features slackened. She let go of Sylvia's hands.

It was very similar to dissociative identity disorder, Sylvia thought, as if the controls of a car had been wrenched from the driver and someone else was now in charge.

But who? Who was coming? Was Burdo about to show himself again?

Outside a blackbird whistled, his song heralding a

single shaft of sunlight across the yard. The atmosphere buzzed, a white noise similar to that of a radio or television out of signal range, as Belinda once more gazed unseeingly into the middle distance.

The sound of the front door clicking open and footsteps marching down the hall towards the kitchen cut into the silence.

"Right, that's all sorted." Mark's voice seemed incongruously loud. "An ambulance is on its way—"

The temperature in the kitchen plunged rapidly. And Mark stopped short.

Belinda's features had become undefined, hovering in a haze of double-exposure, one image superimposed over the other. A pretty if harrowed looking woman struggling to surface over what was a decidedly coarse-looking male, with round black eyes and a large flattened nose.

One Sylvia had seen before. Just now. On the hundreds and hundreds of identical sketches Ralph had drawn.

***

CHAPTER TWENTY-ONE

KEZIA

There was no time to lose. Not a single second, especially on a night like this. He was only three – he could die of exposure. And that was if he'd wandered off on his own. What if the man who'd taken him was a paedophile? God knows there were a few of those in Monkspike.

With one furious backward glance at Tina, his so-called grandmother, who damn well should have been watching out for him, she ran towards the woods screaming his name until her throat hurt. This was her own fault too, and the agony of that truth made it all the worse.

"Gul! Gul! Where are you? Can you hear me?"

All the caravan lights were on now, the sleepers stumbling out with torches, asking what was happening.

"It's Gul," she heard her mother saying. "The lad's gone missing."

At the border of the forest, Kezia stopped and pulled out her mobile phone. The signal was down to one bar but she tried anyway.

"Hello, you've reached Emergency Services—"

Her heart jumped. A lifeline! "My boy! He's three years old and he's gone missing in the forest at

Monkspike."

"Can I take your name, please?" "Mine? Oh, for… yeah, right… Kezia Elwyn, his mother. Look, he was left with my mother at Wolfs Cross and I only just found out. I came over straight away but she hasn't seen him since yesterday evening. She said he went off with a man into the forest. Oh my God!" She raked the sopping hair back from her forehead. "He's gone…vanished…"

By the time she had given a full description and all her details, most of Wolfs Cross were out with flashlights and dogs, and for once she was grateful they were her own because they knew every inch of this place. If Gul was in these woods they would find him. And pulverise whoever they deemed responsible while they were about it.

She broke into a sprint, heading in the direction of the monastery.

A churchman? Why? Who?

Behind her, dogs yelped, bounding through the undergrowth and lights bobbed through the trees. They would search this whole area rapidly, the men familiar with every hide-out and deer-track. Where they were unlikely to look until last however, was where she was going first. St Benedict's had deliberately been positioned well away from the main village and was a considerable trek. The paths from both Monkspike to the west and Wolfs Cross to the east, were arduous and unmarked, and besides - it had that unholy reputation.

It was the reason she loved it and had come here as often as possible ever since she was a child. Drawn to the dark side, it thrilled and excited her. To lie amid the ruins at dusk and watch the bats dipping and diving, hear the ke-wick of tawny owls in the woods, and imagine she, and she alone, had privileged access to the dark courts of the underworld. Until recently she'd revelled in the mystery and the daring of it, never truly believing. But now... well... her heart fair stilted in her breast at the enormity of what she had done. All the old adages replayed: 'Sup with the devil use a long spoon'; 'You can't expect a liar to be true to his word'.

Was all this her fault? Was it?

Panting now, she tramped back up the hill she had so recently sprinted down. Four in the morning and the downpour was torrential. Blue-white flashes lit up the swaying treetops, the forest interior blacker than the night. Thunder cracked and rumbled around the hills, echoing through the valley as the storm swirled overhead, stuck in a never-ending vortex of grumbling discontent. It was becoming impossible to see ahead more than a few feet, rain streaming off branches into pits of mud below. With hands so numb and cold she could no longer feel them, she clutched at each tree trunk and shouted, "Gul!" at the top of her lungs.

Dawn would come soon, but this morning it would be a dark one. The night far too long. Feverishly she pushed herself onwards. Until the sound of shouts and yelping dogs behind became muted, and the dense woods closed in around her. The track was narrow now, the incline sharp and the thicket overgrown. The only trace of any recent presence was that of a deer and that had been a while ago, the cleft of a hoof imprinted where the animal had to grip in order to pull itself up. Breathing hard and fast she climbed steadily, until finally the outline of the scowles appeared at the top. And here, doubling over to get her breath, she could see across the whole valley, taking in St Benedict's and all the land around it. Every few seconds lightning flashed and forked, illuminating the scene.

Holding her arms wide, she filled her lungs and shouted, "Gul!"

Repeatedly she called his name. But again and again it came riding back on the echo of her own voice.

Who or what had taken her boy? *A man of the church…* If she'd only had her wits about her she should have asked why her mother said that. Long robes? Did she mean he was dressed like a priest? Or had Gul followed one of the ghostly white monks people swore they saw here sometimes? Ones she had seen herself only hours ago? But they had been apparitions. Is that what her mother saw?

She shook her head, wishing she'd brought cigarettes. Never in her life had she been so alone. Not lonely. Alone. Ghosts didn't abduct children though, did they? Or cause harm. Why would one come for a boy and lead him away? No, this had to be a real, flesh and blood human. And when she found him she would kill him with her bare hands, then follow him into the hereafter and make sure he was kicked all the way to hell. Her hands balled into fists and her whole face screwed up with overwhelming despair. Tears burned and her throat choked. This is what it was to love someone. To love them more than life itself.

Yet she had believed in spirits herself, hadn't she? Was that not why she was here? Why this had happened? All too willingly she had trusted a blue-eyed handsome demon who told her to go back home; after which she'd worshipped him, brought him libations, invoked darkness, cursed a woman she barely knew, and made pacts. And in amongst all that, had deliberately sought the destruction of another person for no known reason other than she felt compelled to do so. That intent had been so strong, and so all-consuming it had become an obsession to the exclusion of all else. There was a reward coming...she'd been convinced. A good life for her and Gul. And now look...

With that thought every ounce of pain and rage suddenly dissipated. All that was left was a monotony of greyness. A pelting sheet of cruel, cold rain in this, the cruellest and most merciless of hours.

Whatever it was has tricked you. And now it is here. You invited it, gave it strength and recognition in the human world, and now it has all the power, and you have none.

She sank to her haunches and hung her head.

Minutes passed as her misery set in to hopelessness. Raindrops trickled down her neck and her feet sank deeper into the mud. It had all been for nothing. She had become insane. Bad and insane. And now the one person she truly loved had been taken. So what now? What the fuck did she do now? Her very existence spiralled into nothing and her mind floundered in the falling confusion; grief and wretchedness dangerously fraying the cord between herself and sanity.

But, and it crept so gradually into her awareness as to suddenly seem quite loud, someone was laughing; more than that – in hysterics. Her head jerked up. The nasty laughter was everywhere, reverberating through the trees, rustling in the canopy of leaves, floating in on belts of rain. Throaty and hoarse like the caw-caw-caw of a raven.

Her features set to a rigid mask, a great thump of fear banging into her chest. That laugh – the same one she'd heard in the doctor's surgery, the raspy, bird-like screech. *Fuck. It was the demon. He was real. He was fucking real.*

She jumped up. *Holy fuck, what was coming? You stupid, stupid fool, Kezia. What have you messed with? What the hell have you done?*

The velvet blackness seemed to be lifting, becoming steamy and ethereal, the laughter emanating from within the forest sounding like teasing children playing and darting between the trees. Her head began to thud, sickness lodging in her throat. Stumbling backwards, she looked over her shoulder at the view below. At the monastery. Which way? Which way?

Go on…go on…

She put her hands up to her temples. If only the voice telling her what to do would stop. What was it inside her that made her do all these hellish things without even questioning them?

You opened up the doorway… and now you're going to see…You need to…

The ruins below shone white through the veil of rain. And just as before, the air crackled with static. Had it really only been a few hours since she was last here? On what, after all, was a special night. A night with perfect conditions for raising Malphas, giving power and strength to all who came with him. All those who had waited, for so long, in the darkness.

Rational thought receded once more. Her mind thudded in a dull cloud of incomprehension as the pull towards the monastery became magnetic and her limbs moved of their own accord. In a dreamlike state she began to walk down the bank, seamlessly entering another time and another world; one that felt strangely familiar. Gone the ruins. Once more the monastery stood in full majestic glory.

Except this time she did not stand as a watcher. This time the invisible barrier had been removed. The temperature soared, and the air was balmy with the scent of summer. The warm evening was alive with birdsong, heavily perfumed with honeysuckle and wild garlic. Thunder flies swarmed, sticking to her warm, clammy skin, as sweeping through long grass her feet did not appear to touch the ground, but to float above it. Bare feet that knew the way, were taking her swiftly towards the building. A full moon steadily rose on one side of the valley, the sun dipping in a watercolour splash of tangerine and pink on the other. Lambs bleated on the hillside, and the gush of a full river dashed and sparkled over the rocks, gurgling in the reeds.

How could this be? Another dream? Another vision? Yet she was taking part; moving into the unfolding scene, unable to prevent herself from advancing closer and closer to the monastery. Burnished gold in the blaze of sunset, the sculpted arches, rows of windows, courtyards and fountains were dazzling, and her senses reeled. Yet the conviction of having been here before was overpowering, and the excitement tingling inside all too real. On reaching the walls, she lay flat against them, scanning the fields beyond – cat-like, alert.

Good, no one saw me.

She hurried towards a wooden doorway at the side of the building, just as a hypnotic chant began to rise, along with coils of incense, into a sky brushed with faint washes of rose and violet as evening tipped into dusk.

Smiling to herself, almost laughing that the monks were so afraid of the dark, she let herself into the chilly passageway, this the night stair leading from the dormitory to the church. No woman would ever be allowed in a monks' dormitory, but that was not where she was going. While the monks were praying she would be visiting the Abbot, the one who made sure his flock remained petrified of the devil, of the night, of sin and any form of indulgence.

Or you will burn in hell for all eternity, and there will be no God to save you!

And what a good job he had done. Every sin confessed was to Burdo. Every tiny wanton thought or slip of purity, voiced to him. They starved, worked hard and prayed even harder.

While Burdo…laughed. He chuckled, he manipulated, he enjoyed every pleasure, and especially he liked to watch herself when she bathed or danced in the woods…

Still, she must tamp down the disgust and keep him busy this night. Away from the women in the village and away from the children. He was repugnant to her, utterly loathsome: a sinewy, ale-breathed, pox-ridden pig. But on this one last diabolical task she had staked everything. And so mote it be.

Lit candles flickered from inside the dormitories. She

stooped to enter the narrow corridor. Paused to listen. There was something amiss. Her heart snagged on its beat. They knew something. Had they been alerted?

The monks were not so much praying as frantically begging, "Lord help us. Lord protect us. Lord the Devil is with us. Lord help us…"

The chant was increasing steadily in both fervour and rapidity, and a feeling of impending dread filled the air, lengthening shadows and leeching the light. She stood in the dusky passageway, hesitating. The stillness was unnatural. The birds had stopped singing, and what had been a balmy evening now thickened to one of perspiring humidity. What was coming?

Heat. Heat on the back of her neck.

The fear was palpable, sickly and pungent like that of condemned animals waiting in line at the abattoir.

She stood on the threshold.

Then the candles were snuffed out and the chanting ceased.

In the darkness and the silence, she held her breath. Something was badly wrong. Burdo? Should she get to him or not? That he had to be kept here was all she knew. It was her one task.

There came an image in her mind of many pairs of eyes peering out of the window slats upstairs, watching like bats from within a cave.

Inching along the corridor, she moved to where there was a hole in the wall. To see what they saw. And when she did, a part of her died inside.

Held high along the forest edge was a row of fire torches. Not just one row, but dozens…an entire army by the look of it… at least a hundred or more men on horseback. Watching and at the ready. For what? To attack? But why so many and so heavily armed?

And he would know she was still inside!

***

CHAPTER TWENTY-TWO

The shock of betrayal was shattering. Keep him out of the village and out of the forest, was all John had said. She was to keep his attention averted while they carried out a raid on the monastery's stocks and provisions, that was all. He'd said nothing about an attack on the monks.

Panicked she stood with her back to the cool, stone wall, wondering what to do, where to run. The only reason she'd agreed to this was because the villagers had nothing. Her own people slept on straw bales next to the livestock, in huts choked with wood smoke. Banned from hunting so much as a rabbit in their own back yard, they were starving, and all the while the monks here kept cellars full of wine and cheese. Her family would be rewarded, said John, while she…

The memory of his fingertips tingling down her spine, of his velvet soft kisses along her shoulder, made her heart squeeze in pain. Had it all been a lie? All that love, all that passion… and she had lain with him…he had the kind of eyes she had been captive to, had fallen into mesmerised. There had been no resistance to him as he had fallen to his knees before her, and looking up, holding her gaze, pushed up her skirts.

And then thou will be my lady! Just do as I ask…One more time…

No! This could not be, it could not! He would not discard her like this… And he had raised an army. Did he plan to have innocent men torched in their beds? Just to get to the cellars? By now she should be with Burdo in his quarters.

So then, he had left her here to die!

A sudden and violent migraine disrupted all further thought. Sinking to the ground, her mind blacked out. And when she came to, vision after vision flashed before her eyes. Fragments of memory or fractured hallucinations? Was this real or not? She could not be sure of anything, except for one thing – the raw emotional impact was profound, and it was taking her apart piece by piece. What was unfolding here was a truth; a hard, nasty, bitter truth at that. One someone wanted her to see.

Clearly the army had waited all night, because now skeins of rose heralded daybreak. On the hill a row of spruces tapered into a pale sky along the forest's edge, and a low mist hovered over the valley. Still they were biding their time, horses snorting and pawing the ground, waiting for the call to arms.

Why?

Inside the dormitories, the anticipation had stretched across the hours like a spider's thread, becoming ever finer until the gossamer thin strands of expectation and hyper-vigilance could stretch no more. And one by one the monks crept from their beds to look outside. Had they survived the night? It was almost over yet none had slept, and weariness lay heavily upon them. Sunrise Vigils were due and the lonely toll of the bell echoed around the walls. Some were praying aloud by their beds, kneeling with heads bowed.

"Praise God, the creator of light. Praise Christ who has risen, victor over Satan, sin and death."

In one hour light would break through the sanctuary windows and set them free from the horrors of darkness. Yet the bell's toll seemed dull for all that; a death knell for the doomed who knew the end was imminent.

The stench of fear was sickening, the fresh new day ominous. Like the condemned waiting to be led out to the gallows, the dawn preceded eternal darkness and the hell in which they knew they would burn. For who had been pure enough? Who had been without sin? The Abbott's dire warnings revisited each and every one of them as more and more fervently they pleaded with God, remembering a particular moment of weakness or gratification with shame and intolerable guilt.

'Forgive me, Father, forgive me…'

And while they beseeched God to show lenience and have mercy on their souls, high on the ridge the spurring kick to horses' flanks now impelled the charge towards them. Thunderous hooves pounded down the slope – riders whose faces were rigid with hatred, the sound of swords already slicing from sheaths, as wielding fire brands they roared their curses and stormed down the slope.

The army would be upon them in seconds. She found she could not move. Terror struck every nerve fibre, paralysing the muscles, the scream dead in her throat. Even as battering rams broke down the doors and men raced along the corridors, there was nothing she could do to stop the images, to block the sounds of the poor souls crying out to God for their lives, and the slice and crunch of blades puncturing sinew and bone.

She shut her eyes and covered her ears with her hands, yet still the nightmare played out: the close-range terror of faces she would never forget. Eyes rolled into the backs of their heads, tongues were ripped from their throats in one flash of iron, and heads were hacked off using axes too blunt for the job. Many of the monks had been lying on their single iron beds, most were still in prayer, others in hiding. Not a shred of mercy was shown by the assailants as every last one was murdered in a frenzy of bloodlust, after which they ransacked the building, not stopping until it was ablaze and burning to the ground.

The bell had long since stopped tolling.

After what seemed like all eternity, her limbs shakily began to respond again, and the migraine lifted. She tried to stand. The smell of burning human flesh and acrid smoke had cleared, leaving only the clean, sobering scent of early morning rain. Much darker and colder now, the air was wintry clear and the ruins were once again just ruins.

Looking down at herself, she gasped at the state she was in. Had she been lying in the mud? Even her hair was caked in it. One minute she had been looking down from the scowles and the next she was waking up in the dirt.

What was happening? What was she doing here? Had she fallen?

Disorientated and unsettled, she stood up and tried to wipe off the worst of the mud. The light had changed, shafts of silvery grey permeating heavy clouds. She rooted for her phone and checked its torch worked.

How long had she lost consciousness? A second? An hour? Fragments of the surreal dream lingered and she struggled to remember who she was. Before reality struck with full force.

Gul! She was out here looking for Gul. Stumbling around the ruins she began shouting for him once more. Hell, how long had she been out cold?

"Gul! Gul!"

Kitty!

She spun round. Had someone spoken? Was someone here? This was madness. A seriously bad trip. And who the hell was Kitty?

She cupped her hands and shouted again, "Gul!"

Look, Kitty…See…

Once she'd found Gul there was no way she would ever come back here again. Whatever she had done, it was sending her mad. Those scenes were real, almost as if she had lived them herself.

Forcing herself on, she hurried from chamber to chamber among the ruins, examining every pile of stones, every crumbled staircase, and every underground crevice. If he'd wandered this far then he was bound to have taken shelter. Eventually she reached the steps leading down to the misericord, where she had attempted to invoke Malphas the previous evening.

She peered down the steps, shining the torch.

"Gul? Are you in here? It's Mum! Gul, are you here?"

It was such a funny sensation. As she held onto the stone squinting into the darkness of the underground chamber, the same drunken swoon came over her as before, the ground undulating beneath her feet, the oddest sensation that nothing was solid or real. She held onto the wall to steady herself. *No more visions…please, no more…*

One quick look to check for Gul, and then she was out. She took a step down. Just one sweep of the place with the torch…that was all…Then that was it. Never again. Not ever. But if he was here and she hadn't checked…

She took another step, still calling his name. Then another and then another. As before, it was icy and black, wrapping around her back and shoulders in a freezing cloak.

"Gul?"

It reeked of smoke. Had she left candles burning? But that was hours ago! She took the last step and dropped inside the chamber. Instantly it thickened. Her eyes stung and she struggled to breathe.

Get out of here!

"Gul, if you're here please shout because I can't see!"

She ducked her head under the low ceiling, palms flat to the wall as she moved towards the tiny recess at the back, where the horseshoe bats were hanging. Through the smoke it was a struggle to see anything at all, the thin strand of light from the phone doing little to permeate it. Why was it so smoky? She hadn't been here for hours.

"Gul?"

Flicking the torch over the shiny, dripping walls, she did her best to ignore the eerie sight of wrapped bodies hanging from the roof. Hang on a minute, what was that? She shone the light back over what she'd just seen, or thought she'd seen. There was something propped up, quite large, on the far side. Stooping underneath the sleeping bats, she warily approached. It looked like a scarecrow or a heap of clothing. A body? She reached out tentatively, fingers stretched so that only the tips would touch whatever it was.

It was damp. Soft. She tugged at it a little but it seemed stuck. The light barely cut through the thick, sulphur yellow smoke that was wafting down her throat and stinging her eyes, but a terrible thought struck her: this could be Gul, bound and gagged or worse. She yanked off the cloth.

A mummified face contorted in a scream of terror sprang into her own – the cloth a hood, the head impaled on an iron spike.

Kezia reeled back so violently she hit her head hard on the low stone ceiling, then with her hand over her mouth bolted out and up the steps as fast as possible, blindly running across the cloister ruins towards open air.

But outside it was smoky now too, the air suffocating, the sound of fire crackling, and the smell of burning flesh overpowering. What was this? Back into the waking dream again? She had to get out of here right now. People were right - this place was haunted. By a large-scale, bloody massacre.

Look, look!

The one inside was agitated and demanding. *Look!*

She got to the outside walls before she saw gave in, turned around and saw them. The ring of spikes – hundreds – every single one with the head of a monk impaled upon it. Each face wore a grimace of extreme horror, mouth frozen in a scream. Eyes had been gouged out, tongues ripped from their tonsured heads, bloody entrails lying in snake coils on the ground.

She ran. Flat out, and didn't stop. There were only two ways out of here, and she took the one that lead to Monkspike, the origins of the name only now apparent. Was this vision true? No one had ever said the monks were slaughtered in prayer, in bed, their heads impaled on a ring of spikes that stretched around the entire burning monastery. And who the hell was Kitty? Why did Kitty have to look, to see? Why was she losing time like this, when all that mattered was Gul? She had to keep her wits about her, stay in the present.

Her legs ached and her lungs were screaming as she pulled herself back up the hill. Gul wasn't at the ruins, and if he was in the woods at the Wolfs Cross end the family would have found him by now. This track led to the Lodge, Sylvia Massey's place. And dawn was coming. Silver cracks splintered the sky and helicopters droned overhead. Good, they were looking for him. He had to be here. Had to be.

Once in Monkspike she could raise the alarm, get everyone looking. All she had to do was get her breath back when she got to the top then run straight there. He would be found. At least there was help. Help was coming.

She reached the brow of the hill and was about to pause for breath, to turn and look down. Just to see for herself that the vision had faded, that it wasn't real, when her path was barred.

This time he showed himself, stepping out from the trees. Grinning as he threw back a white hood, a rotten-toothed smile spread across his pock-marked face. He smelled of ancient cloth, of rancid breath and mould.

And with him came a wave of revulsion and fear from so deep inside she knew she had felt it many times before. An age-old fear.

The one inside was afraid, too. And angry.

"Kitty." He shook his head sorrowfully like a disappointed parent, his small black eyes hard as flint.

She flinched, unable to look at the hatred burning there.

"Ma cherie. You left me to die."

***

CHAPTER TWENTY-THREE

BELINDA

Her name was being called. There was someone at the end of a kaleidoscope, their face a fragment in the whirling mosaic of colours: orange, brown, green…

"Belinda! Can you hear me? Belinda!"

Another voice. Deeper. "What's the matter with her?"

The kaleidoscope began to slow down, the flying colours lodging into solidity. Like waking from an anaesthetic, she tried to make sense of the world. Old-fashioned orange and brown tiles, bottle green walls, and dark wooden cupboards steadied and settled into reality. But where the hell was this? A woman with a plain brown bob and kind blue eyes was peering through glasses. She looked drawn, tired and pale. Sylvia Massey, of course…And then she remembered. Oh God, yes – this dire kitchen and Ralph sick upstairs. No one in the village must know!

"Don't tell them anyone," she blurted out. "Please - they mustn't know. You don't understand."

Sylvia was shaking her head. "I don't—"

"The ambulance is on its way," said Mark. "Are you alright, Bel?"

"Yes, why?"

"You weren't answering us," said Sylvia. "You seemed distracted."

"Sorry, did I drift off into space again? Essie says I keep doing that. I'm just so tired, I can't function."

Mark was nodding while looking at his watch. "Understandable. Look, it's going to be about twenty minutes, so why don't I take Essie over to ours? She and Molly can walk to school together?"

"Do you think Essie should go to school today?" Sylvia asked. "Do you want her to?"

"Yes, I think so. It's best she has normality and routine."

"Good, I'll give her a shout and we'll get going," said Mark. "Can you two go in the ambulance with Ralph? Brody's expecting him and—"

"Oh God," Belinda wailed. "I can't bear it. What's going to happen to him? I honestly thought it would all blow over, but it's just got worse and worse, and now everyone in the street will see the ambulance. They will know! You have no idea…"

Sylvia reached over to comfort her, gently pressing her hand on top of her own. "No one will think anything other than he's poorly. They don't have to know anything specific."

The effect of Sylvia's skin making contact with her own was sickening. As if a hot claw had clamped onto her, the other woman's blood throbbing heavily, pulsing rhythmically into her veins. She pulled her hand away. "No, but Essie will tell your daughter and then it will be spread around school. The kids will be saying he's gone mad, that he must have seen… well, calling him all sorts…" She raked a hand through her hair, attempting to come to a decision. "I suppose in a way this isn't a bad thing, you taking him away from here – it's better than… I mean, now it's got to this point. Okay, let's go then."

Mark nodded, shouting up the stairs to Essie to get dressed for school.

"I'll see you later, Syl."

Belinda watched him go, noting the way his broad shoulders blocked the light from the hallway, how his long legs strode purposefully towards the front door, hand on the newel post as he looked up to shout her daughter. Something about him leaving, about his back being turned, the front door opening and closing behind him – followed by silence and emptiness after he'd gone – crushed her heart like the end of a painful love affair. One she had in fact, never had.

Sylvia's eyes were on her. And seeing in them hurt and confusion, she flushed under the scrutiny. *Oh my good God, she thinks I fancy her husband.*

She began to shake her head.

Sylvia was nodding, her eyes full of tears. Clearly she was trying really hard not to get upset.

"What's wrong with me, Syl? I feel terrible, I hardly know who I am or what I'm doing. I feel so strange. I keep blanking out then jolting back into life again, and each time I feel a little bit more off-kilter."

Sylvia hesitated, then took a deep breath. "Tell me exactly. Can you describe it?"

"I don't sleep – haven't for weeks, I have chronic insomnia and horrific nightmares that seem so real. And I'm shattered, I can barely think. I can't remember what I've just done let alone what I did yesterday or the day before. And then there are the hallucinations, the vivid and violent waking dreams. It's hard to describe except I actually see a person who isn't there. I know I ought to see Mark or Arran about it, really. That's what you're going to say isn't it – that it's probably extreme stress?"

Sylvia brought her chair round, and adjusting her glasses leaned forwards, watching her intently. "Before Mark came in you were telling me about this person who isn't there - that he was called Burdo. You said he was a monk, dressed in white, that he appeared in these nightmares and you were terrified of him. Do you want to tell me a bit more?"

"Sylvia, you've got to understand that if I tell you anything more you may think I'm insane and act on it. I can't afford to lose my job. I've got two kids who need me more than ever, and that's not the half of it. There are things about this village you don't know."

"Bel, I want to help you and I can, far more than you may believe right at this moment. But I can't do anything if you keep things from me. Look, I promise I will not write you off as mad because you are not. I don't believe Ralph has schizophrenia, either—"

For the first time in weeks, a bolt of light pierced the darkness and her heart lifted. "Really?" You don't?"

"No. And I can help you both. But please, what aren't you telling me?"

"Alright, I'm going to trust you, and I'm sorry I ran out on you at the clinic. I've had my head in the sand for that long I somehow thought given enough time it would be okay, but it isn't, is it? I think I've always done that, just carried on, you know? When Gideon and I were going through a rough patch I cracked on with making beds and packed lunches, going to work, hoovering and dusting, attending meetings, pretending everything was fine and dandy until enough time passed for the problem to have faded away. Then after he died I did the same again – concentrated on sorting out the financial mess, finding a new place for us to live, getting the kids through each day…" She looked out of the kitchen window at the foggy back yard. "I never face up to things. I hide."

"You thought Ralph was going through a phase and he'd come through it? It's hard to know sometimes, especially when you've got a lot going on yourself. But Bel, listen, we've only got a few minutes while we wait for the ambulance, and I have something very serious to put to you. To be honest you might think I'm the crazy one now, but believe me I've been in this business a long time and I've seen and heard things that would make your hair stand on end, so please bear with me and keep an open mind."

"Go on. Because frankly nothing can be crazier than what I've seen and heard over the last few weeks, believe me. And if you knew what went on in this village, really knew, you wouldn't hesitate—"

"Okay, well I'm going to dive in. I don't think Ralph has a mental illness, I think he has spirit attachments—"

"Possessed, you mean? Oh my god!"

"It's not as bad as it sounds. Please stay with this – it's what I do, you know that. I've been practising release therapy for nigh on twenty years and it works, that's all I can say – it works. You've seen the pictures he's drawn, all of one particular monk?"

"Yes."

"And he referred specifically to the name of Burdo – the same person who appears to you. The thing is, if he's diagnosed as having schizophrenia and given anti-psychotic drugs, he will be encouraged to believe his hallucinations and beliefs are not real, but a mental health problem. And this basically gives carte blanche to the infesting spirits to carry on getting stronger and stronger because they are never removed. No one thinks to do it. Meanwhile they stay residing in the host and the host gets sicker. So once we get to the hospital I need to have a word with Doctor Brody. I need time to communicate with those spirits as soon as possible, and get them to move on."

All she could think about was the notorious film, *The Exorcist*. Surely this small, bespectacled woman didn't do exorcisms? "Isn't that done by a priest?"

"The church does perform exorcisms in extreme circumstances, but here's the difference: there isn't much time to explain really, but a priest will assume the spirit is demonic and thus try to force it from the host. Usually, in fact in all my years of practice I've found they are not demonic, but earthbound spirits who need help and guidance to go to the right place. It is no good for them being stuck on the earthly plane, and it's terrible for the host. What we do is move the spirits onto where they should go. We talk to them, explain and convince."

"I can't bear it, this is horrible."

"You wouldn't believe how many cases of this there actually are. I wish society accepted it more and didn't throw the notion away as ridiculous, condemning those affected to a life of powerless exclusion. Anyway, I'm confident I can help Ralph escape that – a life of stigma and more importantly in this case, an extremely poor prognosis. Do you understand me? If he had schizophrenia then he would need the drugs, but I am positive he hasn't. And I don't have much time either. So I need your help."

Belinda looked away. "I don't know. You see, it might be better if he was to stay there—"

"I don't understand why you would say that." She looked at her watch. "Tell me more about Burdo. Everything you know, because I will have to work quickly on Ralph when I get the chance."

Belinda's whole body began to shake as if she had a rigor, her head swam and her throat felt thick and sore. "It's like I've got flu. Sorry, I feel awful. Really ill."

"It's okay. Deep breaths. Come on, Belinda. Whatever you can remember – it's really important."

"Alright. Oh, but I feel I shouldn't say this. It's like I really shouldn't…" The whole room was darkening and getting colder. There was a feeling of impending doom, of being a child who'd done something terribly wrong and was in for the hiding of their life.

"Override that feeling. Have courage. You're doing the right thing."

She broke into a sweat, wringing her hands, forcing out the words which no longer sounded like her own. "Ralph was coming into my room, calling me by this name, Benedicta. His eyes were changing too – the pupils would be rectangular then ellipses then squares, sometimes taking over the iris completely. Kind of like an oil lamp, if you know what I mean? He'd become really aggressive too, playing ear-piercing, thumping music full of expletives and hate, so loud the walls and floors vibrated. And I found blood and knives in his room. I think he's been cutting himself, but Essie said he was killing animals for blood rites or something. Only he wouldn't let me in, wouldn't talk to me, eat with us – nothing. I just didn't know what to do, so I carried on going to work and pretending it wasn't happening. I know I'm a head-in-the-sand person, but it was more than that. I was in a daze, walking underwater, sluggish and not quite with it. I put it down to tiredness and just kept on trying to keep busy and occupied and–"

"Stay with me, Bel. Try to concentrate. So what happened when he came into your room? What was this about Benedicta?"

"He just stared at me, started calling me this other name, walked towards the bed. He…he… tried to… Anyway, after that I put a chair under the door handle." Her chin wobbled and she slammed a hand to her mouth. "I didn't know what to do. I was terrified of my own son. I'd come back here and there'd be filthy dishes and empty cartons strewn about, the music pumping, festering clothes dropped on the floor. Such contempt…and I was so, so tired… I haven't slept in weeks… I don't know…what's…happening…to me…to us…"

"Okay, alright. Let's try to get to the bottom of this. What you can remember about the monk, the content of the nightmares? Try to be specific."

Nausea was rising in her throat and her face flushed hot. Sweat poured down her back. "The monk calls me Benedicta, too. I see his face all the time. Like right now. Oh God, he's glaring at me now, as we speak. He's in my head–"

Sylvia seemed to fade to grey, her voice far away. "What does he look like? Who is he, do you know? Tell me anything you can about him, anything!"

"Sorry…sorry…His eyes are deep-set and black. It's like you're looking into an abyss. Rotting teeth…his face all hard and bony with a flattened nose like a vulture. Yes, he looks like a vulture and I think he's French."

"Yes, I think so too. That would fit."

"Really?"

"Yes, I think Burdo has transferred from Ralph to you, which is possibly why he attacked you that night. Burdo was the leader – the dominant spirit. What I'm not clear on is why…hmm… I wonder why he calls you, Benedicta?"

The sound of a siren wailing caused them both to stare at each other with wide questioning eyes.

"Bel, we have to take care of Ralph in the immediate instance, to make sure they don't medicate him before I can make a full assessment. But please, listen to me, please can we talk again before the end of the day? I don't think you should continue living here alone without help because this is spirit is going to get a grip on you. We need to exorcise him as soon as possible. I'm pretty sure he's singled you out."

"But why?"

"I don't know yet, but it isn't random. I think he's here for a reason and he's not going to stop until he gets what he wants."

"Which is what?"

"That's just it. I don't know."

"Sylvia, I'm scared I'm going mad. You don't know what happens to people here when they go mad, there's a sickness."

"You're not mad—"

"I'm really, truly shit-scared. You're telling me this spirit, this pretty nasty one, is possessing me? And there's a whole lot more possessing Ralph? Oh dear God… This is insane. We don't deserve this. Haven't we been through enough?"

"Exactly. And that's what has made you vulnerable – weakened and susceptible. I know it's a lot to get your head round, but I'm asking you to trust me because the alternatives – staying here and trying to cope; or heavy medication – are both infinitely worse than anything I'm proposing. At least let me try first. It certainly won't do any harm and it might just work."

"I don't believe in spirits or God, though. I just don't."

The ambulance was outside, the sound of boots clomping up to the front door.

"We have to go now. Let me handle Brody when we get there, okay? I'm sure I can help Ralph as long as I get to him before Mark does. And then I will help you. In the meantime, I'm asking you to pray to—"

"I told you I don't believe. I'm an atheist."

"Call on the higher spirits. Surround yourself in white light."

"I just don't—"

"Belinda, now isn't the time for debate. Ralph is threatening to kill the whole village and you've just admitted that this monk is possessing your every waking moment. I don't know what's going on here yet, but praying to a higher power is pretty much all you have."

"It all sounds crazy."

"It always does," said Sylvia. "And the fact most people think that, is the devil's favourite trick."

***

CHAPTER TWENTY-FOUR

SYLVIA

While the psychiatric nurse was checking Ralph into Admissions, Sylvia took Brody into the corridor outside for a chat and quickly brought him up to speed.

"I know Mark won't hear of any spiritual causes, and I am fully aware of the threats to life Ralph's made, but all I'm asking is I be allowed to talk to him before you start with drug therapy—"

Brody was shaking his head, frowning as he listened. A small, wiry Irishman with flame-red hair and alabaster skin, he was beginning to stoop with age and weariness. She'd known him a long time, far longer than Mark had. Brody had been one of her lecturers way back when she was a psychology student, and they'd worked together on many cases over the years. Unlike Mark, he didn't rule out spiritual matters as a cause of certain mental health issues. However, he was a church man and whenever they'd touched on spirit attachment or possession, he'd politely agreed to disagree. 'I know the work Alan Sanderson is doing is successful, and I know in other parts of the world it's well accepted,' he'd said when they last discussed the matter. 'But modern exorcism is not something we can consider here. I can't bring it into practice.'

They'd debated. She'd put forward the argument that we are spiritual beings, that if he wanted to adhere to Bible teaching, then Jesus was reported as casting out spirits. In addition to that there were thousands of documented cases all over the world where spirit attachments had successfully been released with the patient fully recovering as a result. Books had been written by brave pioneering psychiatrists, listing case after case verifying this. Only in the Western world was it dictated that medics and scientists had all the answers and full jurisdiction on the matter, with anything other than textbook classification rejected as ridiculous. And look how recent that was! And besides, what did it matter who believed what, as long as the treatment worked and the patient got better? Surely that's what they all wanted? And it certainly wouldn't do harm to try hypnosis first.

After the discussion batted to and fro over a few drinks in the local pub one evening, he acknowledged that some of his colleagues were now open to the possibility of spirit attachments, soul-carrying and past-life experiences, and had achieved positive results with release therapy. He did however, draw the line totally on offering this himself, insisting that if spiritual attachment was truly the case, then it should be a church matter, and only when all other medical causes had been eliminated.

'But the church assumes the spirit is demonic and simply casts it out. If it's a human spirit where will it go? If it's demonic, where will it go? That's why they won't leave! They're terrified of going back to eternal darkness.'

He'd shaken his head again as if both he and the rest of the world were all doomed and it was beyond him; then smiled, stood up and drained his beer glass. 'Ah, bless you, Sylvia, but you'll not change my mind on this.'

Now though, as she explained what was happening to Ralph and Belinda, touching also on the other cases in the village, he rocked back and forth on his heels, hands in pockets.

"All I'm asking for is one hour."

"He will have to be sectioned first. He's a danger to others and himself. We need to wait for Mark."

"No! I mean yes, I know he has to be detained, that's fine. That's not the problem. Where I need your help is that I have to speak to him before Mark gets here. Please. Trust me. Both Ralph and Belinda have told me things they could not possibly have known, and a few pieces are beginning to fit together. Look, if that boy is started on anti-psychotics the spirits will get stronger, and ignored they'll be free to dominate him further and incite further threats and violence. He won't ever get out of here. And besides, what I propose can't do any harm. One hour. That's all I'm asking for."

In the side room, the admissions nurse was now standing up, looking around for Brody.

"Please!" Sylvia begged him.

He pressed his lips together. "Alright, but when Mark arrives we'll have to section him, so…" He looked at his watch. "Providing he's not held up in traffic I'd say you've got about twenty minutes to half an hour. But if he gets violent, Sylvia—"

"It's not enough time. Can you keep Mark as long as

you can? Tell him to go and talk to Belinda – she's not well herself and she's going to need support. Brody, I can't do this stressed. But yes, if he's violent—"

"I think we should restrain him to be sure," he said as the nurse approached.

"I've restrained him already," she said. "Go on in, Sylvia. I'll be just outside. Here's your panic alarm."

Sylvia exchanged a look with Brody. Nodded her thanks. And walked in.

The room was plain white, the only furniture a single bed by the window, topped with a pale green counterpane. Ralph lay fully dressed, staring at the sky through slatted blinds, his scalp matted with blood, tufts of black hair sticking out at odd angles in a crescent shape around the cranium.

She spoke softly. "Hello, Ralph. How are you feeling?"

No answer.

She pulled up a chair and sat close to the bed, observing him. "Nod if you can hear me."

His eyelashes batted.

"Good. Alright, squeeze my hand if you know who I am."

She reached across for his hand and felt it tighten in hers.

Her heart went out to him. "Hey, Ralph. I think you've had a rough time of it these last few months, haven't you? I imagine you've felt pretty poorly, like you've had the flu? Maybe hearing strange voices or not remembering where you've been?"

His hand squeezed hers again, this time a little

harder.

"You've certainly given your mum and sister a fright. Can you remember what you were saying this morning, about wanting to harm people?"

Slowly his head moved from side to side and a tear oozed from the corner of one eye, dripping onto the pillow.

Damn Mark and his intolerance! Admittedly Ralph had threatened violence, but this assessment should not be rushed. Section and restrain him certainly, but the hurry to sedate him and throw away the key was the worrying part. Why wouldn't Mark listen? Why wouldn't he give credence to what was her lifetime of experience? What the hell was wrong with him these days that he'd become so overbearing and dogmatic. Aggressive, not to put too fine a point on it. God, she needed more time here. Half an hour at most was not enough.

"You had some awareness of it, though?"

He closed his eyes.

"Ralph, unfortunately I don't have a lot of time so I need to quickly explain what I think is happening. I can't be sure but I think you've got into a very depressive state, and you've been with someone who's brought negative energy into your life. As a result, what's happening to you is not, in my view and based on many years of experience, a form of insanity, but spirit attachment. I know this might be hard for you to take in, but I believe you have some low spirits attached to you, and we need to get rid of them. But for that I need you to trust me. I need to put you under hypnosis to deal with it for you. Is that okay?"

His eyes were tightly squeezed, a row of glistening tears along the fringe of his lashes.

His limbs however, were beginning to tense up, and a nerve near his jaw had started to twitch. A change was coming. Those spirits were going to rebel. A feeling of panic was building up.

If he became violent he'd be sedated immediately and she would lose her only chance. She switched on the voice recorder.

"Okay, now listen to my voice and let me know if you understand. I need you to work with me here so we can get you well again. So please, you – Ralph Sully – listen and respond only to my voice. Do not listen to any other voices within you. Listen only to me because I am here to help you. Promise me you will listen only to my voice."

Again he squeezed her hand but instead of the strength of his grip diminishing, this time it increased.

"Good. Okay, first I want you to concentrate on your breathing. Breathe in for a count of ten… let's go…one…two…three…"

His chest rose with each count.

"Good. Now let the breath go very, very slowly for a full count of ten."

As instructed his chest deflated on each count.

Repeated three times, she took him through relaxing each part of his body, which he appeared to do. Her voice became increasingly soporific, each word elongated and dreamy. "Now I want you to picture a beautiful house… with a white door –a big white front door that you are going to walk through into a light, sunny hallway. Can you picture it? The curtains are white and billowing in a soft, summer breeze, the floorboards are polished and gleaming. There's a big log fire in the room to your right, and ahead of you is a wide staircase, with a bannister you can slide right down like you did as a child. I want you to walk up the stairs... up to the top... and looking down at the gleaming bannister... go ahead and slide down it. Off you go. Slide all the way down. Whoosh... Then turn and slide up it – because you can do whatever you wish to in dreams - then back down again. Whoosh! How free and powerful you are to move at will either up or down, to do whatever your imagination tells you, sliding up and sliding down. Up and down... What does it feel like? Nice?"

His lips twitched slightly.

"Okay, now here's the really good part. Slide up to the top and now slide down again. But this time you come to a door, and you push it open. You see a set of ten steps... and now I want you to walk down them. Let's count down them slowly together...one...two...three...four...."

On each count she asked him to squeeze her hand, which he did.

"...and ten. Now you are in the most beautiful, peaceful place you have ever seen in your life. Imagine it: a lush tropical garden is laid out before you - a sea breeze gently caressing your skin, dappled sunlight dancing on the lawns."

He smiled.

"Are you there? What does it look like? Describe it to me. Your dream place, your little piece of heaven."

He began to mumble about a beach and sand dunes.

"What else?"

His voice picked up to one she remembered, the one belonging to an animated boy many years younger. He painted a picture for her, of a turquoise ocean rolling with surf onto sand as fine as talc, and there was a tang of salt in the air mingled with the coconut scent of gorse. He wanted to go surfing, he said, to feel sea spray on his face, to ride the waves.

Good, he had all his senses involved. Still he gripped her hand.

"Now walk down to the beach. You're the only one there. It's hazy and warm and there's a lovely balmy breeze. You're walking along the sand now… and as you walk you find yourself lifting into the air like a kite, flying higher and higher. All your worldly cares are now being left behind. None of it matters anymore. You are a shining beautiful soul glittering in the warmth of the sun, safely floating into the clouds; looking down on the earth and knowing that none of it really matters anymore. You're free. Free of everything. Just let it go… leave it all behind…"

Still he smiled. He was on his journey and oh, how badly he had wanted to go.

"When I call your name you will come back down and we'll go back through the door and up the steps, but right now you are staying up there and enjoying the beautiful view. You can tell me all about it when you come back."

His eyes were fluttering and his response, she had to admit, was thankfully successful. It wasn't always so easy, but he was very tired – totally worn out – and although he would be aware of what was now about to happen it was extremely unlikely he would remember.

In a more severe tone she said, "Now those of you who are using this boy, tell me who you are, and talk in English."

Ralph's eyes flickered to half open.

"What is your name?"

His eyes opened fully, the pupils shifting shapes as described by both Essie and Bel. His body began to twitch at first, then tug at the restraints binding his wrists and ankles. Alarm kicked in. His eyes widened and his face contorted with fury. Yanking at the straps, he started to buck and thrash himself against the bedframe, crashing into the railings. The shape-shifting pupils dilated to totally black and the features began to blur.

"What is your name?"

More than one voice answered in unison. "Bitch, ask your husband who he's screwing. Ask him about Kitteeee…"

"What is your name?"

A chorus of hissing sighs emanated from his throat. The room darkened, and the fluorescent lights overhead buzzed, flicking on and off repeatedly. The tap at the sink in the corner began to drip then gush out in a torrent, and the blinds rattled.

"You don't scare me with your tricks. You won't frighten me. Tell me who you are and what you are doing with this boy."

Shadows chased over his face like storm clouds, transforming his features into one face after another, until a parade of different spirits had shown themselves.

Responses were not always vocal, and although his

voice box was working away with swallows and gulps, the messages were being passed to her through thought transference. Quickly she adapted, closing her eyes and tuning in.

Immediately a series of images bombarded her.

A tonsured monk wearing a white robe was lying prostrate next to a window flickering with stars. His expression was one of paralysing fear. He clutched the sheets, eyes staring into the twilight, other shadowy forms around him kneeling in mumbling prayer. Monotonous chanting droned along corridors, the continuous hum of prayers – no – agonised pleas, begging: 'Please God, please, dear Lord. Our Blessed Father, Almighty God, hear us in this, the darkest hour before the dawn…'

Now she was floating quickly down a long, stone tunnel. A bell was tolling and there was something in the air - smoke, fire. Shouts were raised.

Vaguely the history of Monkspike cut into the images. Yes, hadn't the monastery burned to the ground?

But there was no further time to think before another image, this one far more vivid, shot into her mind. Oh, they wanted her to see alright, and they wanted her to see and feel everything in all its horror. Here was bewilderment, pain, terror and confusion.

Gone now the starlit night. Orange flares lit the sky. Battle cries sounded from outside as doors were battered down and men with iron pikes charged inside. The dormitory was full of fire and an army of men wielding swords. Throats were cut, white-robes saturated with gushing crimson, and heads hacked off with cleavers.

Suffocating smoke filled the rooms and blood-curdling screams rent the air like those of stuck pigs.

Sylvia held her hands to her temples, telling them 'enough'. But no, they wanted her to fully experience this - tongues being wrenched out of throats; bulging eyes that still blinked with life staring out of severed heads rolling across the floor; coils of innards butchered from corpses hung from the rafters. And along with the acrid smoke clogging the air, there was something infinitely worse – burning human flesh.

"Stop! Stop!"

These were Ralph's spirits. French-accented names were shouted into her head lest she ever forget them… *Bernard, Robert, Luc, Henri…* on and on went the list. Dozens and dozens and dozens of names that tipped into hundreds.

Then as abruptly as the onslaught had begun, it stopped.

The smoke cleared.

And one man's face appeared before her.

One man. He sat on horseback looking down from the brow of a hill, coolly observing the massacre, and a ring of burning stakes around the monastery. Each stake had a monk's head impaled upon it. And as the smoke billowed and the building began to crack and fall, he signalled to the men to retreat.

There was something about him that riveted her and she couldn't look away. Swinging a severed head, the tonsure clearly visible, this man was more than simply triumphant. There an air of angry entitlement about him, of callous self-righteousness. The man's face and that of his victim now panned in close for her inspection, in case she remained in any doubt as to their identity.

She caught her breath. Her senses reeled.

Jesus Christ, no! Please let this be a trick…

***

CHAPTER TWENTY-FIVE

Kezia

She fled towards Monkspike. He was everywhere, the smell of his decay filling her senses, his eyes prying into her soul. His presence seemed to fill the woods, the echoing laughter, scathing, bitter and merciless. Malignant loathing reached like the blackest tar to every corner of her being, dragging her into a pit of shame, guilt and wretchedness. Every movement was heavy, her breathing laboured, and sense of reality distorted.

So this is what they meant when they said people had seen him? This was the insanity? There were hordes of them – shapes flitting in and out of the trees as she ran, eyes on her back, a feeling of being violated.

No! None of this is real. I have to find Gul. It's not real, none of it!

Yet the feeling of being followed was immense. At the sound of rushing footsteps in the bracken, she stopped and whirled around, scanning the grey dawn. Mist swathed the trees, cobwebs glinted with jewels of dew, and the previous night's rain dripped from branches. The only footprints were her own. Not a single creature stirred. An owl hooted from somewhere deep in the forest, but the birds were still quiet, the woods devoid of their chatter.

Satisfied there was no one behind, she picked up speed again towards the yew tree and Hangman's Tump. She must get to White Hart Lodge, ask Mark and Sylvia if they would raise the alarm in the village, get the locals on this side of the woods looking for Gul, too. The helicopters were still circling but sounded as if they were further afield. Had they had stopped looking? Were they flying away having given up? Soon rivers would be dredged and teams of officers would comb the woods. Tears pricked her eyes and stumbling, she scrambled up the path. Morning was coming and Gul had been out all night.

Every few yards she stopped to call him, cupping her hands, the echo of his name swallowed by the gloom.

And still the conviction persisted that a presence not only followed her but kept apace, watching from the dark interior of the forest. The one inside seemed panicked as never before. Her lungs became increasingly leaden with every intake of breath; a pressure weighted her shoulders, and a damp and solid load clung to her back like a carcass. The burden increased with every step, the pressure intensifying to such a degree it slowed her limbs, clouding her mind and dulling her senses. It shaded the path ahead and shrouded the trail behind like a tunnel closing in, blocking both progress and retreat. The darker realms she had sought for so long now loomed from every direction, and there was no escape. It seemed as if the very earth beneath her feet was about to open up and drag her down into a deep, dark grave.

What had been done, was not at all what she had thought. Instead she had stepped through to a world from which there was no coming back. What had been seen could not now be unseen, and what had been experienced would remain with her always. Nothing, absolutely nothing, had prepared her for this cold, empty and all-consuming sense of loss. The world appeared in black and white, her sense of self, of the warm-pulsating blood and flesh part of her, turned icy and heavy as the very essence of all that made her human drained away. This was death. Terror clutched her entire being. This was death… a living death…

Hunger cleaved into her stomach, the weight of her own body untenable, and her muscles ached so badly that when a large boulder appeared at the side of the track, she sank onto it. Leaning forwards, she covered her face with her hands. Just five minutes. A few minutes to calm and steady her breathing. She'd had nothing to eat for over twenty-four hours. One thought and one thought only, kept her going. There was no question of resting, at least not for long, until her son was found.

The world faded out until all that remained was the sound of her breathing. The old nightmare flickered into crackling play, the vision of a line of trees on the horizon, of the howling, empty wasteland behind…and the single raven caw-caw-cawing from one of the charred, spiky branches.

When she looked up again however, it was with a jolt of confusion. The morning was foggy and still. A grand oak stood before her, unnoticed when she'd sat down minutes ago, its outstretched arms and knotted jugular roots indicative of a great age. She stared. Shook her head. That it should be so aged…

And what was that? A sack shape silhouetted…?

Her eyes adjusted. From one of its branches a hanged man was swinging by the neck. A freshly hanged man. And next to his still twitching feet, a pile of logs had been kicked away into the undergrowth. His putrid face, lolling tongue and jerking limbs suggested it had only just happened.

Jumping up, she ran towards the man to cut him down. "Sir! Sir!" But reaching for her athame she found it was not in her skirts, and as she neared, the apparition began to dissolve into the ether. Confused she stepped back.

A soft snickering echoed around the glade. Early rays gilded the branches and streamed through the canopy. The night's rain glistened like glass and a shrieking green woodpecker flew between the trees.

The Abbot was there again, wasn't he? Her spine prickled as she scanned the trees. He was the bane of her life. Curse him - always watching, waiting for her to strip for a ritual or to see her bathe… With those soulless black eyes and lascivious grin, he lurked like a plague. Everyone feared the rapist monk, the one who took girls before they were women, who struck terror into men with his talk of the devil, and who richly rewarded those who provided him with his desires. Yet it was herself, Kitty Morse, he wanted the most. The one who possessed the powers he did not, the one who he knew bound and sickened him with her magick.

Alas, he had seen herself and John Rivers. Had seen them and that they had lain together…

A shaft of silvery light lit the glade.

Was he there?

One day he would catch her. One day. Well, tonight she would do a binding ritual under the waxing moon. And invoke the one who would help her.

Turning on her heels she began to run. The hanging man: he was known to her. Yet how could that be? The clothing was like nothing she had ever seen: the shirt a bright dye of green and red. A vision of the future? But if so, why did it resonate so strongly?

Hurrying home, stark images cut into her thoughts yet made no sense: a young man with dark hair and blue eyes, a connection to the hanged man... but what? Why was she here in this spot? Doing what? Had she been gathering herbs and fallen asleep? It was odd that she had been so careless. And the tree! The oak was not so old and gnarled. Increasingly confused and agitated she broke into a run. But from the Abbot she must escape. John wanted her to lie with him but she could not. Just could not - the very thought was repugnant.

But you must... think of the village... think of us. And I will give you everything... I will make you my queen...

The smell of him, the creeping sense he was lurking nearby, caused her to pause again, to examine the angle of light and shade among the tree trunks. Was it him?

Kittee... I have seen you...with him... I have seen you...

A shivering coldness slipped under her skin.

Home was now in striking distance and she sprinted towards it. Every footstep thudded into her bones, the urgency to get there mounting by the second. He would rape her...

But as she drew close, confusion gripped her once more. Something was wrong. The cottage was so much larger than it ought to be, its sweeping pastureland lined with spruce and cedars. On reaching the edge of the garden, she paused for breath with her back to one of the trees and took in the scene. This wasn't right. In fact, it was extremely disconcerting. Frightening.

At an upstairs window a small face peered out. Who was that? And why were they in her house?

Puzzled and annoyed, she walked across the lawns towards the arched oak door studded with iron, just as remembered. So, yes, this was definitely her house. But the rest was unrecognisable, increasingly so as more came into focus through the morning mist. Oblongs of yellow light spread across the lawns, and on reaching the driveway the grass became thousands of tiny stones. She looked down in astonishment. This should be dirt, with sawdust across the front.

Alarmed she looked up at the bedroom windows where the small face had been.

She was still there, observing her with surprise.

In her house! What the hell was she doing?

"Let me in!" she shouted up.

The girl remained motionless.

Thundering on the door she yelled, "Damn you! Let me in! You're in my house!"

About to walk around to the back she swirled around at the sudden sound of wheels on the gravel behind. A cart? But such a noise. A long, bulky vehicle crunched to a halt a matter of feet away and out jumped a man. A man in unusual clothes like the man hanging in the woods. And tall. At a glance quite handsome.

The thing he had travelled in flashed and beeped with red lights as he hurried towards the house, to where she stood by the front door.

Their eyes locked.

"Kezia, what on earth are you doing here? I just heard—" He stopped dead, staring at her, all the colour draining from his face. "What's the matter? What is it?"

She walked slowly towards him with clenched fists, her jaw set to steel and every sinew and muscle in her body tightening to breaking point.

***

CHAPTER TWENTY-SIX

SYLVIA

It took several minutes to recover from what had just been shown. Sylvia flicked a worried glance at the clock on the wall. Half an hour had passed and the horrific visuals had finally finished, with the last scene lingering - a silent end to a horror movie now impressed on her memory for all eternity.

Soon there would be a knock on the door signalling Mark's arrival, and she would know no more than the series of tragic events conveyed. Fortunately the nurse outside did seem empathetic to the delicacy of the situation, so with luck there would be time to do something, because whether the story was true or not, it was clear Ralph's infesting spirits were locked in fury and pain. Had they lashed out, though? Was this personal?

Please, God, please delay Mark. I need more time!

She had to put aside her feelings. It could be a trick to throw her off. It wasn't only the demonic who were bullies, but as in life those who were afraid and insecure often adopted the same self-preservation strategies. It was all about deflection. She had to rise above it even though it had sent shockwaves through her system. A triumphant victor, the man shown to her, the one whose face had been magnified and freeze-framed so she would not mistake his identity, had been holding high the severed head of a monk. His face was rapt with murderous, righteous contempt – the kind that wiped out entire races of people, whipping up mob-rule, torture, terror and annihilation. But to kill monks, men of peace who presumably could not fight back, well that took a special kind of cold-hearted psychopath. Which made the revelation all the more disturbing.

But was it a trick? She had to know. If it was, then it was a powerful attempt at throwing her off balance; if it wasn't, then frankly, it was worse.

She looked over at the clock again. Her decision would alter the course of the exorcism. Attached spirits did not want to be forced out of the host or moved on. They liked it there. The host gave them access to the five senses again, and to earthly pleasures. In addition, they were terrified of being cast back into darkness, or burning in hell for what they had done. So yes, they were bullies if necessary, and would use anything at their disposal to fight their corner.

Okay…she nodded inwardly to herself…What she had been shown was a lie, injecting doubt and weakening her defences. As a result the job of exorcising Ralph just got a whole lot harder. The hate-fuelled victor in the image was not her husband, Mark, but chicanery, and it was imperative not to be manipulated by the effect on her own emotions and ego. A boy's whole life was at stake here. And time was running out. Any moment now Mark and Brody could appear, and the three of them would have to section him, after which he'd be medicated and admitted. And not only that, but others in the village badly needed her help, too. But how did she persuade these badly damaged, angry spirits to go to a light they no longer believed in? To them God was dead. Look what had happened to them – to devout, God-fearing monks!

There had to be a way.

Think…think… Ralph's drawings were those of one particular monk, who fitted the image and description also portrayed by Belinda. In addition to that, St Benedict's Monastery had indeed burned down. That would be what, nine hundred years ago? So why were present day inhabitants being affected? And why the sudden escalation? And why were the old people in Temple Lake Nursing Home so terrified? She shook her head. What was she missing?

Ralph appeared to be dreaming, his eyelashes flickering rapidly.

While he was still under hypnosis she decided to try and find a way through. Hopefully there would be no more sickening images or targeted trickery.

"Thank you for showing me what happened. I have seen how you died and I am sorry for how much you suffered, all of you. But it was a very long time ago and you are in spirit now. Tell me, who is the leader among you?"

A pause. Then a babble of muffled voices worked in Ralph's throat, as if a discussion was going, until one came forward. "Luc. I am the Prior."

"Hello, Luc. My name is Sylvia. I mean you no harm. I understand all you have shown me, and I know you do not want to leave this host, that you take his life force as your own so that you can wreak revenge on the villagers you believe destroyed you. But you must know that the people here today are not the same ones as when you were alive. Nine hundred years have passed. They know nothing of what happened. This boy is innocent and so are the people living here now. You are dead. All of you are dead. And you must go to the light to continue your spiritual journey."

"There is no light, we told you. There is no God and there is no heaven. How can there be? We prayed all day, we worked hard, and we lay in fear of the devil at night. We honoured our vows and lived a pure life, yet when we begged God for clemency in our darkest hour he was not there."

"He was there and He is there now. There is light for all of us. It is on earth that many walk in darkness. Think about it. How could you have found the boy you inhabit now if he had no light to attract your attention? How could you have attached to any of the other humans if you had not seen the light of their being? I believe you were cut down by ruthless, black-hearted people, who wanted what you had and envied your life. This was not God's doing—"

"Yet He let it happen."

"Luc, there are people in the world who are fuelled by anger, hatred, ego and jealousy – this is the corruption of which you speak. You came up against a bad man, pure evil, who incited fear and resentment in people who were starving and desperate. People are what they are. Even the Bible says, 'As a man thinketh in his heart, so is he.' Death doesn't change us, in other words. But everyone, when they pass back to being spirits again, has the opportunity of progression to the light, to be forgiven and to forgive. Always. And this is your chance now. But you must leave behind your rage and bitterness."

"We have been kept in dungeons with no light. We have pain, terrible pain in our necks, our eyes, our tongues. We are blind and deaf, crawling around in the dirt, seeking out those who will help us see and feel and taste the flesh of youth, the burn of liquor, the pleasure of power. We will take their lives as they took ours."

"What century do you think this is, Luc?"

"This is the age of the Cistercians, of the White Monk. And now we will have our revenge. The time is right, a door has opened and we are bringing with us the powers of the underworld to bring them to their knees. Burdo has told us to show them how it feels to see their blood spilled in a place they felt safe, to see their women raped and their children beheaded. And this boy will slaughter every last one of them. We have power over him like never before – our energy is three-hundred fold."

"Burdo was the Abbot?"

"Yes."

A picture of the severed head swinging in her husband's hand – clearly a trophy – flashed before her: the round eyes black, blood dripping down a pock-marked face, the nose wide and triangular...This was the same man featured in Ralph's drawings, the one who seethed with malice inside Belinda. So he was the Abbot. *Fuck!*

"You blindly followed this man?"

"Yes, yes! Of course. He was our Abbot, our leader."

"And you were all massacred in your beds at dawn."

"Yes. And he too."

"Yet Burdo has flown from you now. He goes on to live within other mortals for his own pleasure, leaving you in the dark to sully your souls with foul mass murder."

"No, he looks for one more person."

"To attach himself to, so he can be with a woman."

"Burdo is chaste, the most chaste of us all."

"Yet he knows a woman called Benedicta and another called Kitty. Who were they?"

"We don't know. To be with a woman is a sin. He told us we would burn in hell if we went to the village and lay with the women."

"Yet you blindly followed him and confessed your every move to him and him alone, did you not? You strictly adhered to the faith by reciting prayers and psalms, devoting yourselves to the very last letter without ever having true knowledge of God yourself. Blind faith. Blind religion. Following the doctrine of others. What do you say to what we know now? That the monasteries became rich with land and produce and gold, that the Abbots consorted with local lords and royalty, and accepted gifts and favours from Rome, when all the time the local peasants starved and the monks toiled from dawn to dusk. And when they were not working they were praying. Did you think about your own path to the light? To God?"

"Our faith is the route to God."

"To your blind faith you must add knowledge, and that is what will set your spirits free. You must realise this. The year is now two thousand and nineteen. Nine hundred years have passed with you in the darkness, searching for living beings to latch onto, sapping their light, depleting their health and making them do terrible things to avenge your pain, but nothing has worked, has it?"

"No, this cannot be!"

"And it has not worked because you are not working for your own souls, but for that of another, far darker one. He has made you commit diabolical acts to sate his needs. But now he has abandoned you. He has found this woman, Benedicta. Who, I ask again, is she?"

"We don't know."

"Alright, well he does. He knows who Benedicta is and he knows who Kitty is, and it is my observation that he has left you now he has found them, or maybe one of them. So what of your souls? Your own souls? Do you want to spend another nine hundred years in the dungeons with no light? Stuck and lost and in pain?"

Silence fell for several long minutes, and she held her breath.

"We have nowhere to go," Luc said eventually. "And Burdo. He is our Abbot. We must do as he says."

"You are frightened of him?"

"Yes. We will be taken to the misericord and fastened in irons. One slight transgression and there is terrible punishment – starvation; a cord tightened each day around the skull until it cuts into the brain like a wire; hanging upside down by the toes until one by one…they pop…out of joint…"

The gravity of their fear began to impact badly on the energy in the room. The lights dimmed to that of sulphur yellow and the walls seemed to cave inwards. Scenes of torture and festering wounds endured in dripping darkness, were transferred to her thoughts, and she fought against them.

"Burdo kept you in fear, forcing you to slave for little reward. And he has deserted you now. Your distress, suffering and confusion are the devils of ignorance. Open your eyes. Luc, you are in charge of these men. You can take yourself and all of them to God, to the light, where you will continue your spiritual journey. Or let them ruin this poor young man's life while you remain in the darkness for another thousand years. Or more. Please don't tell me you think he cares about that."

"We have done terrible things. We have committed such terrible acts. To avenge, to hurt, to defile…"

"Yes, and now you have been left to your hellish fate. But it is not too late for you, Luc. Never too late. Look, see with your mind that the light exists for you still. See it now. See other spirits…you have family…"

She closed her eyes tightly, calling on the Archangel Michael for help and support. *Please save these poor souls. Please help them - show them the light. Lift them, exalt them!*

She prayed fervently, repeatedly, using the last of her strength. And when Ralph's tears came they were shocking, sudden and profuse.

His emaciated body doubled up on the bed, knees to chest in the foetus position. She struggled to make sense of what he was saying. It sounded like he was arguing with himself, then crying, sobbing until his body heaved.

She raised her voice. "Luc! Leave this boy now. Leave the fear and pain behind and you will see the light.

Burdo has brainwashed you but will not find any of you again. He has no further use for you except to commit more atrocities through this innocent boy. Look after your souls, the shining spirits God gave you. You must all, every one of you, go to the light now while you can. This is your only chance. Please look. See your relatives; those you once loved. Can you see them?"

"Mother of God, is that my brother?"

Ralph fell silent, his mouth working but no sound emitted. Sylvia glanced again at the clock. Her heart fluttered. That was odd. Two hours had elapsed. Yet there had been no interruptions. Two and a half hours of pleading, persuading, showing, proving and reassuring. It had been successful, she was sure. Watching his face was like seeing the sun chase clouds across a field of corn. Incrementally the feeling of depression and confusion lifted from his aura and her pulse picked up with joy.

This was why she did this. This was why. It was everything.

Elated and exhausted it crossed her mind that higher spirits must have helped her after all, because Mark had been delayed. It wouldn't be the first time - they had assisted in the past. Often there would be no other explanation for the help she received, but she did believe the angels of mercy were here to help troubled dark spirits progress, to eventually pick them up and take them to where they should be. Nine hundred years was long enough.

The soul was a shining, brilliant and remarkable creation which did not deserve to wallow in darkness, ruining the lives of others who were on their earthly journey. Sadly, it was all too common. The deceased often did not know they had died, or they actually enjoyed the lowest of earthly gratifications far too much to relinquish them. These were the lowest astral entities and the first to step in when invited via Ouija or séances, or by those in bereavement reaching out to the loved ones they lost. These dark ones sometimes wished to re-enact heinous deeds such as murder too, and again they hung around the living waiting for a weakness – a drunk, someone chronically depressed or perhaps an emotionally or sexually assaulted teenager, a drug-user, or even someone undergoing anaesthetic in a hospital.

Sadly for Ralph, it had been witnessing the tragic suicide of his father.

About to switch off the digital recorder, she sighed wearily, unhooked the restraining straps and said, "Okay. Ralph, listen to my voice. I want you to come back down now, onto that lovely warm beach. Remember what we said? That when I—"

Ralph sat bolt upright, rubbing his wrists. And a west-country voice, deep, loud and clear said, "What the hell's going on? What are you talking about?"

She nearly jumped out of her skin.

"Pardon? Who are you?"

"Who are you, more like? I'm Gideon. Gideon Sully." He looked around and his jaw dropped. "What am I doing in hospital? I was on my way home. Where's my wife?"

***

CHAPTER TWENTY-SEVEN

It was bothering her. A lot. Driving now over to Temple Lake Nursing Home, she'd ended up spending nearly all day at the hospital.

"What a bloody nightmare of a day! From start to finish," she said out loud.

Her brain could cope with no more, especially not with listening to the news and its non-stop commentary on the current political mess. The arguing egos never failed to rile her, and never more so than today. Snappy and tired, she switched it off. It wasn't that the day hadn't been a success, because it undoubtedly had. It was more a feeling of deep unease: something insidiously sinister was happening and it was impossible to shake off the feeling. For one thing, there was the distinct sensation of being detached from herself. Looking at her hands on the steering wheel they appeared oddly unfamiliar, small and pale, like having an out-of-body experience. On top of that, an icy chill had followed her around like a draught from a crypt.

"Stop it! It's got to you, that's all. It happens. You talk to dead people so of course it haunts you. You have to get home and get rid of it."

All the offloaded negativity had clung to her like a heavy cloud that wouldn't budge along. The countryside was a blur of grey drizzle, wizened trees, and acres of swampy fields devoid of grass. The windscreen wipers squeaked and the car bumped in and out of potholes, as the afternoon weather turned ominous. On and on it rained and rained.

What was it that was making her feel so deeply anxious, though – Gideon's revelation, or the subsequent session with Belinda? Maybe it was the whole emerging picture. One thing was for sure, events were escalating, definitely connected, and intensifying rapidly. This was orchestrated and far from over.

Hellfire, what was she missing?

"You died," she'd explained to Gideon. "You were found hanging from an oak tree in the woods near your home. Your son found you and cut you down."

"What do you mean, I died? Where's this then? God's waiting room?"

"No, this is a psychiatric hospital and you, in spirit form, have attached yourself to your son's body—"

"I don't know what you're talking about. I'm here, aren't I? Talking to you in a hospital. So how can I be dead?"

"Gideon, look at the clothes you're wearing."

He looked down. "These aren't mine. I don't wear stuff like this." His hands flew to his head. "My hair! What the fuck? Have I been in a coma? Had a brain tumour?"

"No, Gideon. You died. You hanged yourself. You are in Ralph's body and he's been extremely ill."

"I feel like I just woke up—"

"What year are we in, do you think?"

"Two thousand and seventeen."

"It's two thousand and nineteen. I know this is a

terrible shock. But you died two years ago and your son has been grieving for you ever since. This can happen, Gideon. When a death is sudden or traumatic the transition isn't made. The spirit is lost and troubled, stumbling around alone in the dark. No wonder you were attracted to a mortal being. And no wonder it was Ralph, who sat and held your body after cutting it down that day. He's been by your graveside ever since, wondering what happened. Missing you."

His head slumped to his shoulders. "Oh God, it's all coming back to me…"

"Take your time. Let's go through what happened that morning. You went for a walk in the woods and—"

"It was too late."

"What was too late?"

"I remember now. For days, maybe weeks, there'd been a continuous whisper in my head. A voice going, 'Kill yourself, kill yourself, kill yourself!' I had this irresistible urge to do it - all the time, every day. I couldn't sleep. It woke me up. And it got louder and louder, more and more persistent. That morning I knew where the rope was, how much to cut, where to do it, and which tree. I was in a trance, like everything was silent and I was floating. I don't know what happened, but the second I put the rope round my neck there was a flash of white like a camera flash, and the logs I'd stood on were kicked away. I knew then. That I'd been tricked. But there was no going back. I was swinging by the neck, kicking and trying to wedge fingers between my throat and the cord…and I was just about to black out when I heard the sound of laughing…sniggering if you like…and my last senses were of the beautiful dappled woods I'd loved my whole life, fading to night, and the sound of this horrible laughter. Too late…"

"What happened next?"

"As soon as I found myself out of my body I saw the cause of my rash act. The white monk appeared. I'd caught sight of him before, but I couldn't say anything to anyone because I know what happens to folk who say they've seen him. Well, there he was standing in front of me laughing. He's got eyes you can't look into – small and round, totally black like the pupil's dilated to fill the whole eyeball. And he's got an 'orrible wide pock-marked nose that spreads across his face when he smiles. Pure evil, he is - pure evil. He kept saying it was for, well, for…I can't use the word in front of a lady…"

"When did you start hearing voices telling you to kill yourself, can you remember?"

"After I got with Kezia Elwyn. She used to follow me round like she'd got a crush. I suppose I was flattered. What man wouldn't be? She was a good ten years younger than me and she's got gorgeous eyes – like Elizabeth Taylor's – violet. I'm not proud of this: I slept with her, but I thought it would be just the once. Thing was, after that I started to see her in my dreams, and I don't just mean see her, I mean she spoke to me, stroked me…I thought I'd die if I didn't have her again, it was that intoxicating. She became an obsession. I lost my head. In the end I went searching for her in the forest, going down to the altar and hoping she'd be there, unable to stop myself. I threw her over it. I practically raped her. And she was screaming and laughing, telling me to do it harder, 'til she bled. It was like she wasn't the same person when she got like that. There was all kinds of bat-shit crazy stuff, sex magick she called it. Blood magick too. I'm ashamed now, utterly ashamed, like the mortification of it all washes through me."

"What do you mean by sex and blood magick? Do you mean satanic rituals?"

"She had this altar like I said, with things burning on it, and a dagger and a cup full of liquor – weird tasting stuff. We drank that, and I'm telling you I was seeing red-eyed dragons in the trees, the canopy was spinning, and this deep, disembodied voice echoed from every direction like a slowed-down vinyl record. She wore masks of animals and drank the blood. I thought it was just drugs at the time, all that calling for demons, but…"

"But?"

"But then it got very sinister. I was addicted and couldn't stop. Every night I got irritable and mad at home, telling them I needed some air. But sometimes she wouldn't be there. Other times she'd be waiting. I never knew what to expect. All I knew was that I was going insane. And my dreams got worse, less erotic, more frightening, with voices telling me to kill myself. I realised then that she was into seriously bad shit. But when I asked her about them, she said my calling was to the dark side and I should listen. It sounds stupid but I believed her. I would've done anything you see, anything she told me to do, that was the hold she had on me. And she convinced me I was chosen, was one of the lucky ones to be invited to the underworld. Even said she was jealous."

"Poor Bel!"

"It was a month, maybe less. She had financial

difficulties, too. I helped her out, gave her our savings. She promised to pay me back but I remember telling her not to worry. She had nothing, see – just that bastard of a husband, and a kid to look after. I felt like me and Belinda had a lot and my kids were spoiled. That's how it started anyway, with me feeling sorry for her."

"Gideon, do you accept you are now in spirit? And residing in your son's body?"

"Yes."

"Okay. The thing is, by residing in him spiritually you are depleting his light and draining his energy. I know you wouldn't want that for him. He's been badly depressed and attracted a whole host of other spirits who've been telling him to hurt himself. He's now very ill, which is why he's here. I know you don't want to hurt him, but you are using his energy and he cannot function. Every life and spirit has a right to be free. You must leave his body and go to the light."

"What light? I'll go back into the underworld where Kezia told me I'd stay. She worshipped this one particular demon – used this name all the time. To be honest I didn't believe in it, I thought all those dreams and the voices were down to the stuff we smoked—"

"What name? Satan?"

"No, Malphas. That's it – Malphas. Is that the white monk?"

Sylvia frowned and shook her head. "No…" So the demonic *was* involved.

"I want to see my wife. I need her to know I'm desperately sorry, and that I love her. I loved my family. I don't know what happened, I guess there are no excuses and now it's all too late. I've hurt them all so much."

"It's not too late to both atone and show full remorse. You got mixed up with something you didn't understand, and your will wasn't your own anymore. But you can start to make amends by leaving your son's body so he can get well again, or he will end up being in psychiatric care for the rest of his life. He's very sick, and so is Belinda. You must not linger here. You must progress to the light."

"You know after I left my body, I saw my lad sitting at the foot of that oak tree holding me in his arms. And I was shouting to him, telling him to look and see what was all around. There were hundreds of them – a long spiralling line of monks in white robes surrounding him, a concentric circle getting smaller and smaller as they moved in on him. My boy sitting alone in the middle…and there was nothing I could do to help him."

She nodded, acknowledging the truth of this. "They've gone from his body now. And so must you. Let him recover, Gideon, and let him live. Hopefully he will remember very little. Open your eyes now and see the light. You have been tricked into believing you have to stay in the dark. See the light now, Gideon, and go towards it."

"I want to say goodbye to Belinda."

"Trust me, Belinda is not herself and it is very dangerous for you to try and find her. But in time you will reconcile. Now you must leave your son's body and go to the light, Gideon. It's the best and only thing you can do for him now."

After much persuading and reassurance, Gideon

finally agreed, apologising profusely for all the harm he had caused.

And by then it was lunchtime. Five hours had passed.

She called Ralph back from his dreamlike state, and signalled to the staff nurse outside.

"Any chance of some coffees in here, please? We're all done in."

It was a different nurse, a guy with a ponytail and a goatee. "Sure, no probs."

Utterly drained, she turned and smiled at the boy blinking at her from where he lay on the bed.

"Morning, Ralph."

"I'm starving."

"We've got some coffee coming. I'm sure they'll bring biscuits as well!"

"Where am I? Why are you here?" His hands flew to his head. "Oh my God. My hair's all shaved."

She nodded. "I'm afraid you're in hospital, my lovely, but you're okay. You've been very poorly. Extremely poorly."

He looked down at the jeans and t-shirt hanging from his spindly limbs. "Fuck, I'm thin. Have I been in a coma? Is that why my head's shaved?"

She cringed, imaging his reaction when he saw the strange attempt at a tonsure, and all the scabs and sores. "No, but it's a similar kind of thing in that you'll have amnesia. What's the last thing you remember?"

At that moment an orderly came in with coffee and a plate of biscuits, and they both lunged for them.

"Oh, thank you so, so much," Sylvia said. The coffee was like a drug hit and she gulped it down scalding hot.

Ralph crammed two biscuits into his mouth.

She held out the plate. "Eat!"

He wolfed down two more and half the cup of coffee before being able to answer her question. "Thanks, yeah, it's odd really. I've got sort of snapshots of things, but the last thing I can remember properly was Me and Ess being in the graveyard. And she was there again – the woman in black we called her – staring at us from under the yews. She's got these amazing eyes, violet, almost purple, and dead white skin. Anyway, this one time she was fixing me with this look and began to walk over. I think she was saying stuff about being sorry for our loss, and that we weren't to think she was being funny nor nothing, but she could communicate with the dead. She told us she could put us in touch with Dad again."

He paused to down more coffee. "Bloody hell, that's good."

"And did she?"

"Ess took off, said she was a spooky cow. But I went with her. She's got this altar in the forest. I was just desperate to know why he did it, see? I mean, my dad, if you knew him, he'd never have done that. He was happy. And he loved us. Like, we did stuff together and he was teaching me how to make guitars."

"And is that the last thing you remember?"

"No. I had dreams about her, like seriously erotic, like she was literally seducing me. I couldn't stop thinking about her after that. I felt doped all the time, like high on weed or something, literally floating. After that I can't remember nothing - just vague flashes of stuff – firelight in the dark, chanting, feeling someone was watching us in the woods, at the altar…I can't think anymore, I'm so tired."

"Okay, have a good rest now and when you're stronger we'll have another chat. I just need to see your mum first because she's been affected too. Have a sleep," she said as he drifted off, "and I'll pop back later."

Brody had agreed, thankfully, to let him rest before asking more questions, and assigned a nurse to keep watch until he woke up. Mark hadn't showed, he told her, and he hadn't rung.

"That's odd. Perhaps something urgent came up at the surgery?"

"Well, we'll keep the lad in overnight for close observations, anyway. I'll go and see him when he wakes up."

Very quickly she'd recapped the session with Ralph while Brody kept a polite, if sceptical frown on his face. Then handing over the voice recorder, she said, "Have a listen and see what you think. Unfortunately, I think Belinda may have a significantly stronger and more malicious attachment. It could be a lot more difficult to exorcise this one as I'm sure he will never go to the light. That said, I don't believe he's possessed her fully yet, but if I don't see her soon I can't say her prognosis is a good one. And she's got two kids who really need her."

Brody nodded curtly. "By all means talk to her. She's in the staff canteen, although I have to say she seemed fine to me." He looked at his watch. "You'll want some lunch yourself, so have a chat with her there and then let her see her son. We'll keep a very close watch on him, don't worry. I trust he's still restrained?"

"No, I took them off. He's better. A hundred

percent."

"Sylvia." He stood up, walking to the door to call for the staff nurse. "It's not a good idea to—"

"Brody, don't worry. He is absolutely fine. But I will leave him with you now – I know you'll be sending him home soon when you've see him. And thank you. I appreciate your trust in me, and I can't thank you enough for giving me the time to work through this with him. But it's worked, Brody. He's going to be okay. And surely whatever anyone believes… well, that's the main thing."

"It is indeed. I can't fault you on that, Sylvia. I just have a hard time accepting that we should be involved in spiritual casting out. It's priests' work." He pressed her hand. "Indulge an old man in his beliefs, won't you?

She nodded, smiled. "It does exist, you know – the dark side. We really do ignore it at our peril. I sometimes feel like I'm a lone voice, labelled bonkers by the rest of society. If only they knew! That's the thing you see, once you know it's real…Anyway, listen to the recording, that's all. Just listen to it. You never know, I might need someone myself one day!"

Belinda had indeed been in the canteen, on her own at the far side by the window. She was staring glassily into the distance, her meal untouched, and only vaguely acknowledged Sylvia's approach.

"Hi, Bel!" she said, sitting down opposite her. "I'm so sorry it's been a while getting back to you, but the good news is…"

Belinda had transferred her attention instantly and fully, looking directly into her eyes. And in that moment a cold rushing feeling came at her as if a freezer door had opened.

She'd stumbled over her words, unable to string any thoughts together. What had she been about to say?

"It's alright," Belinda was saying from somewhere far, far away. "I've been grateful for the time alone, to be honest. It's nice to be out of that dreary house and to have Ralph here where he's getting help."

Sylvia observed the top of her hand being pressed, heard words washing over her as if they were being spoken to someone else. Fighting for clarity of mind, some part of her then, had known that both Ralph and Belinda were going to be alright, and it was now herself at risk. For some reason she did not understand, it seemed the person who was really on the hit list all along, had been herself.

He had transferred to her, hadn't he - the moment she sat down and met Belinda's eyes?

His smile slithered into her mind, the stench of mould and decay filling the car.

Turning up the heater, she flexed her fingers and toes to encourage blood flow. Sweat beaded on her forehead despite the chill shivering up and down her back. Any other time she'd say it was flu getting a grip, but most likely it was a total draining of energy. These things, well they took their toll.

You know better than that though, don't you, Sylvia? Oh, come on...why are you denying it?

Because I'm fuck scared! And evil in life, evil in spirit. Who will help me? Who?

She could almost hear the laughter bubbling up inside.

A single tear dripped down her cheek and she swiped it away. Belinda had a near miraculous recovery. A sure sign of the problem having been spiritual was the rapid return to normal health following the spirit's departure. That and amnesia. And Belinda had recalled virtually nothing about the past few days. All she'd chattered on about was a damp old house that needed painting, and needing to text Essie to tell her to go to her grandma's after school. Fatigued-looking she may still have been, but that woman was back to her normal, speed-dialling, organised self.

So Burdo had transferred…

To me?

Temple Lake Nursing Home loomed into view on the next bend. It wasn't a good idea really, to perform release therapy on the old lady this evening, when her reserves were so badly depleted, but letting her down wasn't an option. The haunted expression in Ivy's hooded brown eyes nagged her conscience. She would do this and then go straight home. Maybe walk back. Get some fresh air.

God, she really didn't feel too good. The big stone house seemed to swim before her as she drove up the long, poplar-lined driveway, the outline rippling as if reflected in a lake. Tiredness was all. She was just so damn exhausted. Actually, as soon as she got home she'd have a bite to eat then go straight to bed. Mark would have to get tea tonight. Which reminded her: what the hell had happened to him all day? Maybe Brody had called him and told him not to bother after all, informed him that his wife had saved the day? Yeah, well that would piss him off. That would definitely keep him away. He'd probably be on the golf course slicing through the turf at this very moment.

Once parked, she glanced at her phone. No messages either. Oh well, stuff him. He could at least have let her know if Molly had got to school alright. She must have been scared stiff after what happened this morning with Essie turning up. Poor Molly, and poor Essie too. At least Essie's mum and brother would be home tomorrow and they could all start to get well again. Maybe a little chat with Essie would be in order too, when all this was over? Just to check she was okay. For sure the darkness had clung to her aura, it was a wonder she'd escaped. Maybe the girl wasn't into the dark arts, after all? Maybe the gothic image and sinister clothing was all a front, and unlike Ralph, she'd run a mile at the first hint of anything remotely unworldly?

She got out and stretched. The rain had eased off and the air was fragrant with rich new growth. It was hard to believe spring was ever going to arrive this year. Ravens cawed in the poplars, but apart from that there was utter silence. A dead stillness.

The drone of helicopters from this morning had long gone.

Oh Christ, yes. That little boy – Kezia's! Pray God they'd found him and the woman hadn't got him mixed up in something nasty. It happened. Sadly, there had been several cases on her books over the years, of demonic rituals involving small children.

What a day, what a bloody awful day…

She hurried towards the main door. But on reaching the bottom step, stopped abruptly to glance up at the windows. Her gaze travelled along the main body of the house until it came to rest on the east wing turret. And from that she could not look away. Her eyes bored into the narrow apertures which had once been the only source of light to those turret rooms. And then to her horror, a grimace began to stretch her features as if pulled by a marionette - a morbid grin over which she had no control.

Appalled, she clutched the stone pillar at the base of the steps, and instantly the feeling of vertigo and liquidity intensified. The ground swelled like an incoming tide, and every sense heightened to screaming pitch. The birds sounded more raucous than they should, the grass shone such a vivid green as to be emerald, and the air froze to Narnia.

This was definitely infestation. Something was doing its damnedest to attach to her while she was weak. An outline of a shadowed face beneath a white hood reared into her mind.

"Dear Lord, please give me strength," she said quietly. Before walking up the steps to a house that seemed to be waiting for her arrival.

***

CHAPTER TWENTY-EIGHT

Kezia

"John Rivers! I've been searching for thee."

Keeping his distance, the man began to shuffle towards the front door. He held up his hands in a placatory gesture. "No, Kezia, I'm not John. I'm Doctor Massey, Mark Massey. I think you're under some misunderstanding."

She shook her head. "I ran straight to the house but could not find thee. The monastery was afire and men attacked the monks. I was still in there, John! Everywhere I have searched for thee…"

Briefly her attention flicked to the young girl hanging back, standing with her mouth open. She too wore strange clothes, and had black smudges around her eyes.

Without taking his eyes from her face the man replied, "Kezia, this is Essie Sully. She and my daughter need to go to school." He began to shout into the house. "Molly! Get your bag—"

"Thou calleth me by another name. Who are these women?"

He shouted again. "Get your bag and get down here, Molly! Now! Both of you go to school and stay there until one of us comes to get you. No questions. Just go."

Molly stood on the threshold. "What's going on, Dad? I'm scared—"

"Just do as I say."

"Why have helicopters been flying over? Where's Mum?"

He shook his head, not taking his eyes from Kezia. "There's a little boy missing and people are out looking for him. It's happened before. They'll find him. Now go to school and stay there like I told you. One of us will come for you later. Same goes for you, Essie. Stay together and stick to the main road."

Kezia's eyes darkened. "Who are these women? What are they doing here at my home?"

"You're very confused, Kezia, and I'm not sure what's going on but—"

"Oh no, I am not at all confused, Sir. You left me there! I was still in the monastery, John, when it was set afire. I fled through the forest to save my own life while those inside were murdered in their beds. I thought there was only to be a raid on the cellars, to ease the hunger in the village, that I was to keep the vile one amused. But now I see I was wronged. I worked the magick for you and I sold my soul to get it."

"Kezia—"

"My name, Sir, is Kitty Morse and thou knowest it well. Have I not made love with thee? Have I not enchanted thee and served thee well? Yet that simpering coward of a wife still shares your bed and your riches, when you promised them to me. I am with child, Sir. Why do you abandon me now, after all you promised?"

"Kezia—" He was walking towards her, getting closer.

She bared her teeth. "Do not touch me. I will never forgive thee, John Rivers." Tears burst from her eyes and her whole body shook. "I will never, ever forgive thee for this betrayal. I loved thee. I loved thee and I got those riches for thee using means most foul and black. I poisoned those God-fearing men and I infested their dreams until they ranted with untold terror. I ran that night to save my skin, but before I did I turned the key on Burdo while he lay waiting, and he burned to his death. I lied to him too, and it disgusted me to say things only a lover should say when I loathed him so. I lay with his vile form, trying not to spew while his sickening black tongue flicked all over my flesh…And all for thee!"

"Kezia, I—"

The man seemed smaller now. A speck at the wrong end of a telescope.

"My name is Kitty. Do not deny me. The truth is there, in thine eyes."

"No."

"Know I will haunt thee, John Rivers, to the grave and beyond. There is no end to this. Forgiveness will never come. I curse thee now: death will come to the big house. Thy blood will be spilled on the stones of thine own hearth along with all thy kin, and no century will ever see the blood stains scrubbed clean. Benedicta will lock herself in the turret and no one will find the key. She will perish to bone, knowing the slow agonising terror of starvation. Your end will be brutal and painful. I curse thee, John Rivers, to the end of thy days and beyond. You are not forgiven and never will be. Rot in hell."

"Kezia, I need to make a phone call." He was backing into the house.

She followed, stealthy as a cat, hands clenched. Into the dim interior.

"Come on now, we don't want anyone to get hurt. You're extremely unwell, Kezia – suffering from delusions, thinking you're someone else. Your son is missing. Your mind is unbalanced…"

She laughed, cornering him in the dark kitchen. "Oh no, my son lives inside of me. I name him, Gulliver. He is thine, John Rivers…"

She paused. A flash of insight as brilliant as sunlight through glass, flared with cruel clarity. That of her own body raped, bloodied and left for dead across a stone altar.

In that moment of confusion and hesitation however, the man shifted position and was now reaching for something.

A glint of metal caught her eye. His fingers were about to curl around it.

Her eyes widened. Hurling herself towards the kitchen knife she snatched it up and pointed it at his throat.

The words that came out seemed not her own, yet the vehemence of emotion came directly from her heart and soul. "I have powers, John. The same powers that sent those monks to madness, that kept them mentally chained, and had them feverishly praying to a God they barely believed in. Powers that made them sordid and sinful, committing foul acts that disgraced their morals and left them withering and shame-faced. And those same powers, my lord, will destroy thee now. They will destroy Benedicta, thy pitiful wife, everything she values, and all of those who drink from the same table and take thy meat and thy coin. Slay me, after all I have done for thee? Take a knife to me? I will take thy soul and feed it to the devil himself."

"Kezia Elwyn. You are Kezia Elwyn. Kezia, listen to me. You have a son. He is missing and I think you are suffering from a terrible—"

A shrill tune played into the darkened kitchen and both of them jumped. A light flashed in her pocket. Puzzled, Kezia withdrew a plastic contraption. The name flashed, 'Clint.'

Clint?

Seizing his moment, the man shoved her away from him with such force she staggered backwards. Then dragging a black bag across the table he grabbed something from inside, before yanking her upright by the elbow and throwing her against the wall.

The tinkling contraption with the name flashing on it, clattered to the floor, just as the name began to vaguely register as one she knew. But by then the man had her in a stronghold, and had stabbed her in the neck.

There was nothing she could do.

She lost consciousness immediately.

***

CHAPTER TWENTY-NINE

Sylvia

It struck her, as it always did, that Temple Lake Nursing Home had once been a truly magnificent house. Flanked by turrets, set in hundreds of acres of parkland and with its own small, private church there was nothing to touch it for miles around. The family must have been pretty grand she thought, trailing the duty nurse across the hall – probably with royal connections.

The two women headed towards the bifurcated staircase, footsteps echoing on the marble tiles. With an ornate balustrade and a pair of classic gilded columns either side, the staircase was accented by an elegant grey carpet running on the treads. Unlike most stately homes however, whether privately owned or not, there were no family portraits lining the walls. Almost nothing of its history remained, bar the skeleton of its architecture and the spectacular stained glass window in front of them. Funny she had never noticed before that it was a mosaic of angels – three – not facing inwards but out, almost if they were protecting the house. Perhaps it was because there was so very little light coming through it today, but they seemed less colourful than usual; quite sombre.

Despite the glare of the overhead chandelier, the house was gloomy, and late afternoon shadows crept across the walls. The window recesses were more than three feet deep, the thickness of the stones keeping the house cool in summer and well protected in winter. But today it was bone cold in the corridors, the stairs creaked, and rain smarted against the window panes. One or two moans emanated from the bedrooms upstairs, and the distinctive odour of incontinence grew stronger as they climbed. Indigenous to hospitals and care homes, it could never be disguised no matter how many cleaning fluids were applied. The smell of decaying flesh, staleness, fear and regret hung in the air. But most of all there was a sense of waiting.

"Ivy's in Room Ten at the end," the nurse was saying as she strutted ahead. "Just down here."

A short, bustling sort of woman with a no-nonsense attitude about her, she opened the door and shouted as she walked straight in, "You've got a visitor, Ivy. The lady's going to hypnotise you to see what these nightmares are all about!"

Sylvia cringed. God, the whole floor could hear. It seemed when people got old dignity ceased to matter, along with privacy and personal belongings. The human being, no longer strong, employed, or heading up a family, was boiled down like a rotting cabbage, engendering little more interest than exactly when they were going to compost back to the soil. What would they leave behind? When would the funeral be?

What a short time we have, she thought, to make any kind of a mark on life. Depression stabbed her sharply in the gut as she walked in, and for a moment she floundered.

The old lady had been staring out at the rain-lashed

lawns, and now turned on hearing the click of the latch.

Sylvia thanked the nurse and closed the door.

There was spirit to the very last, she wanted to scream. The human spirit, that vital spark, was a precious glittering thing and it was still here in this ninety-year-old woman, just as it was in the eighteen-year-old lad who raced around the village in his gravelly hatchback. Far more vibrant in fact. With a lifetime of knowledge, the older spirit burned with insight and compassion. It gleamed in Ivy Finch's hooded brown eyes, glistening with all it had learned and wished to impart. Yes, she could see that now, as she walked towards her with her hand outstretched. This was a lady who needed to tell her things. Badly.

The day's weariness threatened to overwhelm her, and her feet dragged. Nausea rose into her suddenly flushed face and she swallowed down the bile. Call it instinct but it felt like whatever had attached to her wasn't going to like this and didn't want her to continue. The impulse to say she wasn't well and bolt from the room, was overwhelming. Instead, she summoned white light around her and silently pleaded for help. The sooner this was done the better, and then it was imperative to get home quickly.

"How are you, Ivy? Did you sleep any better last night?"

"No, darlin'. I don't sleep in this place. Might nod off in the daytime but I don't get a wink of sleep at night in this house. Never have."

"Really? Have you always suffered with insomnia here, then? That's a few years now, isn't it?"

"Not just me, all of us. We all lie awake at night.

You can hear them, see? And since *she* came to work 'ere, it's got worse. A lot worse."

The white of the old lady's arthritic knuckles shone through her parched skin as she gripped the chair arms. "I'm perished in 'ere. Would you pass me a blanket, there's a darlin'?"

"Yes, of course." She folded the blanket onto Ivy's knees. "Is that better? The radiator's on full."

"Makes no difference."

"Do you want another one for your shoulders?"

"No, I'm alright now, thanks darlin'."

"By 'she' do you mean Kezia?"

"Oh, you know 'er, then?"

"I know *of* her. So what is it that's got worse? And who is it you can hear?"

Ivy met her eyes. "What I'm going to tell you is confidential, isn't it? Only no one, and I mean no one, in this village ever talks about this to outsiders, and the only reason I'm telling you now is because I think you're the one person who might be able to 'elp. Call it a hunch. Anyhow, you need to keep this private and just between us, alright? People won't confess to what goes on 'ere, even on their death beds, it's that bad. I'm frightened, I don't mind admitting. And I mean badly so. Very, very badly."

She faltered, shivering, her hooded eyes staring at a memory only she could see.

Sylvia leaned forward and very lightly touched her hand, "Everything you tell me is strictly confidential, Ivy. And I will help you, of course I will. That's what I'm here for. It's what I do."

"I thought you were the same as all the rest 'til the

last time I seen you. I think you know about spirits, see? And I need to make my peace before I go. I don't want to go to my grave being terrified like most of the folk round here. They don't want to die because they say it gets worse after you've passed. I hardly dare shut my eyes even for a moment, especially someone like me. Do you understand?"

"Yes, I do. You're mediumistic, yes?"

She nodded. "It's going to take some believing, but I swear on my life everything I'm going to say to you now is true. There are people here who need help. I've tried all my life with exorcisms, some successful some not so much, but they torment me now…the spirits…day and night…I don't have the strength no more…"

"That's alright, just take your time. You'll be surprised at what I've heard over the years. There's very little that shocks me now."

"Alright then. Deep breaths, Ivy! This goes way back and you need to know the gist of it first – the grudges and vendettas, all the bad feeling."

"In the village?"

"Regarding the Rivers family!"

Sylvia shook her head, frowning.

"They owned this house - ever since it was built and that's going back to medieval days. I think they were one of the oldest families in Britain. Anyhow, no one wanted them 'ere no more. We'd 'ad enough, and our ancestors before us, of that rotten lot. They'd 'ave people work 'ere and then not pay 'em, see? And in my lifetime too. Oh yes, can you build this and fix that? Then laugh in your face. The last Mrs Rivers went through a dozen cleaners and every one with a tale to tell about how she'd find fault and a reason to dock their wages. Sent her own to private school mind, there was always money for that."

"I heard they weren't popular. Long time ago now, though?"

"People round here don't forget. Anyhow, when the last one left – your 'usband's grandmother, did you know that? Did he tell you? I expect he did. Well, after that it stood empty for a while before it was sold and developed into a nursing home. There were some who very pleased to see the back of 'em and move in, I can tell you. People like us 'ad never seen such grandeur."

"I'm sure."

A knock on the door and in walked an orderly with two cups of tea. After she'd set them down she wandered to the window and stood admiring the view, taking her time.

"Thank you," Sylvia said.

"That's alright," she said, making no move to leave. "Still raining, I see."

"Yes."

Sylvia let the silence lengthen until finally the orderly sighed and walked towards the door. "Right then, if there's nothing else?"

"No. Thank you."

Still the woman left the door ajar, her shadow hovering on the wall.

"Could you close the door, please?"

Ivy met her eyes with a despairing look. "They'll be desperate to know what I'm telling you. Desperate. We don't get visitors, even though most families are only down the road. No one likes coming 'ere, and I don't blame them neither."

She sipped her tea and Sylvia waited before continuing, "You were saying people had been pleased to move into the house when it became a nursing home?"

"Oh yes, at first. But then rumours got out and stories were told. Folk said it was haunted and such like. I know it makes us sound daft, but it's worth remembering that once you've taken up residence 'ere you're stuck: your old house is sold and there's nowhere else to go, and besides, if you tell them you're 'aving nightmares or the place is haunted they'll just give you more sleeping pills. But I'm telling you it's all true, and it's getting worse – a lot, lot worse since that Kezia came 'ere. In fact, call me an old fool, but I'd say it's coming to a head. I can feel it."

"In what way?"

"Well, we've all 'eard the screaming at night, not just me, ask anyone, they'll tell you. And I'm not just talking about the odd scream from someone 'aving a nightmare, I mean grown men screaming for their lives. First time I 'eard it I thought it was vixens in the woods or screech owls – you know, sounds like someone's being murdered? But no, it wasn't that. It wakes you up and then you lie 'ere listening. One o'clock it starts, sometimes going on for an hour or more – men screaming in terror, and footsteps clattering up and down flagstone corridors. All of them floors be carpeted so how come it sounds like boots on stone? There are shouts in the yard outside too, and clattering hooves. You don't see nothing when you look out the window, with your eyes wide and your heart galloping ten to the

dozen. It's black as soot out there, like it is in these parts
– no lights nor nothing. But inside there's an unholy
racket going on, with doors banging and people running
past the door…and there ain't one of us who 'asn't
heard it. Not one. The staff won't believe us, laugh it
off…but the night nurse sits downstairs watching
television, don't she? Smoking, got her music ear plugs
in or whatever they're called. The one before 'er heard it
right enough, though. Left she did, quick sharp as well."

"And since Kezia arrived?"

Ivy lowered her voice to a whisper. "Knew she was a
funny one. There was something of the other world
about her with that white skin and those eyes. You ever
looked into her eyes? Violet they are, purple almost.
And she stares at you, into you, like she's reading your
mind, not saying a word just smiling like she's not all
there. You'll 'ave a thought like, 'I wish she'd hurry up' -
you know, making the bed or something - and she'll say,
'Almost done. Missus Impatient!' But it's not that, it's
the way she hums to herself and runs her hands over
everything in the house. Everyone sees her doing it,
stroking the walls, the bannisters, the pictures. And she's
always in the oldest part, the turret. There's no one in
there, just a spiral staircase now, but they say that when
the Devil Baron lived here, as they called him – Baron
John Rivers, back in medieval days – that he kept his
wife, Benedicta up there in the sewing room. Locked
her up to keep her safe from the mob, only no one ever
let her out again. All dead see? Anyway, that's where she
goes – to the turret, humming and smiling like some
kind of lost soul. And ever since she's been 'ere, there've
been bad things happening, too. Horrible things."

"You mean the creatures you mentioned, the ones crawling into your mind? Do you want to tell me about those?"

Ivy looked away.

Sylvia tried again. "Doctor Massey prescribed you sleeping tablets—"

"Oh, he would. Sorry, I know he's your 'usband and all that, but he's a Rivers as well, and it'd suit him to shut us up about what 'appened here. Anyhow, I've made up my mind I've to tell someone or I'll go mad with it. I wasn't going to. We've kept this secret in our village for a very long time, hundreds of years, but with what that girl's doing. Well, I'm going to my maker 'aving done what I could to stop it, and may the Lord forgive and protect me. I see her, that's what. I see her and the one dwelling inside of her, too–"

"Stop what? You said, 'having done what you could to stop it'?"

Ivy looked out of the window again, at the lengthening shadows of oaks and poplars stretching across the lawns, and her own tissue-white reflection in the lamplight. "What's coming."

"I don't understand."

"There was a terrible thing happened 'ere, did you know? The monks at the monastery were massacred by John Rivers and men from the village. He whipped them into a frenzy."

Sylvia nodded, the graphic images from earlier that day still fresh.

"He'd told them the monks, who were French invaders, didn't have to pay tithes like they did, that they'd taken the best land, and had cellars stocked with wine and cheese while everyone else starved to death. It was a time of civil war and the landowners were given power to do what they wanted while royal troops battled it out. Rivers made the most of it. Got the men to behead nearly four hundred monks. Four hundred. And how did he manage to get in all silent like, then massacre so many? Because he had help!"

Sylvia frowned. "Help?"

"From a witch. Kitty Morse was a black witch. She was a village girl everyone went to for remedies and fortune-telling. But then she went to the bad, fancied herself as Lady of the Manor I expect, and as a favour to Rivers, slept with the Abbot – bewitched him and made him fall in love with her while all the time slowly poisoning the monks. They say she paralysed them with sleeplessness and nightmares, had them so terrified of the dark they were delirious with fear. By the time the mob stormed the monastery they were defenceless and weak, all the gates were open and the Abbot asleep and naked in his bed. They impaled the heads on spikes, raided the kitchens and the cellar then set fire to the place. They say the stench of burning blood and flesh soured the air for weeks, months. No one local ever goes up there to this day, and if they do they don't go again. It's got a, what you'd call, unhealthy atmosphere about it."

Sylvia nodded, trying to keep down the swell of sickness rising inside. Her neck hurt and her insides were on fire. Her stomach burning…

"Anyhow, soon after it happened, Rivers had Kitty Morse slayed on her own altar, in the woods near your place. That's where she lived - her cottage was once your lodge. Had her killed so she wouldn't talk, and so he wouldn't have to move her in or honour his word, I suppose. Used her, if you like. And after that there was a bad feeling in the village. She was feared alright, but she was one of their own. People went to her for healing. She helped women with their babes and made love potions for the young folk. But when they 'eard what he'd done, and found her body raped and murdered on the altar, it all changed, and ever since then the Rivers family was cursed. Rivers never paid those men neither, nor shared the raided food, nothing. Even 'ad those who spoke out against him tortured, and torture in them days was serious torture."

"Yes, didn't they lock them up in dungeons full of snakes and poisonous toads and things? There were some nasty punishments."

"And strung knotted cords round their heads, twisting them tighter and tighter until they entered the brain and festered! Strung them up by the thumbs and smoked them, had rats eating their intestines…burrowing through the stomach while they were still alive."

"They were brutal, no doubt about it.

"Yes, well that's what he did to his own men, his own villagers. And so you can imagine how they felt?"

"Yes."

"And that's what I'm coming to. Rivers, you see, was on both sides with warring royalty – lining his pockets. But it was Queen Matlida who had a stronghold in this area, so word got to her and we won't say how, that he'd been entertaining King Stephen's soldiers. Soon after that, one afternoon while he and his family were eating and drinking in front of their great fire, with a spit roasting, her army burst in and slit their throats like pigs right there and then on the hearth. Benedicta ran up to the turret and was locked in. They say she died up there, of starvation, while he was caught in the tunnel between the house and the church."

Benedicta…

"It must have been a hell of a time to live."

"The thing is though, and hear me out. This is why I didn't want to say nothing because I didn't want no more of your 'usbands knock-out drops, but since that Kezia's been 'ere it's not just the ghostly goings-on you can hear. We've had visitors. Night time visitors. You asked about the creatures I mentioned, well these ain't just bad dreams, these are demons. Demons she's brought with her."

Sylvia fought with the dull headache that pulsed in her right eye, with the tide of extreme fatigue. Her whole body was shivering with fever.

"She's opened a door, you mark my words. I suppose she 'ad her reasons. But in doing so she's given 'im, the one who sends folk mad, life."

"I don't follow."

"There's many lose their minds in this village. One day someone's right as rain. Next they've seen 'im, and then they're swinging from a noose in the woods."

"Seen him?"

"Burdo. The murdered Abbot Kitty Morse seduced. John Rivers brought his head back on a spike and stuck it on the gate out there. It's a pillar now at the bottom of the steps – you'll have rested your hand on it, I expect? That's where he impaled his skull. Burdo's spirit won't ever rest."

"The name Burdo. I heard it for the first time recently. We had an incident in the village—"

"Not another suicide?"

"No, a very ill teenager. But how do you know the name of Burdo?"

"We all know it. There are those who've seen 'im, too. They say he creeps into their minds. His face appears just as they're dropping off to sleep. He introduces himself and after that his is the only face you'll see and the only voice you'll hear. It's usually if they've been in the woods, or got drunk and taken a short cut through the graveyard. Mostly it's those over at Wolfs Cross, seeing as they're the ones out hunting. There's folk who look down on them, call them inbreeds and gypsies but they ought not to. They've suffered the most, and taken in them as 'ave gone mad. Wolfs Cross is where you might say Monkspike keeps its dirty laundry. It's where the badduns go. It's where she's from, too."

Sylvia nodded. "Funnily enough I've a young girl to go and see there tomorrow – Paige—"

"Be careful. It's a rum old place and not what you might think, not at all…"

"And Kezia? Why do you she's brought demons here, into this house?" Sylvia asked, now so cold her teeth began to chatter audibly, despite the radiator blasting out.

"Because she practises the dark arts. And I think Kitty has waited all this time. That's what I'm saying to you - the time is now."

"For what? I don't understand at all." Brain fog was

clouding her thoughts and the need to pass out was so strong the floor kept rearing up to meet her. "I'm sorry, I don't feel great. I get the story and the spiritual unrest, but not what is about to happen - what it is that's coming to a head or why!"

Ivy was getting agitated. "Kitty Morse was a black witch. I told you. She's waited for the right person to invite her and all her demons in with her. They've come for him, you see? For Rivers. The family was cursed, you've only to look at their history and you'll see it's full of infant deaths, tragic accidents, congenital disease and insanity. But it's like she's looking for him, and all that darkness is pouring in with her—"

"Ivy, what demons? What do they look like?"

"There's no form to them. They ain't human, nor have they ever been. Out of the corner of your eye you'll see something slither up the wall, like a fat black rat. You hear your shoes being moved across the floor, or a hairbrush roll along the dressing table. The air gets thick and heavy, and your heartbeat starts to race for no reason. I sit up in this chair all night keeping watch. If I took your husband's smarties I'd be pinned down, paralysed, like some of those poor souls down the corridor there. I hear them crying, begging…screaming if one of these things runs across them. And sometimes I swear if I peer into the darkness long enough there's someone watching me. It's a dark energy she's raised with those satanic rites or whatever the stupid girl does. And because of who I am, what I do - it's worse for me, it's terrible." She clamped a cold, thin hand on top of her own. "They're showing me the abyss… a line of trees all blackened and burned, and behind them a howling wasteland. There's a black wolf waiting for me, head bowed, its coat matted and wet, the eyes red, burning… watching…"

Sylvia squeezed the old lady's age-spotted hand in hers. "You've managed to avoid being infested by these low spirits so far, haven't you? But it's tiring and you're exhausted. I'm going to recommend we transfer you to hospital. It won't be as nice or comfortable, but it will give you a rest, and it will give me time to help some of the others and cleanse the house—"

Ivy managed a weak smile. "Well, you might have managed that once, but not now. It's got a grip and it's far too late." Tears blurred her eyes. "I don't want to spend another night 'ere. Please. I've got a terrible feeling it's all coming to a head. I told you – Burdo infests the mind and makes folk do terrible things, but Kitty - she's a woman scorned and she's brought all of hell with her. I'm telling you, Kezia is one and the same as Kitty Morse."

"What does she want?"

"To destroy John Rivers, I should think. Send him to hell."

"But he's a spirit."

Ivy shot Sylvia a look that jolted her. "Do you believe in past lives?"

"Um, yes. I practise past life regression."

"I thought as much. I've had a long time to sit and think, see? And I believe she's found him. I watched Kezia one afternoon when Doctor Massey came to prescribe my pills."

"You think the spirit of John Rivers is in Mark, my husband?"

"You don't have to believe me, darlin'. But if I were you, I'd watch that girl like a hawk. She 'ad a dalliance with Bel Sully's 'usband for some reason, and look what happened there?"

He called me Benedicta…

"Don't fight me, my lovely. I'm just a lonely, frightened old lady with nothing to lose but her sanity. I had to do the right thing and tell you. We need help 'ere, and I've 'ad this bad feeling for a while. And now Kezia's little boy has gone missing and helicopters are flying overhead all day. I dread to think…"

Belinda. Benedicta. Her reaction to Mark…and his when he heard about Gul, Kezia's child. In a way it made sense.

Ivy grabbed her arm. "You know I'm speaking the truth, don't you? You understand how the dark side works? What I've told you is real, but no one from outside can see it and no one will believe it, so there's no help coming. None."

"Actually, I do believe you. But Mark won't. He won't believe he's in danger from a spirit or a girl in the village who looks like a goth. He just won't."

"It don't matter what he believes does it, if she comes for him with a shotgun? She's Kitty Morse and he's John Rivers, and not only has she just found him but thanks to Kezia she's got a whole legion of darkness with her, too."

"And Burdo? What would he want?"

As Ivy stared into her eyes the strangest of emotions flickered inside. It was odd but her mouth began to twitch into a smile, just as it had on the steps on the way in. She struggled in vain to stop it happening, watching

Ivy's lips move in reply...The old lady's voice was fading out and she only just heard it, as horrified, the grin stretched right across her face.

"Evil," Ivy's lips mouthed. "Pleasure...evil..."

***

CHAPTER THIRTY

Sylvia hurried down the drive from Temple Lake, leaving the car in the car park. The shortest route home would be via the garden path at the back. The climb came out at the top of Cats Hill directly opposite the woods, from where there was a shortcut to the house. But the night was black as pitch, and there was a feeling of dread inside that made her jumpy as a cat. It would be best to stick to the main road, where there were lights, and maybe other human beings.

It wasn't far but she was too unwell to drive and fresh air might help. The migraine that had threatened this morning had developed into a sickly cramp, blinding one eye. Her heartbeat speeded up erratically before slowing to dull thuds that seemed in danger of stopping altogether, before speeding up once more. And it had been almost impossible to concentrate on what Ivy was saying. Much of the story had since vanished into brain fog, and try as she might she could recall little of the conversation. Stupidly, she'd left her voice recorder with Brody. Over-tired probably, just worn out after what really had been an exhausting day.

There was a question mark lingering over her encounter with Ivy, though. Just what had the old lady seen in her that caused such an abrupt recoil?

At the moment the alarmingly inappropriate smile

had spread across her face, she'd stood up to ring a colleague who ran the local hospice. It had diverted attention and happily, miraculously even, secured a place for Ivy, who would be transferred tomorrow morning. But by then Ivy had slumped in her chair, refusing to look into her eyes again or speak, only nodding when she heard of the transfer.

"I will come back tomorrow," Sylvia insisted. "I don't feel well, not at all...but I'll come back tomorrow and work on the house itself, then I will do my best to help some of the other residents. Are you okay, Ivy?"

She'd had to leave straight away. The atmosphere had changed, and the need to get out was intense. She had paused only to inform the duty nurse of the transfer agreement.

"Yes, well she's near the end now," said the nurse loudly.

It was odd though, as she'd listened to Ivy talking, she'd had the feeling that everything was beginning to make sense. But for the life of her she could not now remember a darned thing.

Turning the corner onto Cats Hill, the street lights came to an end, plunging the night into darkness. There wasn't much further to go, though.

Not far...

She set off at a brisk enough pace, the pine-scented freshness of the woods a welcome respite from the stuffiness of the nursing home. Less than half way up however, she was forced to stop and catch her breath, gasping like an old man on Woodbines. The night was chilling rapidly, and so dark that down in the valley even the church spire was indecipherable. How unearthly still it was. Normally, there would be a cacophony of owl hoots, the sound of bleating sheep carrying from distant fields, and the rustling of small creatures in the undergrowth. But this evening nothing stirred. Like an evacuated tube station, all that remained was an empty tunnel devoid of life and light. And it was far from normal.

She reached for the dry stone wall bordering the lane. God, the exhaustion! It was difficult keeping awake.

He's getting a grip. You're too weak...and getting weaker.

This was more than tiredness. More like coming down with something. Hopefully nothing serious or sinister. Molly was still far too young to be without a mother. Jeez, her thoughts were depressing. How come tiredness had suddenly become terminal cancer?

It felt that bad though, it really did, with every step a huge effort and her lungs drum-tight and raspy. It was hard to draw breath. She peered up at the wooded hills with weary eyes. All of a sudden the house seemed so very far away.

The back of her head pounded with sickening thuds.

I feel bloody awful. It's getting worse.

Maybe flu? That and being drained. All the same, it would be best to get home as quickly as possible, then make an assessment in the morning after a good night's sleep. She shivered all over. The temperature was dropping rapidly, a sharp chill slipping under her clothing like a shadow, goosing skin and stealing warmth.

Folding her arms, she hugged herself and resumed walking. Mind you, this had happened once before – on a beach in Bali of all places – and turned out to be an intestinal infection. Yes, it could be food poisoning or something similar, because she hadn't felt like eating all day.

Who the fuck are you kidding? You know what this is. You know!

She paused again. This time with a small stab of fear. Why was her breath misting on the air?

A clammy sweat coated her skin.

She clutched at the wall.

Why the temperature had frozen to that of mid-winter was not a question she wanted to ask herself. The most pressing concern right now was to make it home. This was horrible, although bound to happen in her line of work. If only she could make it home then she could begin exorcising the spirit, and regain strength.

Burdo's ghost will never rest.

She peered up through the woods once more. Not much further to go. Five minutes max. All the same… She turned around and leaned against the wall to rummage for her mobile to dial Mark…it was five minutes too long. Her heart was firing great thumps through her arteries, the rise of nausea surging into her throat.

Oh God, I'm going to throw up!

Breathing through her nose, swallowing gulps of saliva, her hands shook as she waited for the android to spark into life And for the second time in as many minutes the quietness of the evening struck her with its intensity. It was absolutely deathly. With not a breath of air to rustle the leaves. A paroxysm of shivers rippled over her back like a breeze on a chilly pond.

She winged around, certain someone was behind, scanning the black interior of the forest. It was far, far darker than normal. Was someone there?

The back of her neck crawled.

Suddenly the phone pinged with a signal and she turned back, scrolling through the contact list for Mark's number.

Let him be in, let him answer, let him be there…

She pressed speed-dial. At the precise moment a breath was blown into the hair on the back of her head.

Almost dropping the phone, she backed into the middle of the lane, eyes straining into the total blackness. Who was there? Oh, dear God!

The phone was ringing. As in the myriad of trees one shadow broke away from another, and a shape stirred. A flicker of white. An owl? A flash of moonlight on bark? She jumped, hand on heart. Tears burned her eyes.

"Oh, come on, Mark. Answer the damn phone."

After ten rings the call went to answerphone. He'd be washing up, or had left the phone in his jacket pocket. Busy anyway. No option then but to put one foot in front of the other and try to—

Fuck! What was that?

She stood absolutely still, holding her breath. It sounded like a stone dislodging from the wall. Someone *was* there, then! But why were they lurking? What were they doing? No one else lived on Cats Hill. The only other house was a farm that lay a good half mile away, and the old couple always travelled by truck and never at night. A minute passed with nothing further. Swaying on creaking joints, she shook her head, chastising herself. Must have been a small creature.

Get a grip for Christ's sake, woman!

She dropped the phone into her bag.

And as she did so there came the sound of mocking laughter. Nor did it emanate from one particular spot. Instead it seemed to ricochet around the trees, like a sound thrown around by a ventriloquist.

Her heart moved from its normal place and bounced down to her stomach. And through a queasy, muddled blur she began to register just how deeply ink-black the evening had fast become. Not only in the forest, but now the lane, the sky, and the fields beyond. Not a single shred of light and yet it was barely seven o'clock. No stars. No moon. And now – no house.

You know. You know what this is, Sylvia. You do. You know! Think about it – every single symptom…

"Oh, Christ."

The air crackled as if a storm was brewing. And now multiple shadows appeared to rise from other shadows, emerging from the depths as if shedding a cloak from their own substance. She tried to move. But every limb became rigid, locked in their sockets as the shadow shapes closed in, oozing a darkness so total as to snuff out the very light of her being.

Not a single part of her body obeyed her command to run. Her tongue swelled inside her mouth and mind fog blanked out all thoughts.

He introduces himself and after that his is the only face you see, the only voice you hear.

Get out of my head. Get out of my head. Get out of my head.

But this time he reigned supreme. His face loomed into hers as clearly and distinctly as if he was standing in front of her. And his voice, when he spoke, was French accented and scornful, booming into her head so loudly and so clearly it sent shockwaves jarring into her bones.

"Oh, come on, you know I am not going to do that, Sylvia. I have waited a long time for this…"

Who are you? What do you want?

"That's better. Now we can introduce ourselves. Enchanté, Sylvia."

She fell back against the wall clutching her head, mentally pushing away the image of his face. *No, you must leave. I will resist you. You will not infest me. Dear God, please help me.*

***

CHAP+ER THIR+Y-⊕N€

KEZIA

When she woke it was to the feel of wet earth and sharp stones stabbing into her back. Cramped and cold, with a thumping head and her face covered with dirt, twigs and leaves, she blinked grit out of her eyes and tried to sit up. Nothing moved. Her body would not respond.

Okay, okay…take it easy. Keep calm. Where am I, first?

Thick fog obscured everything. She stared hard until one or two clumps of grass emerged, and a couple of tree trunks. They seemed to be higher up, over her head. So was she underground?

Fuck!

Panicked, she dug her nails into the earth and scrambled to push herself up. This was a ditch. She was lying in a ditch! Not an ordinary ditch either, but a deep gully, with tall, densely packed hollies either side. Out of breath already and severely weakened, she tried again to manoeuvre onto her elbows but her body would not respond. After several minutes, with no choice, she slumped back again.

In a nearby tree a squirrel began to scramble around, noisy with its hissing bark, and a woodpigeon cooed. Other sounds carried too, that were as familiar to her as breathing - the drill of a woodpecker, the melody of a blackbird. So she was in the forest then? But where in the forest, and what time of day was it? With no light of any kind it was impossible to tell.

Her throat was dry and sore, and the back of her head ached badly. It must have been a fall. Had she been concussed? Twisting and wriggling in the narrow channel she fought to get onto her side, realising only gradually that her body from the waist down was a dead weight. She looked down, confused. One of her legs was bent at an odd angle from the hip joint. Strangely, there was no pain. Dirt had matted her clothes, and her skin was smeared with mud that caked into the scratches on her arms and legs, no doubt incurred by the brambles she'd fallen into. Had she, then? Fallen? What had she been doing? Nothing, no memory of what could have led to this, would surface.

One thing was for sure, her body was frozen and there was no one around. She had to get out. Somehow. Using her elbows, she began to haul herself along the ditch, inching backwards, dragging the dead weight of her lower body to a point where the gully widened. Soil stung her eyes and she squeezed them shut, blinking repeatedly. It was like trying to crawl out of a grave.

Fuck! I've been buried alive. I'm going to die...

With a huge heave she rolled onto her side and lurched into a semi-sitting position on the unaffected leg. All five senses rushed back in. And with them a searing pain that kicked as hard as a horse. Her bone must have cracked in the fall and with movement, it now hung from its socket like the limb of a raggedy doll. The pain rushed in and she opened her mouth and screamed.

"Help! Help! Help!"

Crying with the agony of it, she forced herself to shuffle further and further backwards, the injured leg jarring a little more with every movement as she searched for a shallow point. Every couple of seconds she momentarily blacked out with the pain. If she didn't get out of this she'd die. Thorns ripped her palms, her elbows scuffed and bled, and the sides of the gully crumbled with more rolling soil and stones.

She blinked and spat out the dirt falling on top of her. "Help! Help! I've fallen! Help, please! Someone!"

From far, far away came the almost inaudible sound of voices.

"Help! Help!"

She stopped, held her breath. No, they couldn't hear.

Tears blurred her vision, her heart was beating so rapidly and so shallowly it felt ready to give out.

I'm going to die.

Someone left me here to die.

She stopped then, the sudden and profound understanding a hammer blow. Someone hated her enough to leave her here to die? And on the back of that thought, came another word… *Again.*

Someone left me here…again!

This time her heart thumped so violently it seemed as if it would be the very last beat. Blackness engulfed her. And she fell back, cracking her head on rock.

Was this a dream? Or had she died?

His face was peering down into hers. The face of the man she loved with all her heart and had sold her soul to be with: ruffled hair the colour of tarnished gold, deep-set green eyes, and a mouth that felt hard and

271

demanding against her own. Overpowering in aura, commanding in presence, he had promised to take her out of filth and starvation to be his own. They had made love on her altar, and bathed naked together in the fresh, clear river. Her skin shivered with the memory of his fingers tracing over her wet, icy skin as they sank into the dewy grass and he declared himself in love, bewitched and enchanted. The very thought of him made her body ache for his, her desire for him all-consuming. Yes, she would do anything... Her heart sang, and the sound of his horse cantering up to the cottage door brought joy such as she had never known. Their love was real, an exalting ecstasy that once experienced could never be unfelt, unseen, unknown. It changed everything. She would never be the same again...

So why then, had he left her here in this ditch? Why had he thrown her away? When he was done!

She had flung open the cottage door. Expecting to feel his arms around her, to tell her she had been left in the monastery... that was right... the monastery was burning...and yes, she had been left there by mistake...hadn't she?

The image of his loving, handsome face dissipated in an instant. And another one took its place. The one where he'd looked at her with loathing and contempt, the mask of beauty sliding from his features as he shoved her aside.

She was nothing.

Had been used.

And with that knowledge she had started to run for her life. Through the forest. A battle cry in her wake.

Men on horses. With swords.

Tears smarted her eyes. A sharp stab to the soul. And floating high above her own massacred body, the scene appeared before her. A young girl with the blackest of hair and the whitest of skin, lay with the sackcloth ripped from her exposed flesh. Ravens pecked at what had once been jewel eyes the colour of violets, beads of ruby now dripping from the sockets, to congeal in the grass. And the soft wash of summer rain pattered onto her altar, rinsing away the carefully prepared herbs, flowers, and small libations offered to the dark ones. Offered for favours, her body sold and her soul exchanged, for Baron Rivers' desires and wishes.

Ah, so that's what happened to me.

The tears dried. And she lay a long time. While the fog seeped further into the trees, a wet layer that deadening all sounds and signs of life.

Kezia drifted in and out of consciousness. At one point, muffled shouts echoed far away, then faded away, until there was nothing at all but the dirt and the dark.

Where I belong…

Once or twice she briefly surfaced, aware on some level of a change in the light. Her heart pulsed weakly, aching in the side of her neck, before a coma claimed her once more, and with it the dark dreams of a more recent memory: an unlit kitchen; something stabbing into her neck… Her right hand rubbed at the site of injury, as delirious in fever she muttered and groaned, her head turning from side to side. There was a feeling of falling, of clutching at kitchen units and thin air, a vague recollection of being carried in a hurry of heavy breathing, of her thigh cracking on impact as whoever it was threw her from a height, then covered her face with twigs and mud... angling her onto her side...*Making it look like a fall?*

"Kezia! Kezia! Kezia!"

A man's voice. Her eyes flickered. Was this life or death? Did it matter?

John...you never loved me. You didn't love me... it was all a lie. I see it now. And I will let you go... I will let you go...I need to be free of the pain, the hurt...

"Kez! Kezia! We're not giving up! You're here somewhere. We're gonna find you! Keziaaaa!"

The man's cry was raw and animalistic, exhausted, panting and desperate. Someone who wanted her alive. Was she this Kezia? Were they looking for *her*?

Different voices now. Another man's voice. And a woman's.

Something else. Dogs. Sniffing, panting, searching dogs. They would find her. Her pulse picked up, lurching sickeningly like the thud in her head. Her voice stuck in her throat, snagging on the dried blood and dirt lodged inside it.

"Here!" The sound was little more than a croak.

The voices were fading, moving away. "Kez! Keziaaaa!"

She swallowed hard and tried again, "Here!"

The calling of her name stopped.

And then the ground was pounding, shaking, trembling. A whole band of boots and crazy-eager dogs were thundering towards her.

"Sam! Over here!"

"Kez! Hold on, they're coming. We've got you!"

***

CHAPTER THIRTY-TWO

BELINDA

At six in the evening, after a couple of hours talking with Ralph, a text pinged through from Essie.

Belinda fumbled in her bag for her mobile. "Oh, thank goodness, it's your sister. I was getting really worried she hadn't replied."

"Is she alright?"

"I hope so. She should be with your gran..." Reading the text, Belinda said, "Mark took her over to his and Sylvia's so she could go to school with Molly."

She rang Essie straight back, "How are you, love? Are you okay? Safely at your nan's?"

"Yeah. Actually Doctor Massey asked Nan if Molly could come back here, as well—"

"Really? Well yes, I suppose he must be busy. Is your nan okay with that? What about tonight – I mean, overnight?"

"She said he'd just asked her to pick us both up from school and bring us here. There've been, like, helicopters flying over the village literally the whole day. It's all over the news about Gul. Anyway, Nan's cool about it. Me and Molly are sharing the spare room and we've just had fish and chips."

"Have they not found the little boy yet? Do you

know?"

"It's on the news just now. We're all sitting here glued to it. Yeah, thank God they found him. He was in the forest – well away from the village, though – over by the monastery, like literally two miles away. But the other weird thing is Kezia's gone missing now. They say she went looking for him in the early hours of this morning and never came back." She paused as the sound of sirens wailed down the phone. "Can you hear it? All the sirens? It's going crazy here. I don't know any more than that."

"Is Gul alive?"

"Yes, he's in hospital being treated for hypothermia. Critical but stable, is what they're saying."

"Oh, thank God. Let's pray he'll pull through. I wonder what happened?"

"We don't know. Looks like his dad left him up at Wolfs Cross and then he wandered off from there, but no one knows any more than that at the moment."

"Honestly, some people don't deserve to have children. What was he thinking? And where was his mother?"

"I don't know. Mum, are you alright? I've been in a right state worrying all day. Are you and Ralph okay? What's happening?"

"Yes, yes we are, love. I've been with your brother these past few hours talking things through, and I've had a long chat with Doctor Brody. We can talk later face to face and I'll explain as best I can, but I believe we owe Sylvia Massey an enormous debt of gratitude. She's helped us both. Hugely."

"You sound normal again."

"How do you mean?"

"Well, you were talking back to Ralph when he was going on about killing people this morning, like you were telling him what to do, to get on with it. You were speaking in a weird voice too, kind of yours but deeper and with a French accent. And he was talking in all sorts of voices at first, then French and then English again. I've been trying not to think about it. I mean, has Ralph got schizophrenia? That's what everyone's saying. And then there was this girl at school from Wolfs Cross, who said a lot of people go mad in this village, that there's a curse, and if you see the white monk you'll go insane."

Belinda took a deep breath. The curse of the white monk was a story as old as the hills, the same one she'd heard at school too, and it was kept tightly under wraps. The truth of it was something she had never chosen to believe, but right now it sliced into a raw wound and she flinched. That, and the part about herself speaking to Ralph in a French accent were all too sharp reminders of the day's trauma.

"I've been scared, Mum. It was like you were both possessed."

There was a vague recollection of sitting at the kitchen table this morning, telling Sylvia about a horrific dream, about not feeling herself, that someone was making her say and do things. But possessed?

"No, Essie. No, we mustn't use dramatic phrases like that. But it's very hard to explain on the phone. I'm exhausted, as well. I think the best thing to do would be for the three of us to sit down and have a good talk when Ralph has made a full recovery, which he will, perhaps with Sylvia present. Then we can try and make sense of it all. He doesn't have schizophrenia, though, and neither of us is mad."

There was a pause on the other end. The background noise faded away, followed by the sound of a door closing.

"I'm just stepping out of the lounge while they're watching the telly. Right, I'm on the stairs now. The thing is, I don't get it though, Mum. Why were you both talking like that? It was really scary. I kept thinking of those high school massacres where they said a voice told them what to do; but worse - you were telling him to get on with it!"

"Oh God, yes. But you need to know there was something else going on, and this is what we'll talk about when we're all together. Ralph and I are sitting here at the moment trying to understand it. He and Kezia were into the occult you see, and Sylvia convinced me that he wasn't mentally ill at all, but badly affected by, well, how can I put this...?"

"The dark side?"

"Yes. Dark spirits."

"Right. Okay Mum, this is freaking me out. I've had these black shapes, hooded things following me before, only I didn't want to say because of what the kids said at school about the monks coming for you in the woods. I saw the way Sylvia looked at me sometimes, as if she could see them around me. I felt really nervous going through the forest. And Molly said they were in the corridor outside her bedroom at night. I thought we were just scaring each other, that it wasn't real...but it is, isn't it? Oh my God, I'm so scared.

"I know, I know. But–"

"And then Ralph this morning, when he started mocking me, he knew… he knew what I was scared of and what I'd seen. He said they were clinging to my back, that he could see them and they would poison my mind and make me do terrible things, and I'd end up in Wolfs Cross."

"Essie, stop. Listen to me. Sylvia was right about there being spiritual attachments. But none of us are mad or ill. Ralph made a rapid recovery, and mine was instant because she knows what to do and how to help." She closed her eyes for a second at the lie, at the acknowledgment of the moment Sylvia sat opposite her in the canteen and a weight lifted from her… "We were lucky, so very lucky, to have Sylvia here. And I can promise you I am perfectly well, and so is Ralph. Honestly, if you could see him now you'd see the light back in his eyes, although the Lord only knows what he's done to his hair!" She smiled at Ralph as he grimaced. "The important thing is we've got him back and we're all going to be fine. In fact, we're so fine we're coming home tomorrow."

"Back to that house?"

"No. Molly can go home in the morning, and Ralph and I will stay at your nan's for a day or so until I can sort out a rented flat. I'm not going back there and nor are you. We'll sell up. It isn't the house itself, it's the memories and the darkness. I can't face that and I don't want you to have to, either. I think we should move out of the village altogether. You'll have to get the school bus but we'll find a nice flat full of light. I promise."

"Okay."

"Don't worry, Essie. It's going to be alright, we'll

choose a nice place and it'll be a fresh start for all three of us. And I know Sylvia will help us understand and deal with what has happened."

"Yeah."

"Oh, and by the way, you're much stronger than you know. Stronger than Ralph and me."

"How do you mean?"

"In spirit, Essie. The dark spirits didn't get to you like they got to us. Stay strong and don't be afraid. Have you heard of white light?"

"No."

"Well, imagine you are surrounded with it. Weird I know, but it works. The darkness can't get through."

"You mean like God?"

"I mean white light, divine light, whether you want to say God or you want to say the universe. It works. It keeps the darkness at bay and protects you from fear."

"Okay. And you're sure it's all over? That you're both normal again?"

"Yes, we're both normal again."

"Okay."

"Right, now don't stay up too late and I'll see you after school tomorrow. Can you put your nan on a minute please?"

"Yeah. Night, Mum."

"Night, love."

A moment later her mother was on the line.

"Belinda? What on earth's going on? I don't mind having the two girls, that's not a problem, I'm just worried sick. Are you alright? Is Ralph alright? Is what's happened tied up with all the rest that's going on? I knew Ralph was mixed up with that Kezia Elwyn. I knew it wouldn't end well. Mary Clingbine said she'd seen the pair of them in the woods at the witch's altar—"

"Mum, stop! Ralph's been extremely poorly, but he's okay now. We've been chatting all afternoon and we're both really tired, but the doctor says he's going to make a full recovery—"

"Well, what's been the matter with him? You know what this village is like. You know what the talk will be when they find out, and what happens to folk who've seen—"

"No, he's fine. I've told you. He's been given the all-clear. I won't say he hasn't been very ill. He has. Look, I'll explain better in person, but his recovery has been rapid. Sylvia Massey worked with him and… Oh look, I'll explain best I can tomorrow. Is it alright if we come straight over to you? Only I don't want to go back to that house, not ever. I'll find a rental within days. We won't be under your feet for long—"

"Of course it is, you know that. Stay as long as you like. Alright, well that's me told, anyhow. I'll have to wait 'til tomorrow then to hear the full story. I'm guessing Sylvia will want Molly home, so in that case you and Essie can have the spare room, and Ralph can sleep on the settee. You will still be here in Monkspike, though, won't you?"

"No, I don't think so, Mum. It's been bad. We won't go far, only to the next village, but it's so very dark here…and I need to see the light."

After ringing off, she closed her eyes. Oh God, she really did. She really did need to walk in the light. Stroking her son's forehead as he fell into a deep and peaceful sleep, she blinked back the tears. The white monk had gone. Of that she was sure. But the memory of his coal black eyes, so devoid of humanity it was like staring into the howling emptiness of eternal damnation, would never quite leave her. The abyss, once seen, could never be unseen.

***

CHAPTER THIRTY-THREE

SYLVIA

There should be a moon but there wasn't. The night was a black-out without a single visible outline. She forced herself to keep going up the hill, fumbling for the drystone wall, every step wading against a tide. It couldn't be much further now. It felt like hours. The gatepost for the lodge should be here…any moment now. Where was it?

Dear Lord, please let me get home, I just need to get home.

Every laboured breath threatened to be the last. Her lungs ached and her legs dragged, the impulse to give up and fall to the floor overpowering. Like the worst kind of virus her head pounded and her energy had drained, rendering her weak and shivery. But she could not, must not, give into the exhaustion.

Deep inside, the tiny pilot light of her spirit waxed and waned like a candle in a high wind. Focusing internally, she latched onto the vision, willing it to shine brighter, to extinguish the mocking, dark presence threatening to suppress her existence.

With every step and breath she took however, he gained in strength, surging into her mind as the dominant force. His image burned onto her retinas, the charnel smell of ash, mould and putrefaction suffocating. She staggered against the wall, clutching at the moss with her fingernails. If she lost sight of that flickering light inside, for the merest moment, he would step right in and take over.

Dear Lord, please help me!

Dear Lord, and the Archangel Michael, I call on you for your divine love and help...to surround me in your beautiful white light and protect me from evil. Please take this dark spirit from me...

Falling now, into the bottomless wells of his eyes, a cool rushing feeling ensued, like entering an abandoned railway tunnel. It began to close in around her, the aperture becoming narrower and narrower. Soon it would close altogether and the light would go out forever.

*Our Father, who art in heaven...*She faltered. Began again. *Our Father, who art in heaven, hallowed be thy name, thy...* She could not remember the next line. Christ, what was it?

You don't know the words. You don't believe. You don't believe... ha ha! No one does...no one really does...

Burdo's grin spread widely, gleeful and triumphant, as slowly, inevitably, her feet began to shuffle forwards through a tunnel that echoed with the moans of lost souls and the soughs of a winter wind.

Desperately she tried to re-conjure the tiny flame of her own spirit; tried so hard to picture a lone candle burning at the far end of a cave. It was there. It had to be... faltering and flickering...

And then into the darkness a memory surfaced, of herself as a child with her grandma, who had taught her the Lord's Prayer. They were sitting in front of a coal fire after she'd had to pretend to know the words at Sunday School and been brought out in front of the class to be shamed. The lines now came to her in full, and after she had cited them she mustered all the strength she had and stood her ground, stopping in the tunnel to turn around and face her nemesis.

Her voice was small, echoing around the dripping walls. "I am stronger than you, do you hear? I am alive and you are not. I am alive and you are dead. You are dead and you are to go to the light. You are to go to the light and complete your journey. You have no business here on earth and I reject your presence. I have not invited you. Get out of my head."

He appeared to fade a little, and reality filtered in like mist through the cracks of an old building - enough to see the drystone wall beside her, to feel its solidity beneath her fingers. This was the gatepost to the lodge. It was here. *Oh thank you, God. Almost home!* She grabbed onto it and hurried down the drive, with hands out in front of her like a sleepwalker.

But as she drew closer it was clear something was wrong.

Why were no lights on?

The house reared into view suddenly, its stones luminescent, the windows unlit.

Puzzled, she stopped in the porch, clinging onto the cool stone walls while scanning the grounds. A layer of fog hovered over the grass, causing statues and shrubs to look as if they were floating. Where was Mark? Where was Molly?

She shivered with the pinching coldness, damp

pressing into her spine. Was this death? Had she died and become a lost soul, wandering aimlessly around in the fog trying to find people she knew?

A soft sigh breathed into the nape of her neck. "Did you think I had gone, ma cherie?"

This was death…

"I won't be going to the light, ma cherie. And nor will you. Ever. Now please, go into the house."

An automaton, she turned and obeyed. There was no part of her able to resist the command. It was her own hand which pushed open the door, and her own feet that moved swiftly inside, gliding or flying was how it felt, down the hallway. Eyes not her own began to search for someone, doors crashing open by her own volition, excited breath rasping heavily in her ears as she flew from room to room. Like a burglar she found herself rampaging through the shadowy house. He was here. The sweat of his skin and the stench of his fear rose in the air like the pheromones of a wild fox. Typical of a bully, he must be lying low. Hiding.

The excitement inside built to feverish.

"Rivers!"

The name rang out, a hollow note into empty rooms. Searching… searching… always in the dark… searching but never finding. But now… so close. Her footsteps clattered down the corridors, each room inspected. The fog was now so heavy it steamed at the windows in a quiet hush, adding a strange, bluish hue to the night air. Nothing here was familiar though, the layout all wrong. Confusion rose and along with it a surge of rage. Kicking at the doors, drumming the walls with her fists, the voice within her yelled, "Where are you, you quivering coward? Come out and face up to what you have done!"

Thump, thump, thump! Her fists pounded the oak panelling.

And then suddenly there he was. Cowering on the floor, whimpering like a shamed child in the corner of an upstairs room. Head in hands, his face was smeared with dirt and tears.

She stood in the doorway, aware of the grin distorting her features.

"So there you are! Well, well. I have waited a long time for this moment."

At the sound of her voice he looked up and met her eyes. Trembling, he seemed to be handing something over. Something glinting and sharp.

A nasty snicker cackled inside her head. Disbelievingly she took the offering, closing her fist around its bone handle. "And you even arm me?"

Slashing the blade of steel down the inside of her arm she licked the blood. "That tastes so good, oh delicious, alive and salty. But not as good as yours is going to taste, or look. When it hits the wall." She drew back her arm.

Mark jumped up. "Christ, Sylvia! What the hell are you doing? It's me!"

She hesitated. Who was Sylvia?

Do it! I command you. Do it.

"Sylvia? It's me, Mark! What are you doing cutting yourself? Are you mad?"

She swayed on her feet.

Do it! Do it!

A flicker of awareness sparked in the darkest recess of

her mind. A tiny light in the back of the cave. Fleetingly her limbs became heavy again, and the knife wobbled from her grip. A voice from far away, one that sounded feeble and thin, despite the fact it was shouting as loudly as possible, said, "Mark, get help. Ring Brody. Ask if he listened to the tape. Tell him it's urgent. I told him he might be needed."

Mark hesitated. His boots, she saw now, were muddy. There was soil in his hair, smeared all over his hands and face.

Do it!

"Mark, ring Brody. Now!" Her body crumpled to the floor. "I don't care what you believe. I'm begging you."

He picked his phone up, then tossed it aside. "I can't. You don't know... You don't know what I've done."

"Mark, I'm really ill. Badly... not joking... serious... get Brody..."

Burdo's image roared into her head and she fell back against a chest of drawers as if physically shoved, shifting in and out of consciousness.

I know what he did to you. Your name is Burdo. I know what he did. I know the story and I will make sure it is outed. But you must leave this anger and hatred now, and go to the light.

Never.

I will not kill my own husband. John Rivers is long dead and so are you. You were violently murdered while you slept, but it was nine hundred years ago. You were betrayed by the woman you loved, but she too is long dead. You must go to the light.

Loved? She's just a whore like all women. I feel no love. Only contempt, ma Cherie. Contempt.

That's a disgusting thing to say.

It's a delicious thing to say. Besides, I like it here. I like what the people have – the young girls, the young boys, the drink and the things they smoke. Yes, I like it very much. Besides, I am with you now and you have such…um…access…

Mark was kneeling over her, enfolding her in his arms, crying into her hair about not being able to stop himself from doing what he did, from taking the girl into the woods and leaving her for dead. Not understanding why he did it, not making sense of anything anymore…

She struggled to understand what he was talking about. But his grip was strong. He had her arms pinned to her side, and the knife he had been intending to use on himself, now dropped from her hand with a clatter.

"Mark, you must phone Brody. I need him urgently."

Laughter bellowed inside her head.

"And then, tell him…that you do, too…"

There was no way she could stay conscious for another second, and rapidly now she began to slip away. "Brody…"

Images flashed before her, of young patients lying on the couch being violated by her own hand; of her own voice softly instructing spirit attachments to harm and cut and bully; of her own face laughing at a woman under hypnosis, a woman covered in bruises and weary with violent abuse.

Burdo's round black eyes bored into hers, and this

time the magnetic pull was too great.

I'm going to fall!

Yes, yes you are.

Somewhere in the darkest part of a dream, she thought her hand was being squeezed.

"Brody's on his way now, Syl."

A tiny flicker very far away that looked like a fairy light, twinkled in the darkness and she focused on it.

Is that my spirit?

"Stay with me, Sylvia."

He was stroking the hair from her forehead, his voice far, far away. "I phoned him because you were talking to yourself, saying the strangest things. He told me he heard the recording, that he's spoken at length with Bel and Ralph, and that he's on his way."

She thought she squeezed his hand back but found she had no voice, no notion of time or space, and could only watch and hold on to that tiny twinkling fairy light – a fishing boat out at sea.

"He said they found Kezia and her little boy. I never got a chance to tell you what I've done. And I don't know why I did it…" His voice broke. "I had a rush of being angry, of needing to shut her up. She turned up here speaking to me in old English, and the funny thing was it seemed to resonate. I just lost it and I don't know why, Syl. I don't know why…"

Burdo's energy must have temporarily weakened. There was still a chance she could be saved if Brody got here, if he knew what to do, if he had the stamina and the persuasive skills to make him leave her. Yes, there was still a chance.

"God, I'm so sorry." Mark's voice was fading in and

out. "I haven't listened to you. And what's worse is that I knew things were all wrong, I feel like I've been wading through water for weeks, months even. I just don't feel like myself. I can't stop myself from doing or saying things that are totally out of character."

At times she wondered who was speaking, and who the man was. What was he talking about? His voice droned on and on. Sometimes the small light on the dark ocean flickered and wavered, faded and flared. But it was still there.

"Please be okay. Oh God, Sylvia. Please be okay."

Yes, her hand had definitely squeezed his. Her lips moved and she hoped the words had formed. "Make him exorcise me."

The laughter bellowed inside her head. *Ah, ma Cherie, you are trying my patience. You are difficult, perhaps too strong. But this Brody who is coming…yes, he is weaker…and perhaps more interesting. Yes, I will wait for this man. Let us wait for him.*

Her hair was being stroked, her forehead softly kissed. And the bobbing orb of light on the ocean, although still elusive, grew and burned brighter.

Somewhere deep within her subconscious, long before she surfaced again and began to drift towards it, she thought, *I must pray for Brody. Yes, I must pray for Brody…or Burdo is going to get into the wider world…*

***

CHAPTER THIRTY-FOUR

Kezia

Sometimes it was dark, with amber slats projected on the wall, the hush of night velvety and comforting. Other times the light was harsh and bright, with busy noises from beyond the door. Overhead the steady beep-beep-beep of a machine kept pace with her heart, and occasionally a trolley would rattle down the corridor. After two days she noticed the needles butterflied onto the back of her hand; then the weight of an entire leg cast in plaster.

"Thought you weren't ever gone wake up," he said.

She struggled to focus. He leaned over, the stink of nicotine and whisky wafting across her face.

"Sam?"

Under the glare of the lights his skin was a crisscross of deeply etched lines. His throat hung in pinches of skin and his eye-whites had yellowed.

About to answer, he broke away to cough violently, his wiry body doubling over. His chest sounded tight, the cough unproductive yet clearly exhausting him. "I had to wait and see you were going to be okay, Kez."

She nodded. Of course, he'd found her, hadn't he? He must have been out looking for Gul and then herself… nearly twenty-four hours in the rain.

"Is Gul–?"

"Yeah, he's grand. He was ice-cold but they've warmed him up, and he's eating now, asking for his mum."

A tear smarted at the corner of her eye and she swiped it away, the memory of her frantic search surging back. "They find out what happened? Why he vanished like that?"

"Little lad's not talking. The police have sent a special children's officer to see him but so far he'll only say he wants his mum, so my guess is they're going to wait for you to get better before trying again. Clint, Kade and Tina have given statements, but the police have gone after Ralph Sully for some reason."

She shook her head. "Why?"

"He'd been out that night, been seen. He's not the only one been taken in for questions, either. That Doctor Massey has, too."

"My brain can't take it in, Sam. I feel so tired."

"That's right, you rest. I'm not feeling too good myself, to be honest with you. Smoker's cough playing up."

He looked grey, haggard, she thought, and sunken. "You been 'ere all this time?"

"Like I said, I had to make sure you were alright, and now I know. You're a strong one, Kez. Always were. I remember when you ran away from Wolfs Cross. No one ever did that before: every kid comes out of there is born broken - you know, in the mind. Not you, though. It's like sometimes, well it's like you're possessed of a stronger spirit than everyone else."

She began to drift off, dragged away on a tide of

drowsiness. "Where's that son of yours? After what he did?"

"Packed and gone. And good-riddance, though I say it myself. Even that tart down the pub wouldn't give 'im the time of day after he left the little one with Tina, knowing damn well she was pissed out of 'er 'ead. But worse than that, when me and Kade went to fetch him that morning Gul went missing, he told us he'd be there in a minute and shut the door. Never turned up, did he? Probably went back to bed."

She turned her face away. There were no words.

"Anyway," Sam squeezed her arm. "There's not a soul in the village, or in Wolfs Cross, who'll even look at him. Not even his drinking buddies. No, he's dead to me, he is. Dead."

She heard little more, the image of her husband splayed out in a drunken stupor, interspersing with other memories – those of his quirky lop-sided smile as he lit a cigarette and called her 'darlin' the first time. It had not she knew, ever been love, but briefly the emotion had caught her heart and blocked out the pain.

When exactly Sam finally left her side she couldn't be sure, but she thought she heard a message. It was to be the last thing he ever said to her, and maybe one day it would make sense.

"Oh, and Kade told me to tell you something, Kez. He said it was safe for you to come back to the forest. I don't know what he means by that, but it's what he said to tell you. That the one you fear has gone."

***

EPILOGUE

Six Months Later
Kezia Morse

Kezia hummed softly to herself as she wandered around the conservatory of White Hart Lodge, watering herbs and plants. All of them had a specific purpose, as did those in the garden, from mandrake and henbane, to aconite and valerian. Love, lust, protection and hexes – this is why the people came to her, as they had always done. Business was good, and life was getting better.

Mabon: she bathed in moonlight and practised the oldest religion, safe in the knowledge she was well protected. The villagers never walked in the woods, and made sure to keep others well clear with tales of terror and hauntings. And those in the darker realms advised her well. Most of all, here she was – back where she belonged – home again after all these years. Thanks to Sam.

Six months ago, Sam and his men had combed the forest, eventually finding Gul in an underground stairwell at the monastery. Although Gul refused to tell anyone else how he got there, one night he whispered into her ear, that a man in a long white-hooded robe had come for him with cheese and apples and dark red juice. He'd been hungry, and followed.

When Sam and Kade found him he was on the floor in the freezing cold, laughing and talking with his invisible host. There had been no one else there, Kade said, but the atmosphere wasn't nice, not nice at all, and the lad was mottled blue with skin like ice. They tried to find her, to tell her Gul was alive, but could not.

"You'd vanished," Kade told her. "We got your footprints and the dogs got your scent, but we couldn't find you for the life of us. It was Sam who kept looking. Sam who wouldn't give up…" His eyes had searched hers.

In answer to her silence he simply shook his head. "None of my business, o' course."

She had been lifted out of a ditch on the north side of the small private chapel adjacent to Temple Lake House. Few ever visited the place. Even fewer wandered around to the north or devil's side, which bordered unconsecrated ground. Reputedly, Kitty Morse had been buried there, her neck pierced with a knife, the four quarters of her body hidden at various locations, with only the dislocated skull in the unmarked grave.

She had a fractured femur, a dislocated knee, and was in a diabetic coma thanks to an insulin injection directly into the carotid artery. After a week in hospital with hypothermia and pneumonia, she finally recovered, but Sam, who had a smoker's chest, had not fared so well and died before she could thank him. Clint, good-hearted to the end, had immediately set about divorcing her when he saw the Will, but, and here she began to hum and smile to herself again, a binding ritual had kept him from venting his fury on her. The beeswax hexing poppet had a photograph of him stuck to it, the mouth sewn together; and it now lay in the bottom of her freezer. It seemed to have worked. Vilified by the locals for having left his young son that night, for failing to join the search team and only staggering out of his bed the next day to ask what happened, he didn't bother pursuing paternity rights and the Will had not been contested. He hadn't made so much as a squeak.

It came naturally now, the study of herbs and libations, hedge-riding and flight. She wrote a journal each day, monitoring the phases of the moon, planetary alignments, and when each plant would come to fruition. There were ways of practising this most ancient of crafts and the affinity for it excited her as if born to it. For the first time in her life she belonged, was valued, and the one inside seemed purringly content.

Yes, she thought, I have everything I asked for. I have Gul, the lodge, the woods, and rich abundance. The house had been a good price too, with the Masseys upping sticks and leaving in a hurry. Their solicitor had been instructed to accept the first nearest offer. She'd offered half what it was worth and got it.

Most of the information came from locals who bought tarot readings. They inhaled sweet incense, and drank the kind of tea that loosened tongues. Afterwards they could not recall what they'd said. But she knew every detail of the gossip most salaciously imparted.

Paige Morse had been over just yesterday.

"I'm sorry you lost the baby," she'd said, cutting the cards. "What happened?"

Paige shrugged, her lop-sided face blank of expression.

"Was it Kade's?"

Paige shook her head.

"Whose?"

She shrugged again. Then tears formed in her eyes. "They got me in the woods, some lads."

Kezia saw who it was immediately. Saw through the girl's eyes, felt the pang of her humiliation, heard the taunts, the mockery, the jeering. "I'm sorry, Paige. You got to take care and not go around alone, you know that?"

She nodded.

"What did you do with the body? Did you bury him?" For certain it had been a 'him' – the spirit of a young boy hung around them. "Ah, he's not happy. What did you do?"

"We burned him."

It was said quite matter-of-factly, and Kezia flinched. That's what some folk still did. A miscarriage, an aborted foetus, would be burned and the death unregistered.

She shook her head. "You must give him a proper burial. You have the bones. Bury him properly, with respect. I will take you to my special place in the woods."

Paige smiled and a light flashed in the dull eyes. "I was going to call 'im, Gul, after your lad, Kezia."

After the reading, she gave her more brew and a smoke. "Doctor Massey's going to court, you 'eard?" Paige volunteered.

She nodded. No longer practising as a doctor he was pleading insanity. He and Sylvia had both paid a high price for living in Monkspike. Well, outsiders tended not to do so well here, she thought. Never did. Best not to come, then - meddling with what they didn't understand.

"Where's Sylvia Massey? Your therapist? You see her, do you?"

Paige nodded. "Couple of times I seen 'er. But then she left and I don't know where she went. They just said that he was in the papers, facing charges for what he did to you. Folk are saying he went mad."

"Runs in the Rivers' family," said Kezia. "Big shame for them, really."

She grinned and Paige grinned back.

"What about Bel's son, Ralph? You ever see him about?"

The girl shook her head and giggled. "You put some stuff in this smoke, Kez?"

"Course, I did. So tell me about Ralph Sully. Did they find out where he went that night Gul disappeared? I just want to know what the police said."

"I ain't 'eard nothing. They're saying he'd been out looking for you, that he used to spy on you at the altar." Paige shot her a sly grin, started giggling and flushing red. "They say he used to watch you doing naked dancing."

."Yeah, well he won't be doing that no more, will he?"

Paige shook her head. "Belinda Sully's still doin' 'er nursing and that, but I think 'er kids don't come 'ere no more. I think they all left."

Kezia nodded, satisfied that Ralph had nothing to do with Gul's disappearance that night. That it must have been the one whose name was never even whispered around here, lest he appear once more in nightmares and dreams. Sometimes she wondered where he had gone. The eyes that once watched her in the woods no longer did so. The odour of musty cloth and decay no longer pervaded the sweet, forest air. And the one inside no longer seemed edgy and alert. Perhaps he had travelled far… gone with the Masseys…or beyond into the wider world? One thing was certain, he wasn't here. He no longer plagued these woods, although the fear remained.

She bent to tend the plants. How wonderful to be alone. There would be no need for another man in her life. Not ever. After all, there was more than enough to cope with on that score.

He came to her nightly. Sometimes it would be in the forest on one of her midnight forays to the altar. She would arrive home barefoot with twigs in her hair and bloody scratches all over her legs and arms. The level of euphoria was beyond anything a mortal man could ever provide, albeit wild, unpredictable and at times frightening. She went to lean against the wide-open door leading out to the lawns.

The gilt-edged forest seemed all the blacker for the dying sun on the horizon, a smoky nip to the air now as showers of leaves fluttered in golden breezes to the floor. Yes, he had wanted her back here, and for good reason. Kitty had sealed her fate nearly nine hundred years ago, with an infernal allegiance that had passed down through ancestral lines and could never be broken.

"So you had me all along, Malphas – mind, heart, body and soul. You are my master and I your servant."

At that moment, Gul looked up from playing with one of Loki's new puppies, on the lawn. They had taken all four before Kade drowned them. The look in the dog's eyes as she wrapped the warm, whimpering bodies in a towel and took them home, had been one of acknowledgement. A debt repaid.

The burnished bronze of the late afternoon sun caught like fire in her son's hair, his eyes as stark and dazzling as wild violets. She lifted her hand to wave. The sky darkened, and the picture flicked to black and white. Static buzzed in her ears. Another vision was coming. While some were welcome, others were not.

This was not.

The trees became a thin line of five or six, the trunks black and wizened, the branches giant thorns. Behind Gul, a howling wasteland stretched into eternity, and a large raven cawed in a shimmering blue haze.

Gul was waving back to her.

It had all been for him, of course. Kitty had made sure of that. For the child who never got to live. And now here he was, beautiful and alive.

"And mine," screeched the raspy voice of Malphas. "Mine."

***

ACKNOWLEDGEMENTS

1. With grateful thanks to Wendy Adair… www.modernexorcist.com …for all her help, knowledge and advice regarding spirit attachment therapy, modern day exorcism and the presentation of symptoms. A brave lady and a true inspiration. If you are interested in reading more on this subject, Wendy's latest publication is: www.intotheunder.world.com : 'Immersion in the ancient Greek Underworld, including God and Goddess invocation, intuitive/mediumship development and the shadow world'. I find it endlessly fascinating!

2. And my profound gratitude to Raven Wood, a traditional witch of Germanic and Celtic roots, who lives and practices the craft in Wisconsin, USA. Thank you for providing me with your invaluable knowledge on the herbs and plants used in witchcraft, not to mention your personal insight. I am most grateful, as always, for both your help and your precious friendship. Find Raven's authentic, handmade products on: etsy.me/2L6rVih

More Books by Sarah England:

FATHER OF LIES

A Darkly Disturbing Occult Horror Trilogy:
Book 1

'Boy did this pack a punch and scare me witless..'

'Scary as hell…What I thought would be mainstream horror was anything but…'

'Not for the faint-hearted. Be warned – this is very, very dark subject matter.'

'A truly wonderful and scary start to a horror trilogy. One of the best and most well written books I've read in a long time.'

'A dark and compelling read. I devoured it in one afternoon. Even as the horrors unfolded I couldn't race through the pages quickly enough for more…'

'Delivers the spooky in spades!'

'Will go so far as to say Sarah is now my favourite author – sorry Mr King!'

***

Ruby is the most violently disturbed patient ever

admitted to Drummersgate Asylum, high on the bleak moors of northern England. With no improvement after two years, Dr. Jack McGowan finally decides to take a risk and hypnotises her. With terrifying consequences.

A horrific dark force is now unleashed on the entire medical team, as each in turn attempts to unlock Ruby's shocking and sinister past. Who is this girl? And how did she manage to survive such unimaginable evil? Set in a desolate ex-mining village, where secrets are tightly kept and intruders hounded out, their questions soon lead to a haunted mill, the heart of darkness...and The Father of Lies.

http://www.amazon.co.uk/dp/B015NCZYKU
http://www.amazon.com/dp/B015NCZYKU

***

TANNERS DELL
BOOK 2

Now only one of the original team remains – Ward Sister, Becky. However, despite her fiancé, Callum, being unconscious and many of her colleagues either dead or critically ill, she is determined to rescue Ruby's twelve year old daughter from a similar fate to her mother.

But no one asking questions in the desolate ex-mining village Ruby hails from ever comes to a good end. And as the diabolical history of the area is gradually revealed, it seems the evil invoked is both real and contagious.

Don't turn the lights out yet!

***

ᛖAGDA
BOOK 3

The dark and twisted community of Woodsend
harbours a terrible secret – one tracing back to the age
of the Elizabethan witch hunts, when many innocent
women were persecuted and hanged.

But there is a far deeper vein of horror running
through this village; an evil that once invoked has no
intention of relinquishing its grip on the modern world.
Rather it watches and waits with focused intelligence,
leaving Ward Sister, Becky, and CID Officer, Toby,
constantly checking over their shoulders and jumping at
shadows.

Just who invited in this malevolent presence? And is
the demonic woman who possessed Magda back in the
sixteenth century, the same one now gazing at Becky
whenever she looks in the mirror?

Are you ready to meet Magda in this final instalment
of the trilogy? Are you sure?

***

THE ⊕WLMEN

If They See You They Will Come For You

Ellie Blake is recovering from a nervous breakdown. Deciding to move back to her northern roots, she and her psychiatrist husband buy Tanners Dell at auction – an old water mill in the moorland village of Bridesmoor.

However, there is disquiet in the village. Tanners Dell has a terrible secret, one so well guarded no one speaks its name. But in her search for meaning and very much alone, Ellie is drawn to traditional witchcraft and determined to pursue it. All her life she has been cowed. All her life she has apologised for her very existence. And witchcraft has opened a door she could never have imagined. Imbued with power and overawed with its magick, for the first time she feels she has come home, truly knows who she is.

Tanners Dell though, with its centuries old demonic history…well, it's a dangerous place for a novice…

http://www.amazon.co.uk/dp/B079W9FKV7
http://www.amazon.com/dp/B079W9FKV7

***

THE SOPRANO

A Haunting Supernatural Thriller

It is 1951 and a remote mining village on the North Staffordshire Moors is hit by one of the worst snowstorms in living memory. Cut off for over three weeks, the old and the sick will die; the strongest bunker down; and those with evil intent will bring to its conclusion a family vendetta spanning three generations.

Inspired by a true event, 'The Soprano' tells the story of Grace Holland – a strikingly beautiful, much admired local celebrity who brings glamour and inspiration to the grimy moorland community. But why is Grace still here? Why doesn't she leave this staunchly Methodist, rain-sodden place and the isolated farmhouse she shares with her mother?

Riddled with witchcraft and tales of superstition, the story is mostly narrated by the Whistler family who own the local funeral parlour, in particular six year old Louise – now an elderly lady – who recalls one of the most shocking crimes imaginable.

http://www.amazon.co.uk/dp/B0737GQ9Q
http://www.amazon.com/dp/B0737GQ9Q7

***

HIDDEN COMPANY

A dark psychological thriller set in a Victorian asylum in the heart of Wales.

Warning – contains highly disturbing material!

1893, and nineteen year old Flora George is admitted to a remote asylum with no idea why she is there, what happened to her child, or how her wealthy family could have abandoned her to such a fate. However, within a short space of time it becomes apparent she must save herself from something far worse than that of a harsh regime.

2018, and forty-one year old Isobel Lee moves into the gatehouse of what was once the old asylum. A reluctant medium, it is with dismay she realises there is a terrible secret here – one desperate to be heard. Angry and upset, Isobel baulks at what she must now face. But with the help of local dark arts practitioner, Branwen, face it she must.

This is a dark story of human cruelty, folklore and superstition. But the human spirit can and will prevail…unless of course, the wrath of the fae is incited…

***

http://www.sarahenglandauthor.co.uk

***

CPSIA information can be obtained
at www.ICGtesting.com
Printed in the USA
LVHW081732290120
645192LV00031B/1269

9 781693 405631